Acea and the Adventure Thru Time

Mock Family –

You guys rock!

Go Link!

SLCC 2016

Kyle L. Shoop

The Acea Bishop Trilogy:

Book 1: *Acea and the Animal Kingdom*

Book 2: *Acea and the Seven Ancient Wonders*

Book 3: *Acea and the Adventure Thru Time*

For more information on the author or this series, please visit www.KyleShoop.com

ISBN-10: 1532882122
ISBN-13: 978-1532882128

Cover art by Chris Brewer (www.behance.net/chrisbrewer/frame)

To my mother, and the loving memory of my father.

TABLE OF CONTENTS

Chapter I

Newton's Apple

I quickly duck down beside a short stone wall, trying desperately not to let my heavy panting give away my location. I'm so exhausted that I cover my mouth with my hand just to muffle the sound of my breathing.

I really should get out of the library more to exercise.

Though my breathing isn't as audible now, I still hear the thumping of my heartbeat and hope that whoever is searching for me can't hear it.

Should I move? Are they close by?

I remain motionless with my back against the stone wall, listening for where the guards are on the other side.

"Anything yet?" I hear one guard yell out to another. The sound of barking by eager, angry dogs echo from the man, telling me that I must have given them quite a scare when I scaled the gates of this place to break in. Knowing that they're using search dogs to hunt me down only makes me that much more worried about the sound of my heartbeat giving me away.

"No, not here – you?" The other guard yells back.

"Me neither. Let's try over in this direction. I'm sure it's just some type of prank. It's just a university after all – what's of value that could be stolen anyways?"

I wouldn't say it's going to be *stolen*, but more … *prevented*. At least, that's how my father describes it. Vesuvius will always tell me that we have to prevent bad things from happening, or to instead facilitate good things happening - and that's why we do what we do. I don't question my father. I never ask what it is that we're specifically trying to prevent or facilitate because I … well, I just don't question my father.

Why would I? He is my father, after all. If I can't trust him, who can I trust?

But I do know one thing: the guards are wrong. Whatever it is I'm preventing this time is of value – *much* value.

Years ago, I actually did begin to question my father about the things we'd been doing. "Acea," Vesuvius had responded, "do you trust me?"

"Yes, of course, father."

"Then do not question me – but know that it is imperative that we do what we've been doing."

"And what is it that we are *actually* doing?"

I can still remember the look that my father had given me

when I continued to question him despite his instruction not to. It was a look of scolding disappointment that I've never since wanted to receive again. But he nevertheless replied with words that have given my actions purpose and motivation to this day: "What we are doing is the most important thing in the world's history. We are preventing evil from occurring. There is nothing more valuable than that. And only we can do it."

Those words still echo in my mind while I wait for the sound of the guards to disappear into the distance on the other side of this stone wall. When I think they're gone, I glance cautiously over the wall to make sure the path is clear. I watch the guards and their dogs retreat down a grassy knoll, walking toward the other side of the university's campus.

I'm glad it's early morning, otherwise there would certainly be students outside to help find me. But on this specific morning, on August 29, 1666 – there's no one around. At least, not yet. Maybe soon, but think I'm in the clear for now.

I reach into my pants pocket and pull out my pocket watch. It's a beautiful but simple-looking watch with a golden cover. I crack it open and smirk to myself for a second. To any other person, this would look like a normal pocket watch. But not to me - I know better. There are two secrets about this watch that not even my father told me when he gave it to me as a gift. And he didn't have to. When I just touched it for the first time, I could tell what this little device was hiding – as if I had already owned it before.

I don't know which secret is more useful, but luckily they're both revealed with the same spell. I used to need to say it out loud, but now I only have to think it.

"Aperi oculos meos."

Suddenly, an etching appears on the inside of the watch's cover on its left side. It changes automatically with every assignment Vesuvius gives me, as if he's somehow the one who magically does the inscription on it. For my current assignment, the etching on the inside of the watch's cover reads:

AUGUST 29, 1666, 07:34
CAMBRIDGE, ENGLAND
GET THE APPLE

Because I never really know what to expect on one of these assignments, the watch's second secret has always proven to be just as useful as the first one. To everyone else, the right side of the opened pocket watch would appear to be just a normal watch. There is a minute hand, second hand, and hour hand. But after I manifest the spell, another hand appears – a red hand that is obviously unrelated to what time it is because it's constantly moving. It initially took me a couple assignments to figure out what it is. But once I did, it was extremely useful.

A compass! So, as I'm moving through areas which are completely unknown to me, I'll at least have some frame of reference for where I should be going. Over time I realized that the compass doesn't lead to north. Instead, I learned that it points me to the location where I need to go to complete the assignment.

Between this helpful use of magic and the instruction inscribed on the inside cover, I'm set.

But when I examine the direction the needle is pointing me in, I'm not very enthused. It's pointing me toward where I just ran from – on the other side of the wall where the guards were just standing.

I really hope they've left already, otherwise I'm in trouble.

. . . I should have looked at the compass immediately after I arrived here, instead of waiting until now.

I peek around the edge of the stone wall I've been leaning against, and exhale in relief. I think the guards – and, luckily, their dogs – are gone. Just on the other side of the wall, across the field, is a large brick wing of the university. I'm not really sure what part of the college this is, but its size is impressive.

. . . or maybe I've just been holed up in the Great Library for too long. . .

Because my instructions say to "get the apple," I'm guessing that there's a courtyard just on the other side of the university's wing. And I'm guessing that's where I need to get to.

The sun had been rising while I scaled the campus gates, so I don't have much time at all. I need to get to my destination very soon. If I miss it by even a second, I know exactly what the consequence will be – evil will not be prevented. And even more pressing is the fact that the longer I wait, the more students are likely to arrive and interfere.

I'm about to move from behind the wall, but I suddenly hear the echo of a dog bark from off in the distance.

Great.

I'm now no longer sure if the guards have totally given up their search, but I don't have time to wait any longer. After glancing around to ensure the coast is clear, I move slowly from the stone wall across the field and up against the bricks of the university's wing. Holding my wand in my hand, I cautiously inspect the campus grounds for anyone who may spot me. Unfortunately, there isn't anywhere to hide other than just keeping as close to the building's wall as possible while I move across the field and into the courtyard on the other side. As I pace against the university's wall, I duck down to avoid being seen through the wing's large windows.

If I had my way, I'd be invisible right now – but Vesuvius forbids it. He says that magic is only to be used in the human world when it's absolutely necessary as a last resort. If humans were to realize the existence and power of magic, as Vesuvius taught me, then our task would be insurmountably more difficult. He also taught me to try to avoid interaction with humans as much as possible. So, I don't know why I'm actually gripping my wand right now – perhaps it's for comfort or out of habit after all these years.

I cautiously round the edge of the building's wing and glance into the courtyard on the other side. Luckily, it's completely empty. And even more luckily, I see exactly where I need to go. In the far corner of the courtyard, kind of up on a hill, is a tree. From where I'm standing, I can even see that it's not just any tree – it's an apple tree.

Bingo. Found it.

I glance down at my pocket watch to confirm that the compass is pointing me right at the tree.

Yep, that's it alright.

Next, I look at the time - to see how long I have until the deadline that's etched into my pocket-watch.

It's 7:22 a.m. and the watch says to get the apple at 7:34 a.m. I've got twelve minutes left – piece of cake.

I start to get cocky thinking about how easy this assignment was, especially compared to others. But as I get closer to the tree, that cockiness quickly disappears.

There are hundreds of apples in the tree! Which one am I supposed to get?

I look back down at my pocket watch, hoping that it'll somehow give me more directions - even though I already know that it won't. But something strange stands out to me. Why do my instructions include an exact time if I'm just supposed to "get the apple?" Couldn't I find the right apple and get it before the specified time? Some instructions for prior assignments haven't even included a specific time, so this one must have for a reason.

Having now reached the tree, I stare up into its branches and realize I just don't have time to spare. I don't know which apple I'm supposed to get, so I might as well start collecting as many of them as I can.

Boy, am I glad I brought my backpack with me.

I quickly climb up into the tree. I furiously begin plucking as many apples as I can off of branches and shoving them into my backpack.

Hopefully one of them will be the right one . . . my backpack can't hold them all.

I'm not even in the tree for two minutes when out of nowhere a young man comes and sits underneath of the tree directly below where I'm perched. I try to be as quiet as possible, but I've got to continue collecting as many apples as I can.

The man is just sitting beneath the tree reading a book. I'm flabbergasted.

What type of person comes to the courtyard and reads a book all alone this early in the morning?

After a minute or so, the rustling of the tree branches must catch the man's attention. While looking distracted, and even annoyed, he glances up into the tree and yells up at me.

"Hey, who's that up in the tree? Can't you see I'm reading? I'm doing very important work down here you know. Could it wait until another time maybe?"

No, it certainly cannot wait until another time!

Though I don't want to talk to the man in fear of altering the past too much, I don't see any way around it. Thinking quickly, I just blurt out the first excuse that comes to mind. "Sorry, sir. I'm just a gardener and … want to harvest this tree … before the apples over-ripen and fall to the ground."

It hits me. I know exactly who this man is, and why I have to find the right apple at the exact time. What the man says back to me confirms my thought.

"Well, fine gardener, allow me to introduce myself. My name is Isaac Newton and I'm working on the problem of motion. You see, for years I've been grappling with the idea that ...."

Newton's tone isn't really demeaning, or even self-important. It's more as if he's thinking out loud and has made the wrong assumption that I actually care about his idea. The only thing I really care about is finding the apple. Over the years, I've learned not to question the connection between my assignment and how it actually will prevent evil. For all I know, I'm just removing one domino in a whole line of important events. But in this case, I know the importance of the apple: when it falls, Newton solves his problem and becomes a foremost thinker in human history. I don't know how this leads to evil, but I know I must find the apple that will drop. Newton's very influential ... somehow.

I pretend to care about the dissertation Newton is giving me from below, by diverting his attention away from me with a series of inconspicuous "uh-huhs." I furiously pick as many apples as I can off of the surrounding tree branches, and throw them into my backpack. The minutes tick by, and I have no idea if I've even succeeded yet in this assignment.

I guess the only way to know if I've completed it is by picking apples until the time on my pocket watch - how nerve-wracking!

As if not being sure whether I've picked the right apple is suspenseful enough, I'm becoming even more worried at how many students I'm suddenly seeing slowly begin to arrive on the university grounds around me. This situation is quickly becoming more complex than I want.

When the space inside of my backpack is full, I panic for a moment. I glance at my pocket watch and almost drop the bag of apples when I'm surprised that I only have about fifty-five seconds left until it's 7:34 a.m.

I instantly pause when out of the corner of my eye I see what I *know* to be the apple I'm supposed to grab. It's out on a branch towards the outside of a tree – too far out of my reach!

What am I going to do?!

I fight back unexpected tears of sadness when I realize this is going to be the first assignment that I'll fail.

What will I do? What will my father think of me?

I close my eyes for a second, hoping I'll come up with a plan. But when I reopen them, my heart stops. The sight in front of me is not only surprising, but unbelievable.

A golden key? What?

I absolutely cannot believe my eyes when I momentarily see a golden key dangling from the edge of the tree branch. I am so confused that I again close my eyes for a second and then re-open them – thankfully to see the apple there again. Only now the apple is dangling on a thread of its stem!

Wait. . .it's about to fall!

I panic - I won't be able to reach it in time!

Anger wells up inside of me. Intense, aggressive anger.

This is all Newton's fault. I want to punish him. Because of him, my father will now think less of me. It's all his fault.

I decide to punish him by destroying the inspiration of his ingeniousness.

The apple breaks free from the branch and begins falling. I watch it descend, as if the apple is moving in slow motion. My hatred for the apple and Newton lead to only one outcome. I stare at the apple in disgust. When I wince, I use my powers to crush the apple in mid-air, before Newton is even aware of it.

There. Assignment completed.

I feel liberated, and my emotions are freeing. However, this ecstatic feeling only lasts a fleeting moment until it's interrupted by several passing students.

"Did you see that?" One of them exclaims, pointing in my direction.

"I did!" Another hollers. "That guy just . . . I don't know, it must have been magic or something!"

Suddenly, a crowd of gawking students quickly accumulates - each of them staring in my direction.

I have no idea what to do, so I do the first thing my instincts tell me to: run. I jump out of the tree, throw on my backpack, and take off. I need to get back to the portal-doorway through which I'd initially came. And the fastest way is not around the university wing that I hid by before. Rather, the fastest way back is *through* the middle of the university. I jet toward the large crowd of staring students and run right through them. Books and backpacks fall to the ground when I brush past several of them and into the main building of the university. Many of the students begin chasing after me, causing me to speed up even faster. I have no idea how I'm going to get out of this situation without being caught!

I race through the halls of the old, brick university and speed into a classroom – hoping I could lose the students that way. No luck. Instead of losing the students chasing me, I run right into a classroom full of students!

Who has class this early in the morning?!

I jump through the rows of desks, causing even more commotion than I had even thought was possible. Students leap up from their desks, pointing at me as I run through the class and out a door on the opposite side of the classroom.

"Hey! Get back here!" I hear the professor yell from right behind me. Many of the students are in an uproar, and I think the amount of students chasing after me has actually gotten substantially larger.

I'm now sprinting through the halls, courtyards, and buildings as fast as I can. The uproar on campus has spread like a wildfire, and I don't even know if my legs will last long enough for me to get back to the exit. When I suddenly hear barking, I know the guards are again after me as well – just more sets of legs added to the chase.

"That's him!" I hear the guards yell while running. "That's the same guy!"

I finally make it to last building on the edge of campus, which is unfortunately a library. I find this out the hard way when I erupt into it. If there was anyone actually studying in here this early in the morning, they no longer are.

I glance back to see that the group of fifty or so followers are only behind me by about thirty feet! I see an exit door out of the library facing the direction where I'd climbed over the university fences before. I spring towards it and burst out into the edge of the campus lawn facing the fence. But rather than running to where I'd left the portal open, I dart over against the side of the building and quickly mutter "*Absconditus!*"

If ever there was a last resort requiring being invisible – this is it. All of the students, guards, and university faculty chasing after me reach the campus lawn and are mystified.

"Where'd he go?"

"He couldn't have gone far."

"Is that him over there?"

"Maybe he really *is* magic," I hear one of them say. I can't tell if he's serious or cracking a joke, but I now know the reason for Vesuvius's instruction to not use magic in the human world.

Soon enough the crowd dissipates while I'm still panting behind them against the building – safely masked from their view. When everyone is gone, I climb over the fence and retreat around a group of tall bushes where I'd left the portal-doorway back to Lemuria open.

Just as I reach my hand out to touch the portal, the ferocious barking of a dog that had gotten through the fence approaches me from behind. I'm not sure if it's barking at me or the unusual – and barely noticeable – shift in light that the doorway creates. But to have fun, I mutter the invisibility spell again and immediately re-appear right in front of the guard dog.

"Boo!" I exclaim, laughing at how I'm now the one making the other afraid. The dog quickly whimpers and retreats back toward campus.

I turn and reach out to the portal, instantly being transported back to Lemuria.

Ugh. Not this place.

I hate Lemuria. It's so … bleak and … I don't really know the word other than to say "in between." Though I know Lemuria can't actually do so, I always just think to myself that it should "make up its mind" to either be the human world or Terra Fabula. Stupid, I know, but I just don't like the "in between" feeling. That – and being here always gives me a vague feeling of having been through something … something … I don't know. It's a feeling of hurt and loss, but I don't have a specific memory. Even though I know I'm probably just over-reacting to this place, I try to be here as little as possible. Unfortunately, it's the bridge between the two worlds, so I have to travel through it for each assignment.

Over the years I've created the portal-doorways from a room I found in an abandoned building in Lemuria. I don't know why I describe it as abandoned, though – everything is abandoned in Lemuria because no one actually lives here. Over time, I've come to use one specific room as my only point of contact with Lemuria for my assignments. It's the place from which I'll create the doorways to the different points in time in the human world, and which contains my doorway back to the Great Library.

All around this room are tables and items that hold memories to a time from before I discovered it. Torn paintings, random writings, and broken gadgets are all strewn about the room and laid on the tables. I think the reason I've come to gravitate towards this room is because it's really the only place in Lemuria which I've discovered so far that isn't just grey. All of these prior artifacts are obviously from one of the two worlds, since they actually have color – even if it's faded or chipped.

I dump the apples out of my backpack and onto the table. Though I've been using these tables as kind of a trophy room for all of the artifacts which I've obtained from my assignments, I figure that it's probably good for me to keep some food in this room. But with the apples now being dumped out, I absolutely can't wait to get back to the library.

I turn to the large painting showing the Great Library and step through its doorway.

I'm home.

Chapter 2

The Birthday Present

For the past six years I've been a student. Since the first moment I remember meeting my father, I've made the Great Library my home. I've mined the shelves and enclaves of the library for knowledge. I don't really remember the days beyond six years ago, and I never really get to see my father, but that doesn't bother me. The library is my home - from the wealth of knowledge stored within, I'll become the greatest sorcerer that has ever lived. My father says so.

Even though I have an actual room out in the Capitol, I rarely ever visit it. There's really nothing in the Capitol for me – or anyone – anymore. It's just a tomb of well-preserved marble buildings enshrined in the past. It's not the future for me. Instead, most nights I drift to sleep with my nose in a book or map. When I discover the next great adventure from an ancient wizard or sorcerer, or when I've finally perfected a new spell, I feel like a newborn child whose life has just begun.

Interestingly, the wizard stories have never really appealed to me just from the stories they tell. Why would they? The stories are the past, not my future. Rather, what intrigues me about the stories are the mistakes the wizards will make. Those mistakes always end poorly for the wizard, and I often scoff at how I would never have done the same thing. So if there's really one thing which I enjoy about the past that keeps me reading book after book, it's the lessons I learn from them – knowing how other wizards have fallen makes me even stronger. This keeps me reading, or rather *devouring,* the books in the Great Library.

It didn't start out as my idea to study so much in the library. Vesuvius told me to. Then, over time, it became my only real companion between assignments. Just when I think I've finished reading all of the books in one nook of the library, I'll discover another hidden section containing even more fascinating stories. Time after time, it's like certain books have been hidden, yet still preserved for those who are meant to find them. That enduring mystery has also motivated me to continue reading. The floor-to-ceiling shelves and concealed enclaves of books have always been there for me when no one else was. In the last six years, my only real interactions have been with my father. And even those have been . . . inconsistent.

Vesuvius will often only appear when he has a new assignment, or when there's specifically something he wants to teach me. He'll walk through his painted black canvas from his Kingdom with pointed instructions, and without any small talk. He's very direct, and I know that everything he does has a calculated purpose. Though he's not very good at pretending to visit me for any reason other than assignments, that's okay – he's my father and he's very busy with important work. I just like his company and know that he'll help me achieve my full potential as a sorcerer one day. He tells me that he's cultivating me to one day take over his empire. Just like a son should.

The only time that I recall him visiting me for a reason other than an assignment or lesson was one year ago today on my seventeenth birthday. Though just having my father remember my birthday was a gift enough, he outdid himself by giving me the pocket watch as well!

With the pocket watch coming to my mind as last year's treasured birthday present, I look down again in excitement at how much the present has come to mean to me. Now that my last assignment is over, I open it up and just appreciate it for its non-magical purpose: a gift to a son from his father. I trace my finger over the cover and feel its smooth simplicity.

I wonder where Vesuvius got it from.

I'd never really thought to do this before, but I carefully

inspect the outside for any identifying marks that could tell me of its origin. I squint when I see some very small scratches on its top dial.

Though not being an engraving, the scratches are still obviously intentional, rather than being something that could have happened during one of my assignments. The scratches look hand-carved and I squint again to see what the design is:

VB

"VB?" I can't help but question skeptically out loud once the letters come into view.

Like - Vesuvius Bishop? How fitting that he would give me a gift with his name inscribed on it.

With the value of the pocket watch momentarily diminished in my opinion, I just put it back into my pants pocket. But when doing so, my thumb rubs against the smooth, plain surface of the front cover. I can't help but briefly think how the simplicity of this watch is odd – it doesn't really seem like Vesuvius's style. It's origin thus still remains a mystery to me.

My thought process is suddenly interrupted, though, by the surprising and welcome sound from the tapestry leading to my father's Kingdom.

"Son!" My father directs. I'm not really sure if his tone is a greeting or a command for me to come to him. But either way, it doesn't matter.

He's remembered my birthday again!

After not remembering my birthday for the first four years, I'm totally shocked and excited that he's now remembered to visit me on it for two straight years. I run over to where he's at in the upper circle of the library surrounded by the tapestries to each of the Kingdoms. When I run up the stairs to greet him, I first have a hard time actually seeing him among all of the charred-black books and tapestries painted black in the upper circular-room. Vesuvius's dark black cape blends in all too well to the environment.

"Over here, son."

When I hear his words, I jerk my head to the right and finally see him standing in front of one of the tapestries. He stares into the blackness of the doorway facing away from me, and I can't help but wonder what he's thinking about as he stares.

"What are you doing staring into the black paint, father?"

He snarls for a second to himself, as if me having pointed out the blackened tapestries reminded him of something he didn't want to be thinking about. "Remember," he says emphatically, "it's not paint. It's a very powerful spell. We're safe with it – for now."

"So, why do the tapestries still have to be blackened? Especially yours - I wish I could see your Kingdom more often – even if just through the doorway. It was an amazing place."

It's been six years to the day since I stepped through Vesuvius's tapestry and into his Kingdom for a brief moment. Since then, I've yearned to go back, but he has refused to let me do so for some unknown reason.

"It's a line of defense. You'll understand one day. Besides, it's changed since when you were there. I've … added additional … security." The mysterious way which he says that catches my attention, leaving me yearning even more to see what his Kingdom now looks like. But my curiosity is suddenly interrupted when my father turns around and looks directly at me, with an awkwardly crooked smile.

"Happy birthday, son. Six years ago today, you came to me… and I …. I gave you the present of seeing my Kingdom on the first birthday we shared together. There were some years there where I was … preoccupied. But last year, I gave you the pocket watch. And now you are eighteen years old."

My hope builds up into excitement. Again, he doesn't have to bring me a gift - just having him visit me for something other than an assignment is special enough. But I'm, of course, still excited when I see him reach into his long, black cape to reveal something he's obviously been hiding from me the entire time.

"This year," he continues, "I've brought you this."

He pulls from his cape a leather, hard-bound book the size of a large atlas. Its aged binding and worn pages tell me that this has been passed down through the ages.

"Wow," I mutter to myself in amazement as he hands it to me.

But very suddenly, and completely unexpectedly, my heart skips a beat when the book in front of me flashes and changes appearance! For a brief moment, I see a different book than the one that Vesuvius just handed me. I see a book with the same leather, hard-bound cover but with a different symbol on it – it's the same symbol I've seen inscribed many places as the seal of an abandoned order of wizards. I blink, wondering what just happened and if my eyes are playing games on me. When I reopen my eyes, the book has changed back to the one my father brought me. Though the vision of the other book has left, the image is seared into my mind, leaving me with a strange feeling of familiarity.

"Where did you get this from?" I ask, trying to get my mind off of the unusual vision I just experienced.

Vesuvius stares straight at me, as though he's deciding whether to tell me the full truth about its backstory. "Oh, very well," he gives in. "Since I am now entrusting this important guide to your care, I suppose you should know where it came from."

Vesuvius begins pacing casually around the circular room, pretending like he's inspecting the room while he divulges to me the ancient book's history.

"It is among the oldest known books belonging in the lineage of Sorcerers. It was lost for many years, but its creator resurrected it from the ashes. He travelled through time to give it to me. And now, I give it to you."

Unsatisfied with the vague response I just received, I try to pry a little more into its backstory. "And who was its creator?"

Again, my father stares at me, probably wondering why I would care so much for more information. I can see his hesitation in giving me more information recede, though, when he looks down and sees the book in my hands.

"Well, like I said – it's yours now, so the more information you have the better. The man's name is Cadeyrn. He's been a trusted ... advisor of mine for some time."

The manner in which Vesuvius says Cadeyrn's name is as though he's interested to see if I've ever heard of him. And, surprisingly, I haven't. For all of the books and stories I've read here in the library, none of them have ever mentioned anyone with that name. At least, not that I can remember. But before I can ask who Cadeyrn is, I'm enthused when Vesuvius continues telling me more about the book.

"Open it up," he says excitedly. In fact, I don't think I've ever heard him with such an eager tone.

I put the book down on a charred, wooden stand in the middle of the room and crack it open.

Dates!

Many dates line each page. On each line next to the date is an instruction. Some of the lines are randomly crossed out, but many of them aren't. I have a feeling that I know what this book is, but I ask my father just to be sure. "Are these...."

Before I can even ask, Vesuvius is all too eager to tell me more. "That's right! This is the book where your assignments come from! We call it the *Book of Historiarum*. And now it is yours. I am entrusting you to complete the assignments on your own. I believe you are ready."

"But there are hundreds of them. How will I know which ones to do?"

"No, no. There's no need to do them in any certain order. And there's no need to complete them all. Think of it like a building. The building is made of bricks. If you want to tear it down, you can just start to do so by breaking down one brick at a time. Eventually, the house will then crumble to the ground once you've removed enough. It's time that you took over these assignments on your own. I have other equally important work I must be doing now. Besides, you're ready."

I have a sinking feeling in my stomach when he says that. I haven't yet told him how poorly my last assignment went, and that I'm afraid I screwed it all up by using my magic and talking to too many people.

"Wait, father, there's something I have to tell you."

His eyebrows rise as though he wasn't expecting me to say that. "…and?" He waits for my answer with intrigue and skepticism.

"Well, it's just that … my last assignment didn't go so well."

"How so?"

I divulge to my father the entire events of the embarrassing encounter. My description sounds so much like a confession and a justification for my actions that I feel like even smaller of a child before this great Sorcerer.

When I conclude, Vesuvius just pauses for a moment while thinking about how he wants to react. The silence in the air is humiliating. But before I try to end the silence, he asks an obviously calculated question.

"And how did you *feel* when you thought you would not complete the assignment?"

"Angry. Hateful. Despising." My tone sharpens as I recall exactly those emotions, as if I felt vindicated in why I felt that way. Those were the same emotions I felt when I crushed Newton's apple as it was falling.

"Well, then, you're even more ready than I thought you are."

My father's response is surprising, and I'm instantly elated. "You see, son. The book is not the only present I have for you."

Really!?

"You are ready to be appointed a Sorcerer. Being a Sorcerer is a step beyond being a Wizard. A Wizard is afraid of their feelings, and seeks to shun them. They say they don't, but they really only care about a limited spectrum of feelings. A Sorcerer, however, cultivates and harnesses his fully array of emotions – both the good and the bad. He harnesses them for an ultimate purpose. Wizards have no real purpose – they merely maintain the status quo, no matter how pitiful it is."

"And what is the ultimate purpose for us Sorcerers, father?" I ask.

"For now, it is to complete as many assignments as possible in the limited amount of time we have left before my full plan comes to fruition. I will tell you – no, *show* you – more later. But for now, I will bestow the appointment of Sorcerer upon you when you get back from your next assignment."

I'm beyond thrilled. The day I'd looked forward to, and studied so hard for, has finally arrived! It's the best birthday present I could have asked for. And the fact that it was so unexpected has left me even more excited than I can contain. I flip through the pages of the book of assignments.

"Which one should I do next?" I ask myself out loud in excitement.

My father's hand reaches down and holds my hand still on the book's pages.

"This one - we will do it together. Father and son."

Chapter 3

The Wright Brothers

Vesuvius is pointing down to a line in the *Book of Historiarum,* but out of habit I instead open my pocket watch to see what and where our assignment is:

DECEMBER 17, 1903, 10:35
KILL DEVIL HILLS, NORTH CAROLINA
STOP THE FLIGHT

My father sees me use the pocket watch and smirks. "You won't be needing that for this assignment. Just follow my lead."

Even though I've gone on probably a hundred assignments over the years, I'm both excited and nervous to have one with my father. I hope I live up to what he expects of me. But then again, I suppose I shouldn't worry too much. After all, we want the same thing: to prevent evil. However, I'm also still very curious about several things, and hope that I can use this rare experience as an opportunity to learn even more from him – especially since it sounds like I'll be more on my own once I'm appointed as a Sorcerer.

"So, now, where do you keep the doorway to Lemuria?" He asks.

"Oh, it's in the library downstairs. Follow me."

Vesuvius turns and looks down at the rest of the library, as if he's looking at a part of history which is inferior to the present day.

I couldn't agree more. . .

As we walk down the staircase, Vesuvius examines around it. "So, you're still living here, then?"

I just nod, not sure if living here meets his approval.

Vesuvius continues, "I don't know why you wouldn't. The library's better than the Capitol, at least. The Capitol has become worth nothing more than a pile of stones."

Whew – I'm glad he approves!

Vesuvius pauses while glancing down at the whole library below. As if he's not sure he should even be mentioning it, he asks: "Have you found . . . oh, never mind. . . ."

His mysterious tone instantly catches my attention. "No, father, what is it? Have I found what?"

He again hesitates before deciding to continue what he started. "There's a secret . . . er, *special,* area within this library which has been used by Sorcerers. It's unknown to Wizards."

"But, why haven't you told me about this before?" I exclaim. The idea of there being a treasure trove of knowledge used by Sorcerers for millennia is instantly intriguing.

"Because you're not a Sorcerer. Well, you *weren't* a Sorcerer."

"So, where is it?" My excitement is about to burst out of me.

"Patience, son. One thing at a time. If you haven't found it yourself by now, then perhaps you're not meant to find it yet. Now, we have an assignment to complete. Where is your pathway to Lemuria?"

Disappointed that I'll have to wait until another day to discover this mysterious hidden section of the Library, I focus on the assignment at hand. "It's just over here." I signal to a stone enclave containing several books that I had fallen asleep studying before my assignment to obtain Newton's apple.

The tapestry to Lemuria hangs in the enclave. Even though I don't tell Vesuvius that it's where I often sleep, I think he can tell. Ignoring this, though, he stops to admire the doorway to Lemuria.

"You know, such a simple doorway took ages to create. Don't take it for granted. The pathway to Lemuria is not simple without it."

Ouch!

Immediately, I feel a pinch in my chest that I can't explain. But just as quick as it comes, it also goes away just as fast – almost like it was meant to remind me of something.

Strange...

Vesuvius inspects me cautiously when he sees me wince and rub my chest. Ignoring my momentary pain, he just continues: "Wouldn't it be great if we didn't even need to travel through Lemuria to get to the human world? Wouldn't everything be so much easier if we could just bridge the two worlds?" I'm not really sure if he's actually talking to me or just thinking out loud, though, since he stares straight at the tapestry while speaking.

"You mean, bridge Terra Fabula and the human world?" I ask. "How would that even be possible?"

Vesuvius turns from looking at the doorway and smiles right at me like he knows a secret that I don't. "We shall see. Now, let's get on with our assignment."

We step through the doorway and into my room in Lemuria. For a moment, I'm embarrassed at all of the "trophies" I've kept from my assignments which lay strewn around. I feel like a kid whose parents just came home from vacation to find the house trashed.

"Relics, huh?" Vesuvius says while examining the room, graciously describing them as something more than trophies. He smiles in amusement. "I suppose it does add a certain amount of … *color* to the place." I think this is the first wise-crack I've ever heard from my father, and I honestly don't even know how to react.

The awkward moment of silence ends, though, when Vesuvius interrupts. "Funny that you found the same room which I had used in my younger days to complete assignments. In fact, it looks like some of *my* old souvenirs are still here as well."

Vesuvius used to complete assignments as well?

When I hear my father talk about his younger days, I realize just how very little I actually know about his past. His prior silence in discussing his past, and vague way in which he just brought it up for the first time, leaves me with a mysterious feeling.

"Well," Vesuvius continues, "since this will be my last trip through time for quite a while, I suppose I'll create the path."

Vesuvius then holds out his wand and recites a spell that creates a shimmering circle of light suspended in the air. "*Tempus initere 12-17-1903, Kill Devil Hills, North Carolina, 10:25.*" I've done this exact thing numerous times myself, after having learned it from him. I know that it's the spell to create a doorway to a certain place and time in history. And each time I've wondered the same thing...

Is this a tempore nuntis that I've read about in the books?

I seize this learning moment as an opportunity to be taught more about sorcery. "Father, is this a *tempore nuntis?*"

Vesuvius scoffs. "No, Acea – a *tempore nuntis* is a child's game. Those are just a window to a place in time – a child's game. *This* is a *tempus initere."*

"*Tempus initere?*" I repeat. "I've never read that term before in any book."

"No, you wouldn't." I look quizzically at Vesuvius, who interprets my look and continues to explain. "That library was written by a bunch of Wizards. They're afraid of *tempus initere.* What did I tell you before? Wizards have no purpose, they just maintain the status quo - so they don't have *tempus initere.* But Sorcerers do – *we* do."

My father's emphasis on "we" excites me and gives us a united purpose. "Well, father, let's prevent evil from occurring!"

He smiles devilishly back at me – just like he had forgotten until now how he had explained things to me long ago, but that he's nevertheless impressed I remembered it. We both look ahead to the shimmering light in front of us. "After you," I say.

"Grab your wand," he responds. "You're going to need it."

My father's grin increases as he holds out his wand and touches the doorway, disappearing instantly. I take a moment to myself before I enter the doorway, just enjoying this rare opportunity with my father. I take a deep breath and stare straight ahead - the same devilish grin that my father wore is now adorning me as well. I touch my wand to the doorway and travel back in time to 1903.

I appear through the shimmering doorway of light leading to Kill Devil Hills in North Carolina. My father is waiting for me restlessly. "What took you so long?" He asks, wand in hand and not really wanting to hear an answer. Rather, he's looking toward a hill in eager anticipation. "Come, that's where we're headed – let's get going!"

The fact that we appeared in the middle of nowhere – just a field of tall grass – is surprising. I glance around to see if there's any possibility of this being a trap, but really – there's nothing around. I feel a strong breeze signaling that we must be close to the ocean, but otherwise there's nothing here. My father is far ahead, marching toward a tall hill. The wind blows his long black cape behind him, and I enjoy the sight of my father's dominant, confident presence before I run to catch up to him.

"So, father, what's the plan?" I try to not let the excitement in my voice show too much. I'm eighteen now, after all – I don't want to sound like I'm twelve or something.

Very directly, as if he's been looking forward to this moment for quite some time, Vesuvius responds: "We're going to show mankind that *only Sorcerers fly.*"

"Fly?" I almost interrupt, "But we can't fly."

Vesuvius stops in his tracks, his eyes wide in disbelief. "What do you mean, you don't know how to fly?" I don't even get to try to justify myself (even though I have none), before my father just continues. "Well, what have you been doing in the library for all of these years? Have you learned *anything* useful?"

"Well of course I have, father. I learned about..."

"Acea, we are Sorcerers *not* historians. You must be learning things which are *useful* – spells which you'll need in the *war*...."

War? What war?

I don't have a chance to interrupt him, though, as he continues to scold me. "So I just guess that this time, I'll have to teach it to you myself. I'll even teach you the old verbal command. *Ascendet indignation caelum.*"

Just like that Vesuvius is immediately whisked up several feet into the air. He levitates with such ease that undoubtedly he's conquered mastering this spell.

I pull out my pocket watch to secure it around a belt loop, just to make sure it doesn't fall out while I try to learn to fly. Out of habit, I pop it open to briefly see what time it is. My heart sinks, though, when I see the minute hand move from 10:33 a.m. to 10:34 a.m. Immediately, I hear cheers and hollers begin to echo from the other side of the hill.

Only one minute left! We're going to miss the time – we'll fail this assignment!

I begin to yell this up to my father, but he's already well aware of what I'm thinking. The same devilish smirk he adorned earlier reappears before speaking to me. "We won't fail the assignment. I want us to be late."

"…but why?"

"To make a statement."

"What statement?"

"Only *Sorcerers* fly," He repeats. "Now follow me."

Without even waiting to see if I can fly with the spell, Vesuvius begins slowly gliding to the top of the hill. I take his lack of waiting as a sign that he's just confident in my abilities to quickly master the spell as well.

Ascendet indignation caelum.

Just as my father, I'm immediately pushed up high into the air. And flying is not a problem. Rather, I feel as though I belong in the air – not because I'm meant to fly, but because I'm meant to conquer my abilities in magic. Flying comes as natural to me as magic does – which means that it's almost intuitive.

I quickly catch up to my father. Side by side, we fly in tandem over the hill. With our wands in hand, our presence is powerful and direct. We have a statement to make to these humans.

It feels good not to have to hide my magical abilities during this assignment, and I briefly wonder why we don't have to – contrary to what my father has told me before. But my thought is interrupted when I see Vesuvius raise his wand.

Just as he raises it, we ascend over the top of the hill and the view of the other side comes into focus.

Crackle!

Immediately, a lightning bolt of power zaps out of my father's wand in a thunderous crackle of light.

As soon as I see where the bolt is going, I realize what he hit: a simple, primitive aircraft manned by one pilot laying in the middle. The bolt of magic doesn't bring the plane down, though it obviously creates a tear in its wing.

"Ahh!" The pilot yells unexpectedly while trying to maneuver in hope of avoiding crashing to the ground. "I've been hit!"

Vesuvius and I are descending the hill behind a group of people watching this first flight of man.

I know who these people are. They've come to watch the Wright Brothers' first manned flight. How dare they – how dare the humans think that they can fly.

In anger I point my wand and shoot at the airplane as well. I don't even bother shooting just one bolt, though. No – I need to teach these humans a lesson.

Instantly, my repetitive bursts of lightning send the aircraft crashing to the ground in a pile of sticks and smoke. I see the pilot limp away from the burning crash site, leaving me smiling in pride.

That'll teach him.

By now the cluster of onlookers – no doubt being a select group of news journalists and other influential minds – have all begun scattering in fear. Their screams ring off of the hillside before retreating into their cars to escape the chaotic scene. Vesuvius and I send a couple more bolts down to the ground – just to emphasize who is in command.

My father nods down to the two Wright Brothers and I follow him over to where they stand hopeless in the grasses.

"Who… who are you?" One of them trembles while gazing at our magnificence up in the air. "Why did you do that?" He's attending to his brother, who looks too injured to do any talking.

"Only *Sorcerers* fly." My father says emphatically. Every time I hear Vesuvius say that I feel more and more like I, too, am close to finally being a Sorcerer.

Soon enough…

Vesuvius shoots a threatening look toward the two brothers before flying off - his terseness leaving a forceful demand ringing in the air to these humans.

Well, that definitely was the exact statement he wanted to make!

I glance over to the pieces of wood strewn about the ground which used to be the Wright Brothers' first successfully manned airplane. I look back at the brothers huddled together in fear. While looking at them in the eye, hovering above them, I point my wand at what remains of the airplane and shoot it with one last lightning bolt. Flames jet up into the air and I bask in the sight of the horrified looks on the brothers' faces.

Assignment completed.

When I turn around, I see that my father has stopped briefly at the foot of the hill to witness what I've done. I quickly fly off to him. As I approach, I hear him speak.

"Well done, Acea. I have no doubt that you are ready for what comes next."

I know what the answer is, but I still ask him – wanting to hear him say it again out loud. "And what's that?"

"To become as I am – a Sorcerer. It's time."

Chapter 4

Cadeyrn

We storm into the Great Library, fresh from the victory of the last assignment.

"Ahh, that felt great," my father exclaims while moving the wooden stand from the middle of the tapestry-lined room. "Almost just like the old days for me."

"Old days?" I ask. "You mean you once also...." I begin to finally ask about my father's old days completing assignments but he interrupts me.

"Well, of course," Vesuvius says sharply. His tone tells me he wants to boast about his past, but that it's something he still keeps guarded. "I too was young once and learned from a very skilled Sorcerer just as you are." He grins, knowing he just referred to himself as being very skilled.

The idea of my father being anything other than a skilled, experienced Sorcerer is something that I never thought of. Though, I suppose, the more I think about it – the more it makes sense. He must have learned sorcery from someone, too, I guess. But the thought of my father being a young Wizard only makes me more curious.

Why did he become a Sorcerer? What was he like before he became one? Is he the only Sorcerer in his lineage?

I'm about to ask my father more about it, but I'm surprised that I don't have to. It's almost as though I've opened the door to a golden period of my father's life that he's enjoying recollecting… now that he's finally let his guard down a little to share it.

"You see, I was just about your age when I realized that wizardry wasn't … complete. The lack of full expression of my feelings was unsatisfying." While Vesuvius talks, I notice that he's continuing to re-arrange the middle of this part of the library – tidying it up for some unknown reason. "I happened upon sorcery at the right time. I'm not sure if I found it or if it found me, but the completeness of its practice and … philosophy … seemed natural to me. Then, *he* came to me. And after many years being trapped in … well, never mind that. Anyways, here I am today, ready for you to assume it."

"Assume what?" I ask.

"Well, the Oath of Sorcery, of course."

My father stops re-arranging things in the library and the room is now generally clean. I have no idea why, though – and I really don't even have any idea of what's going on or what Vesuvius has been talking about.

"Vesuvius, father – what are you talking ab...."

Before I can finish, though, immediately there's a flash of light in the center of the room where the wooden stand used to be. It's so unexpected that I jump back in a defensive stance with my wand drawn. The flash recedes and now in the middle of the room there appears to be a barely noticeable shift in the light.

Almost like a ... wait, it is ... we're on the receiving side of a tempus initere! Someone is travelling thru time to visit us!

I can't stop staring at the portal, wondering who is going to appear. But out of the corner of my eye, I see my father bow to one knee. I'm not sure exactly what's going on, but I figure doing the same thing as my father would at least be prudent.

Bowing to one knee, I lower my head to the ground as my father is also doing. I hear footprints appear from the doorway. Still staring at the ground, in part out of my nervousness for the unknown situation that's unexpectedly occurring, I hear the footprints first move toward my father. Then, suddenly I see pointed shoes right in front of me.

Without any warning, a finger touches my bowing chin and moves it upwards. Two piercing green eyes stare straight into me. Not at me, but *into* me. For a split second I have another one of my unusual flashbacks to another unknown experience where I've seen these eyes before. But I have *no* idea where from.

What's going on?

The flash quickly disappears, thankfully, and I'm now left focusing on the eyes staring straight into me.

The man doesn't even make an expression, rather his eyes say everything. He knows who I am, though I have absolutely no idea who he is.

In a menacing voice, the man speaks: "I have been waiting for this exact moment, Acea."

Am I his enemy? I certainly feel like I am. Who is this man?

"Who ..." At the risk of sounding nervous in front of my father, I clear my throat and start again more confidently – hoping my nervousness isn't exposed. "Who are you?"

The man looks over to my father. "Are you sure he's ready? You were much more ... mature at his age. And much less nervous."

"Oh he's ready," my father says, luckily. "I assure you of that. His feelings, and *powers,* are much more advanced than mine even were at such a young age. Besides, we're running out of time. We need him. War is upon us."

The man glances back at me, still calculating whether I meet his approval. "Well, what do you have to say for yourself?" When I get over the fact that he's still staring straight at me with that same piercing look, I realize he just asked me a question. I may not know who he is, but I do know he's asking me if I think I'm ready to be a Sorcerer.

"If you're asking whether I'm ready to be a Sorcerer, I am. I have completed every assignment that I've been given and…"

"Enough about the assignments," the man interrupts. "Are you *ready*."

"Ready for what?" I respond. To be honest, I'm getting impatient with his vague questions and not having a clue about what exactly is going on or who this man is.

"I will ask again, are you *ready*?" The man says, even more menacing than before.

By now, I'm furious. I want answers and instead this stranger is playing a game with me. I'm just about to answer, when he doesn't even give me a chance – instead asking me the same vague question *again*.

"Are you *rea…*"

"That's it!" I yell, having been thrown over the edge. Any shred of my initial nervousness is now long gone. I rise up quickly from having been kneeling and pull out my wand. Pointing it directly at the man, I speak firmly and threateningly. "Don't you dare ask me again! If I say I'm ready, then I am! Now, I want to know right now who you are and where you came from!"

For the first time, a grin adorns the man's face. "Well, there you are. *That's the Acea I remember.*"

Remember?! Who is this man? What is he talking about?

The fact that I had some type of flashback or something when I first saw his eyes is haunting. I feel like there's something I should know, but I absolutely have no clue what's giving me this strange feeling. Fortunately, the stranger continues before I'm forced to reveal my uncertainty with what's going on.

"I am Cadeyrn, and I have been waiting a very long time to meet you again."

Cadeyrn – I know that name! He's the man who gave my father the Book of Historiarum.

. . .And what does he mean he's been waiting to meet me again?

"Acea," my father says, "Cadeyrn was the man I told you about who came to me and taught me how to be a Sorcerer. He is here to appoint you a Sorcerer."

Cadeyrn holds his wand up and flicks his wrist. Instantly, a black cape appears in front of him. He holds it out to me and speaks. "Today is your ceremony where you receive your cape. You may now bow."

With that, I bow again before Cadeyrn, completely excited that this is the very moment I've been waiting so long for. I will now become a Sorcerer! Cadeyrn lays the black cape around my shoulders, and I instantly feel as though I've graduated from childhood into the same ranks as these two great, powerful Sorcerers.

I see the black, silk-like material of the cape flow down to the ground around my shoulders and I'm prideful in now being among the few who get to wear one. I've stared so many times at my father's cape, looking forward to the day when I too would have one – knowing it represents respect by others toward the high rank of Sorcerer which I've achieved.

Cadeyrn points his wand down toward me. "Now, Acea, join your wand with mine and repeat the Oath of Sorcery after me."

When I touch my wand to Cadeyrn's, I feel something … strange. It's powerful, but not in a fulfilling way. Rather, the power running through my wand and into me gives me a strong sense of emotion – every emotion from pride to anger. I focus on Cadeyrn's intense stare and try to collect myself so as to ensure I accurately repeat the Oath as he says it:

"Omnia spondeo sequi te, et ut pugnarent contra illos qui rejiciunt plenum usum magicae. Totum me huic trado omnino omnis autem affectionis meo. Vivat Sorcery!"

"Now rise," Cadeyrn directs.

Having taken the Oath to join their exclusive status, I stand up - not knowing what to expect.

"Your father will now instruct you on the rules."

Rules? What rules?

Vesuvius walks over to me, and Cadeyrn takes a step back – watching carefully to ensure the rules are accurately conveyed.

"Son," Vesuvius begins. Though he was unusually cheerful previously, his usual direct tone of voice has now returned. "There are three time travel rules which you must swear to abide by before you are adopted as a Sorcerer. The first: you must never time travel to visit Cadeyrn – he will come to you, if he chooses to come to you. The second: you must never time travel to visit members of the Order of the Nine in the past. It is fruitless and a waste of time."

Order of the Nine . . . I've read about that group in the library.

I had always assumed that this ancient Order was disbanded or extinguished over time. So, I have no problem agreeing – traveling to the past to visit an abandoned, failed group of Wizards with lesser power than myself seems like a waste of time.

"And, perhaps most importantly – the third: you must *never* time travel to look at your own past or future. With regard to the past, it is not meaningful – the only thing that matters is what you will do, not what you may have done. In regards to travelling to your future, everyone's future is fluid – it is not carved into stone yet. Therefore it cannot be trusted and will only deceive your belief of who you really are."

This last rule is troubling to me. I've always been curious about what my future held and often figured I'd get around to sneaking up on my future-self one day when I have enough time. And as to travelling to the past, I've been especially curious about seeing what things were like before I met my father six years ago. That far-away time period is so fuzzy to me that it's almost like it didn't even happen. And especially with my sudden and unexpected flashbacks I've been experiencing lately, I've been wondering if there's something in my past which could help explain them.

But, just as Vesuvius instructed, I know that my past is nowhere near as important as what I am capable of accomplishing: greatness. Knowing that, and along with my desire to finally become a Sorcerer, there isn't even really a decision to make.

"I promise," I say.

"Ha ha," Cadeyrn laughs shrewdly. "You don't really think all you have to do is say that you promise, do you?"

. . . Actually, I did . . .

Cadeyrn shoots his hand out and grabs my left arm, holding it out in front of me. His intense grip around my wrist almost cuts into me, and the pain is excruciating. I grimace in pain and close my eyes, wondering what he's doing and why whatever he's doing is taking so long.

Is this a trick? Is he testing me?

I open my eyes and stare directly into his face, trying to decipher his motives.

"Your will power is strong, I can tell you have much inside of you waiting to burst out." Cadeyrn says to me. I still can't tell his motives, but seeing my father calmly standing behind Cadeyrn reinforces that this is not an unusual part of the ceremony. "As a Sorcerer you will learn to harness this potential and will be of much value to our side in the war."

Just when I think the pain couldn't become any more intense, it magnifies greatly. Cadeyrn holds up his wand and points it at my wrist. When I feel an immense burning sensation in my wrist, I again close my eyes and grimace out loud. I've been trying to not make a sound, so as to not show any weakness in front of my father, but I'm unable to hold it in.

Flash!

When I open my eyes, though, I'm now seeing another image of something else.

My eyes must be deceiving me from all this pain. What's been happening to me lately?!

I don't have any more time to focus on why these flashes have been happening. Rather, the warmth I feel from what's in front of my eyes help me cope with the immense amount of pain I'm experiencing.

Instead of seeing Cadeyrn and his wand searing something into my left wrist, I see another person. This person is comforting, like an old memory of something good which I've long forgotten. Like seeing an old friend. The man has a short white beard and is old – kind of like the Wizards I'd read about in the Great Library. He, too, is using a wand to brand something into my wrist. However, whatever he's branding leaves in me the impression that it's something I want, not something that's being forced upon me. I look down at the brand in my wrist from this unknown man and am shocked to see a quick glimmer of the same seal I saw on the leather book in my prior flash – the one that's the seal of an abandoned Order of Wizards.

Suddenly, I know what the seal is!

This is the seal of the Order of the Nine.

Just as I have this realization, the pain in my wrist ends. The flash quickly dissipates and I see Cadeyrn staring into my eyes. Thrilled, he exclaims: "It is complete - you are now a Sorcerer as your father and I am." The sly smirk that comes across Cadeyrn's face gives me the feeling that he's won a victory of some kind. And rightfully so - I have, too. I have worked so hard to achieve this moment of finally becoming a Sorcerer like my father.

Immediately, I'm overcome with an overwhelming sensation from everywhere inside of me. The feeling's just as though every emotion of mine has been lit on fire, each stirring separately and wanting to burst out of me. Though I should feel confused by the wide array of feelings I'm suddenly experiencing, I'm not. Rather, each of those emotions is directed toward one purpose: to prevent evil. And right now, from what my father has directed, the method of doing this is to complete as many assignments as I can.

"I must get going onto the next assignment!" I burst out, both in excitement, anger, and haste.

"Yes, that's it," Cadeyrn exclaims from the corner of the room, smiling. "That's the Acea I remember – that's the Acea we need."

Cadeyrn then looks over to my father and nods as though his task here is completed. He walks slowly over to the shifted light of the *tempus initere* to return to wherever he came from.

"Wait!" I yell out loud to Cadeyrn. Though I was initially nervous at the sight of the old man, something about taking the Oath of Sorcery has united me with him. I now feel as though his purpose is engrained in me, and that I'll miss him once he leaves. "Where are you going? Why are you leaving so quickly? . . . I have so much I want to learn from you!"

My father just stands next to me, grinning as though he's won the lottery with my instant connection to his mentor.

For the first time since I've met him, Cadeyrn's expression changes from menacing to one of pity towards me. "You must now fully understand the Oath you just took. *You are now the same as I am – in all things.*"

With that, Cadeyrn turns toward the *tempus initere* to leave. But before he does, he turns back to me and issues one final thought. "Remember your time travel promise. Do not come find me. I will come to you."

"You will?" I ask almost desperately, wondering when I'll see him again next.

He just winks at me and vanishes through the doorway in time.

Vesuvius turns to me and speaks: "Congratulations, son. You have *no idea* how *long* I've waited to see this moment happen. You are my son. Now go and fulfill your full potential as a Sorcerer!"

Vesuvius walks over to the tapestry leading to his hidden Kingdom. Before he steps through, though, I ask the one question that's been on my mind since our trip to the Wright Brothers. "Father, why is it okay now to reveal our magic and the existence of Sorcerers to the human world?"

"No, no, Acea – it's not that it's now okay to do so, it's *necessary*. Perhaps we were more obvious with our magic during that assignment than we needed to be – I was testing you back there. It's still important to show some restraint so that we don't rely too heavily upon our magic. Nevertheless, we are in the eleventh hour before the war. We must step up the pace to ... prevent evil. We must ensure that the building blocks of the human world crumble faster and faster, for war is upon us."

"What war?" I finally ask. His mention of a war during our last assignment was the first time I'd ever heard him mention such a thing. Since then, both Vesuvius and Cadeyrn have mentioned it several times. I'm glad I remember to ask about it before my father retreats back to his Kingdom for some unknown period of time.

"What war?" He repeats, almost scolding. "Oh, my son – how I forget that you truly know so little. Focus on your assignments for now. When the time is right, I will show you what I am talking about."

He's just about to step through his tapestry-doorway when I ask one last question. "But how will I know which assignment out of this whole book is the one I should do next?"

"That, Acea, is up to you. For you are now the same as I am, in all things. Use your feelings."

With that, my father disappears through the tapestry back into his Kingdom. I run up to the tapestry to try and see if anything is briefly visible through the doorway. As always – no luck. Just complete blackness.

One day I'll get to see my father's Kingdom again.

I stop, though, and just peer into the blackness. It hits me. I'm a Sorcerer now. Finally, after *all* of these years, I'm a Sorcerer!

That means . . . one day, this will be <u>my</u> Kingdom!

The feeling of power and pride wells up inside of me almost to the point of it being uncontrollable. I feel the brand on my wrist and look at it for the first time. It's a circle with one line through the middle. One line – not surprising. Us Sorcerers are all the same now, as if we are one in the same. I trace the brand with my fingers – it still hurts due to being a fresh wound. I can't help but stare at it, though, without having the uneasy recollection of my prior flash with the seal of the Order of the Nine. Since I feel that I'm having these flashes for a reason, I decide to keep an eye and ear open for anything that can shed light on what's happening to me, as well as anything about this ancient Order of now-defunct Wizards. Until then, I'm going to enjoy my newfound status as a Sorcerer – I've earned it!

With a large smile on my face, I turn to the *Book of Historiarum* laying on the wooden stand. I flip it open and just stare in excitement at all of the dates written inside.

Which one will I do next? Which one do I want to do next?

My new freedom to adventure through time at will is exciting! I glance down at an assignment instruction that says "Shoot the First Shot."

That sounds cool.

I recite the spell to Lemuria and enter my trophy room within. In full confidence of my power and magical abilities due to now being a Sorcerer, I don't even stop to plan for what I may find on the other side of the *tempus initere* before I travel there.

"Tempus initere 4-19-1775, Lexington, Massachusetts, 6:02."

Here I go!

Chapter 5

Paul Revere

Bang!

. . . . Wait, what was tha. . . .

Bang! Bang! Bang!

The portal-doorway has dropped me in the middle of a field of tall grass. It's the evening and almost dark, but I think that all around me. . . .

Bang! Bang! Bang! Bang!

Yep, those are definitely gun shots! I've been laying low on my stomach, hiding among the grass so as not to be seen. To my left is a large group of men constantly firing at something to my right. While trying not to make a sound in the grass, I reach down to my pocket to get my watch – hoping it'll tell me where I need to go.

Yuck. I'm lying in several inches of mud.

The ground is so muddy that I'm covered in it. I open the pocket watch, but even have to try to clean the inside off due to how dirty my hands and fingers are. It's nearly dark outside, so I have a tough time reading the inside of my watch. But my hopes sink when I see what it says.

What? Are you kidding me?

I've been brought to April 18, 1775, and *not* April 19, 1775. I know this because the inside of my watch is engraved to say "April 19, 1775, 6:02 a.m." However, the sun is going down and it's almost dark outside. That means I've been brought to sometime just before the event where I need to "shoot the first shot." I've often wondered how the spell knows exactly where and when to transport me for each assignment, but I don't have any time to think about that now – there's gunshots being fired all around me!

Laying on my stomach, I reach around and put my pocket watch into the back pocket of my muddy pants. It's time now to find my way out of here.

"Gentlemen, well done!" One man yells from the group. "Keep practicing, for we march to Lexington early tomorrow morning!"

"Yes, sir, Lieutenant Smith!" I hear several men respond eagerly.

I'm in the middle of a field being used as a practice firing range! I've got to get out of here before they find me . . . or worse yet, before I get shot!

I cautiously glance up from my hiding spot, hoping to find a way out of this dangerous situation. Peeking just above the top of the grasses, I see a forest to my right. I turn and look at the large group of men practicing shooting with their rifles, and am amazed at how there are hundreds of men in red jackets camped at the outskirts of the field.

"Hey, what's that?" One man suddenly yells.

"I think it's some kind of animal," another yells.

"Well, whatever it is, I bet I can shoot it!"

"Ahhh!" I yell out instinctively in fear of my life. I yelled out loud without even thinking about it, but maybe it'll help them realize not to shoot at me.

"Look, it's really a rebel spy – shoot him!"

Immediately, gun fire rapidly rings out from behind me. I dart off running at full speed to the protection of the forest, still yelling out loud. "Don't shoot, don't shoot! I'm not a spy - ahhh!"

It's no use. I hear banter from the group in back of me saying things like "I don't see a red jacket," "if he's not a spy, then why's he running," and "well, why was he hiding in the field then?" Gun shots continue flying all around me, and I initially have no time to think about what to do other than to run for my life.

But with my wand in hand, I suddenly remember that it's okay to use magic now. I go to shoot back at the group, but just as I do an intense sting hits me from behind! I fall to the ground, pain instantly piercing into my backside.

"We got him, let's go!"

The men rustle through the grass and slop through the mud, getting closer to where I lay maimed.

"When we get him, let's bring him to Lieutenant Smith – he'll know how to get information from him."

Through the darkness befalling the shooting range, I hear the rustling of the men moving closer. I reach to my backside to feel how much blood there is. But to my surprise, there's none! However, sharp pain is still shooting through me. I don't know why there isn't any blood, though, since I know without a doubt that I've been shot. Through the distraction of the immense pain, I continue to hear the men talking as they search for me.

"Well, if he's not with Britain, then he's got to be against us."

"And if he's not with us, then he must have heard our plan."

"Yeah, and there's only one thing to do if he heard our plan."

The situation is getting worse. Trying to think clearly, I realize that I only have two options: either lay low and try to hide among the grass and mud, hoping they don't catch me, or try to run for my life. The only risk to running is that they could keep shooting at me if they've still got their muskets with them. But, really, if I hide here there's little hope that they won't find me. The pain is so intense that I have a hard time thinking straight through my deliria. All I know is that I want out of this situation.

I'm running for it.

I jet up and run as fast as I can toward the forest about twenty yards in front of me. Every other step I take is more of a hobble, but I just focus on the trees to try and distract me from the agonizing pain.

"There he goes!"

"Let's get him!"

"I'll shoot him from here!"

"Ahhhh! No, don't!" I yell again, trying with everything I have to make to the trees for cover.

They do still have their muskets!

Bang! Bang!

I hear bullets wiz past me, and I know it's just a matter of time until they hit their target – me!

Wait, I can use my magic to turn invisible. . . . Oh no - Where's my wand?

In the rush to make it to the forest for safety, I had dropped my wand into the mud back in the grass. There's nothing I can do right now. I feel naked without it.

Bullet after bullet continues to zip by me and strike the trees in front and to the side of me. I can't believe how lucky I am that they're not better shots.

I don't know how they're ever gonna win a battle – I guess that's why they were practicing when I got here.

I reach the forest. Rather than immediately jumping behind a tree for cover, I continue to scurry into it – hoping that they'll give up once they see how deep I've gotten into the woods. I zig-zag among the trees so as to try to make them lose track of my direction of travel. The fact that my back is covered in dark mud is certainly an advantage. I'm a dark figure moving through a dark forest. Unfortunately, I'm not moving very fast anymore due to my injury.

After several minutes of this, I can no longer ignore the intensity of the pain in my leg. When my hobbling turns more into a slow limp, I stop behind a tree and just listen for a moment – hoping I'll be able to decipher whether the men are still hunting me down.

Several minutes go by without a sound.

I think I've lost them.

I exhale out loud from the pain I've been enduring and go to examine my wound.

Snap!

...what was that?

Something just broke a tree branch on the ground. I instantly duck to the ground, covering my head with my arms for safety. I should begin running, but the pain is just too much. I can't even take a step with that leg.

They've found me.

When several more branches snap, I *know* they've found me – the sounds come from directly in front of where I'm huddled down. I can tell they're approaching – they're probably circling around me.

I'm toast. Even if I could run, they've likely surrounded me.

I'm about to look up to confront my captors head on, when I'm surprised by what I hear next.

"Psst – hey kid!"

What?....

"Look, we don't have much time – they're close by. Can you hop on?"

I look up, shocked by the lucky turn of events which appears to be happening.

"I … I think so," I say, obviously in pain. If this man is my enemy, he undoubtedly knows I'm in a compromised position right now due to my injury.

I have no other option, though, but to trust the man. He's riding a horse and extending a hand down to me. "Climb on up – we need to get out of here. Quickly, now."

I limp over to the horse and grab the man's hand. He pulls me up so that I'm sitting in front of him. I get the feeling that he knows how weak I am right now, and wants to make sure I don't fall off the horse.

"Okay, hold on tight – and don't worry, I've got you as well... Yaw!" The man says while spurring his horse. The horse jolts forward and begins running through the forest. I hear the men behind us catch on to our escape and begin firing in our direction. We weave through the trees at an alarming rate, and I know we're now clear of the group that was hunting me down.

I still feel delirious from my pain, but I know I should find out as much as I can about the stranger I'm entrusting myself to. I'm about to start asking questions, but he does first.

"So, are you a Brit or rebel?"

"I . . . I don't know what you're talking about." Still not having a clue as to how I'm supposed to "shoot the first shot" on this assignment, I decide to not risk taking a side.

"Well, are you with the British?"

"No." I say concisely in pain. I figure I'm telling the truth. I'm not a redcoat or a rebel – I really don't even know what those are.

"I guess that's good enough for me. Now, did you hear anything about their plans?"

"Yes," I admit. Again, I'm not deciding to take a side, so I figure I should just be as useful to this man as possible right now.

"Well, boy – tell me everything you know!"

"They said something about marching to Lexington..."

The man gasps and interrupts me mid-sentence in anticipation. "When? Did they say when?"

"Early tomorrow morning." I'm not sure if it's the pain or the galloping of the horse, but my head is now hurting immensely. The only thing that seems to help is if I close my eyes and drift off to slee....

"Boy!" The man yells, startling me awake for a moment. "Wake up – I need to know if you heard any names."

My head begins getting woozy and I have a hard time thinking. The bobbing up and down through the woods isn't helping, but I seem to remember one of the men saying that their lieutenant would get information out of me.

What was his name... what was his name... Oh, I know – Lieutenant Smith!

I blurt it out to the stranger, and he can tell I'm drifting off uncontrollably.

"Hang on there, son – we're just riding into town. You have no idea how much you've helped us. We'll take care of you."

Just then I see lights up ahead from a town. The man veers out of the woods and rides through the dirt road into the middle of the town. Initially, there's no one else along the streets. It's long been dark now, so they're probably all inside for the night.

At the sight of safely reaching the town, I again start to drift off to sleep. With my eyes closed, I hear the stranger begin yelling out loud: "The British are coming! The British are coming!"

Instantaneously, the town comes alive. I hear doors to the houses open and men come running up to us. The man stops his horse and flops me back into his arms. Before handing me off to someone, he consoles me. "Young man, my name is Paul Revere. We're in Lexington, and we'll take care of you now."

Chapter 6

The Shot Heard 'Round The World

I open my eyes, dazed at my surroundings. I'm lying on a well-worn mattress in a bed off to the side of a large room in an old wooden house.

This feels incredible.

It's been years since I've actually slept in a bed. Most of the time, I fall asleep on the library floor with blankets and using a pile of books as a pillow. I'd once thought about going to get a mattress from inside the Capitol, but never got around to it.

I move to get up, but a woman notices my movement. She's standing by a group of people huddled around a table. But when she notices me, she runs over to me with a worried look on her face.

"It's okay – you're okay. Easy now," the lady says. "You're fortunate, you know. You weren't actually injured from the bullet…"

It certainly felt like I was!

"The bullet hit this – your pocket watch protected you," She continues. "Without it, you'd be much worse off." The lady holds it up and my heart jumps.

My pocket watch! What time is it? How bad has it been damaged?

I grab it from the lady and examine it to see whether it works or not. There's a large hole in the middle of the front cover, with it essentially being blown open and shredded. Worried that it won't work for me anymore, I open it to see if it's still ticking. The glass covering is cracked, but luckily that appears to be the only thing broken. The hands still move. Unfortunately, the inscription inside of the cover is useless from the front cover's damage.

5:36 a.m. – less than thirty minutes until I'm supposed to complete this assignment. I wonder what I'm actually supposed to do.

"Oh good, the boy's awake." I hear one man say to the group of other men around the table.

They all walk over to me, and I see that Paul Revere is among them. "How are you feeling?" He asks.

I just nod as if I'm alright and stare at the group in front of me. Paul breaks the ice by asking. "So, is there anything else you remember overhearing the British say about their plan?"

"No, I think I told you everything. Mainly, I just wanted to run for my life."

The first man chimes in: "Well now, speak up – who are you, then?" He asks sternly, trying to determine if he can trust me.

There's one thing I know: I want to complete my assignment,

and I need to do it soon. I figure the best way to do this is to fit in with their group somehow. Responding confidently, I answer: "My name's Acea. I was just on my way to town to warn you of Britain's plan, but they caught me."

"You're a Patriot, then?" Another man says.

I nod my head. "You don't see a redcoat, do you?" I hope the group believes me. Fortunately, I'd seen that all of the British men were wearing red coats.

"Well, then," the first man says. "You're going to need a gun!"

Someone else from the group hands me a gun, and the first man continues to explain the situation. "My name is John Parker. This here group is one of the Massachusetts Militia. Son, you may have just helped save several of these men's lives with the information you gave Mr. Revere."

I look at the group behind John Parker. For the first time I realize that the group's much larger than I even realized. I'd guess that there are about seventy to eighty men armed and ready to fight. But, from what I remember seeing of the British army, I have an uneasy feeling.

"Mr. Parker, I don't think there's enough men here." I say meekly, breaking bad news to the man who seems to be their leader.

"What? How many men would you say the British have?" He

asks.

"From what I saw, I'd say several hundred."

John Parker grunts, looking toward another man. "Sergeant Munroe, did you hear that? Make sure each man is armed and understands the stakes – we'll need every last one of them."

"Yes, Captain," Sergeant Munroe responds.

Captain Parker then turns to Paul Revere and the two other men to his side. "Mr. Revere, I need you and your two other scouts to begin riding toward Concord at once. When …. er, *if* … the British break through our militia, they will then undoubtedly march toward Concord."

"Yes, sir," Paul Revere says. He turns and winks to me just before leaving immediately, as ordered.

The group of men around the large open room of this old house had been in an anxious uproar when word spread that I'd seen several hundred British redcoats. But when Captain Parker turns to everyone and begins speaking, they quickly fall quiet and listen to his speech.

"Men," Captain Parker instructs with stern authority, "the redcoats are almost here. I don't know how many of us will fall today. Some of you are farmers, and some of you are trained militiamen. But there's one thing we all have in common. We are all

Patriots. And when we leave this tavern, we're united in one cause – to revolt against the crown that seeks to tax and punish every hardworking colonist and their families on this new continent. We will not have it! We will obtain our freedom from such oppression!"

The group of men cheers in support. "So what's the plan?" Someone yells from the back.

Captain Parker quiets the crowd before divulging his strategy. "We may not have an advantage in numbers, but we can surprise them."

The feeling of excitement is quickly buzzing from the electric crowd, and everyone is quiet so as to hear the specifics of the plan.

Captain Parker continues: "Like I said, most of us here are simple farmers, and that's exactly what we look like. We'll leave Buckman Tavern and walk over to the Lexington Common Grounds in town square. Once there, we'll be in parade-ground formation – in plain sight but not blocking the redcoats' road to Concord. Stand your ground. Don't fire unless fired upon, but if they mean to have a war, let it begin here."

With that, the militia of ordinary-looking men all leave the tavern and walk towards the Commons as the Captain had directed. Being among the last to leave, I hear Captain Parker lean over to Sergeant Munroe and comment: "Sergeant, I believe this is where the Revolutionary War will begin. Whoever shoots the first shot, it'll be heard around the world."

That's it! That's what I must do to complete this assignment – shoot the shot heard around the world!

Undeterred by the expectation of being outnumbered, the men arrive at the Commons in the heart of the town. They do exactly what the Captain ordered and assume the parade-ground formation around the square. I also line up along the exterior of the Commons, knowing that I'll somehow have to be involved in this battle if I'm going to successfully complete this assignment. Holding my musket tight with one hand, and wishing instead that it was my wand, I grab my pocket watch with the other.

5:57 a.m. – exactly five minutes until the time for my assignment to be completed.

. . . But – where are the redcoats?

"Psst – hey solider," a man next to me whispers. "What's the deal with your black cape anyways?"

But just as I'm about to make up some explanation, the British approach down the main street at an alarmingly fast speed! The front section of the company is led by many men on horses, while two different companies flank in from both sides. They all converge at the same time to the middle of the Commons, drawing the surprise of the Patriots. The Patriot soldiers are all alarmed by how fast the situation has evolved, but none break the commands given by Captain Parker.

One redcoat on horseback rides to the front of the troops. Several lines of horses are behind him, and a line of redcoat men on foot march up to be right behind the leader. They each draw their rifles and point them toward the surrounding militia to reinforce their leader.

The man at the front draws his sword, waves it out to the militia, and commands: "I am Lieutenant William Sutherland of his majesty's British army! Lay down your arms, you rebels, and disperse!" To say Lieutenant Sutherland looks threatening is an understatement. He means what he says.

The air is tense between the militia and the large, intimidating British army who vastly outnumber the Patriot militia. Every soldier on both sides has his rifle drawn, just waiting for someone to shoot the first shot.

I don't even need to look at my watch – I know that I'm within a minute or less of the deadline for my assignment. Not wanting to be late, I draw my rifle as well. I'm standing on one side of the Commons and have a great shot at the line of soldiers who marched up on foot behind Lieutenant Sutherland.

Should I actually shoot one of them?

I suppose the only way I have to kick off the war is by aiming for one of the redcoats, so that's exactly what I do. Just as every other soldier has already done, I pick my rifle up and aim it toward the line of redcoats. Staring down the long barrel to aim it, I pull back the lock and squeeze the grip hard.

Man, I wish I had my wand - it's such a superior weapon.

The standoff between the armies is still on edge. No one is being decisive to fire the first shot of the battle, knowing it will spark a much larger war. I squint one eye, aiming to just shoot it at the group of redcoats.

Wait!

My heart jumps for a second, and I blink to make sure I'm not seeing things.

I . . . . know that man.

There's a man who is completely unlike the other redcoats – instead of remaining still with his rifle drawn, he's moving among them. Towards me! As he weaves in and out of the line of troops, the entire time his stare is fixated directly on me! The realization of this man singling me out sends shivers down my spine and makes me feel uneasy.

Who is this man? I recognize him somehow, but can't place who he is or where I've seen him before. Why is he singling me out? Not only am I back in time, but I'm in the human world – how could this stranger know who I am?

The eeriness of this situation startles me. It's almost as if the stranger is waiting for *me* to make a move before reacting to it. Without even thinking about if the deadline for this assignment has passed yet, I momentarily put my rifle down. I want to see how this stranger reacts.

As soon as I lower my rifle, the man stops and curiously inspects me – as if he didn't expect this to happen. But in the speed of a blink of an eye, he raises his rifle at me and shoots. He shot the first shot of the war – not me!

An intense flash of light flickers from the barrel of his gun, which radiates in my direction as the bullet flies through the air right at me. I don't understand what's happening, but for some reason everything around me begins moving in slow motion. With the speed of my environment slowed down, I look straight at the bullet to try to dodge it. But what I see is not a bullet!

I keep blinking out of disbelief of what I'm actually seeing, but the vision still won't go away. Flying right at me is a red ball about the size of my fist!

Where's the bullet? I keep asking to myself. The ball moves through the air in my direction inside of a flash of light – the same type of flash I'd experienced with my other visions.

What is going on?

As the ball moves closer and closer to me at a quick speed, the sight of it is also familiar. I just don't know where from.

What is going on?!

Something stirs inside of me trying to awaken, as if the red ball is trying to force me to remember an experience that I just have no memory of.

I have no time to think about anything else, though – the ball is about to hit me! In panic, I reach my hand out toward the ball without even thinking about it – just to try and shield myself from it. I close my eyes for impact.

A couple of seconds go by and I'm surprised to not have been struck by anything. Wondering why, I open my eyes. Everything around me is again moving at a normal speed, and the men all around me are now distracted by the battle which has commenced. They don't even notice what just happened.

The red ball has disappeared; rather, suspended in the air right in front of my outstretched hand is a bullet. My breath is taken away.

I just stopped a bullet in mid-air with my magic, and without my wand!

Immediately, the vision returns and I now instantly see a red ball stopped in mid-air in front of my out-stretched hand. Indeed, the vision has returned long enough for me to notice more than just the red ball. Incredibly, I notice that I'm now standing on a field in the middle of a stadium full of observers. I absolutely cannot believe my eyes. There is a part of my history which I can't remember – and that now wants to be remembered. Certain events are recalling these memories randomly, but that's all I know. I don't know if I've hidden these memories for a reason, or the motive behind why they seem to now want to be recalled. But I also can't dismiss the possibility that someone could be giving me false memories as a way to deceive me. Until I know more, I decide I can't trust these "memories" the visions seem to be giving me.

Right now, all I know is that the redcoat that shot at me is still several yards away staring at me.

He shot at me and wanted to hurt me. He'll regret that.

With my hand still outstretched, I close it to clench into a fist. Just as with Newton's apple, the bullet in front of me implodes and falls to the ground. My rage toward this hostile stranger quickly intensifies.

I'll make him pay.

I can tell that the fight around me is more of a massacre of the Patriots than an actual battle. But I don't care. This isn't my battle.

For some reason, my assignment was to start the war, and surprisingly, this stranger was the one to do it. And it didn't just start randomly – he meant to shoot me.

I run toward him, now staring right back at him to give away my intention for revenge. The man actually looks surprised about my hostile response and quickly runs back into the crowd of numerous British soldiers. In the blink of an eye, I've lost him.

I stop, sad that my chance for revenge was missed. But I have a feeling that I'll see this man again. If his intention was to hurt me, I know this won't be the last time I'll see him.

I'll have to be very cautious on future assignments and look out for this guy. What if he can move through time like me?

I certainly don't want to be massacred along with the great majority of other Patriots, so I pick up a redcoat from a nearby fallen soldier and put it on over my cape. With my assignment completed – even if it's at the hand of someone else – I jump onto a horse whose prior owner is among the victims. I may have been delirious when I rode into Lexington with Paul Revere, but I know the direction from which we came.

I ride the horse out of Lexington, lucky not to even be shot at while I escape. Along the way, my thoughts begin racing about the stranger and his motive.

Who could he be? Vesuvius and Cadeyrn both mentioned a war. Could this man be part of the war? But if so, who is on the other side?

There's obviously more information I need to find out from my father about this war. And now that I'm a Sorcerer like him, hopefully he'll be willing to provide me with this important information. The more and more I think about the timing of this whole catastrophe of an assignment, the more I can't help but think the timing is odd. I just became a Sorcerer, and someone tried to assassinate me on my first assignment alone as one.

Did the man know I was a Sorcerer? This whole thing couldn't have just been by coincidence, could it have been?

Still riding the horse along the dirt road, I try to be practical and think rationally for a moment. I *was* the only person in the militia wearing a black cape, so I must have stood out visually.

Could the man maybe just have been singling me out because of that?

Maybe, I suppose. But something just seemed calculated, like he had motive to shoot at me. It doesn't feel like just a coincidence. And then the way he was surprised that I tried to retaliate against him . . . I don't know why he'd be surprised by that, but it was almost as if he knew me well enough to be surprised by it.

I can't stop thinking about how unusual, and personal, the attempt felt. I finally ride up to the field where I'd hid previously from the British shooting range, and decide to just keep the threat in mind for future assignments.

I hop off the horse and walk into the field. Luckily, it's no longer as muddy as last night, so I begin searching everywhere for my wand. I know I should get back to the portal-doorway, but I desperately need to find my wand. I dropped it somewhere in here last night and have felt naked ever since without it. Sure, I'm learning that I can use my powers without my wand, but just holding it gives me a lightning rod for the intense amount of emotions I've been feeling ever since I became a Sorcerer.

I scurry through as much of the field as I can from where I think I was last night, searching intently for any sight of it. No luck. I'm not sure if it got pushed into the mud, which has since dried up, or if a solider found it, or what. But regardless, it's gone.

Having decided any more searching is fruitless, I give up and walk back dejected to the location of the doorway. I pass through it back to Lemuria.

Inside my trophy room, I take off the redcoat and throw it onto a table. I'm too sad and embarrassed by what's happened to even think about the redcoat as a trophy from that assignment.

"What will father think?" I ask aloud to myself in frustration. "It's bad enough that I screwed up my first assignment as a Sorcerer, now I've also lost my wand. Good going. I even damaged the pocket-watch he gave me as a gift." Even though I know I should be happy that the watch saved me from getting shot, verbalizing my frustration doesn't seem to help anything. Instead, my worries only increase.

Can I even get another wand? If so, how and where?

There's no way I'm going to tell Vesuvius about this mishap yet. I need to do something to impress him first to even things out.

I know. What if I complete several assignments in a short period of time? That would impress him.

I scroll through the *Book of Historiarum.* Though I don't know what the assignments actually mean, since I don't really know the context of each assignment description, it doesn't matter. I just read through the pages, looking for three which seem to be ones I can complete in a short period of time.

Got them.

Not wanting to have to remember each assignment's information, I tear out the books pages holding the assignments.

Here I go. Three assignments – I can do this!

I'm strangely excited by the idea of racing through time to complete several assignments in a short period of time. In my mind, I see it as a game to test my abilities. But I also hope that doing this will help in the war that my father and Cadeyrn mentioned.

Not having my wand to create a *tempus initere,* I'm left curious to see what the full extent of my powers can be without it. I point my finger in front of me, and begin circling it in the air while reciting the spell.

"Tempus initere August 3, 1904, St. Louis, Missouri, 2:05p.m."

When the light appears to shift in front of me, I go to touch my finger to the doorway, wondering if that will work instead of my wand. When I touch the doorway, a bright light flashes. I must be more powerful than I even realize - it works!

Chapter 7

The St. Louis World Fair

Instinctively, I look down at my pocket watch to see the description of my assignment.

That's right – it's blown apart.

"Hey! Watch it kid." A large, gruff man rumbles at me after bumping into my shoulder as he walks by me. "What'd you do, come out of thin air? Scram - this back alley of the fairgrounds is for vendors only."

Vendors? What's that?

The man doesn't even look back at me, instead continuing to rush off to somewhere important. I notice that he's carrying a tray strapped around him of some things which are brightly colored. I don't know what they are, but part of me certainly wants one just from the sight of them!

The man reaches the end of the alley where it intersects with a road containing a crowd of people walking by. I curiously walk down to follow him, wondering if wherever he's going is important enough that I should also be going there. The man stops at the intersection and his demeanor changes slightly from being gruff and unhappy to gruff but salesman-like.

"Cotton candy! Get your cotton candy here! This fluffy, yummy new candy invention is unlike anything else you've ever tried. Love it as it sticks to your tongue and then magically melts. Comes in two flavors. Get it first here!"

Cotton candy? That sounds delicious!

Observing several people stop to buy some from the man, I hurry down the alley to the intersection before he runs out. I reach the intersection and have to instantly dodge between all the people who are quickly walking along the street.

This place is packed . . . whatever it is.

I remember the man saying that we were on "fairgrounds," but don't give it another thought once I reach him.

The man is busy passing out a cone of the cotton candy to whoever is assertive enough to reach for it. I'm glad I got here so quickly – he's sure to run out fast.

I reach my hand out to grab a blue cotton candy cone. The man is just about to hand it to me when he looks down to see that I'm the one grabbing it.

"It's you," he growls at me.

"Well, yes, sir – I'd like one please. I really am sorry about what happened back in the alley."

I'm actually not sorry, but just the sight of seeing the brightly colored cone of deliciousness is enough to make me say whatever I think will get me one.

The man looks me up and down suspiciously. "Alright, fine. But just like everyone else. It's one nickel."

"A … nickel?" I ask naively. "What's that?"

"A nickel. You know, money? These aren't free."

"Right, right … a nickel," I say, trying to sound like I had known what he was talking about. "Well, I haven't got one."

"Then scram."

He looks up to hand a cone to the next customer, but another man comes to my rescue. "Here, I've got a nickel to buy one for the young man. He looks like he could use a treat."

I'm so surprised by the sudden change of events that I don't even know how to react. I see a hand giving the salesman a nickel. But when I turn to say thanks to the stranger, he's passed by and has gotten lost among the crowd.

Wow – I sure got lucky!

The gruff man hands me a blue cone, mumbling while doing so. "You must have a guardian angel or something. Today's your lucky day. Now move along, you're blocking my other customers."

The only thing I see is the cone of cotton candy in front of me.

I really hope it tastes as delicious as it looks and smells.

Plucking a piece off, I stick it on my tongue in delight.

Yum!

The next couple of minutes are a war within myself of savoring each piece and succumbing to the temptation to scarf it down. Finishing my last piece, I toss the cone in a trash bin and begin licking my fingers to capture each crumb of this amazing new invention.

Now, let's see about this assignment.

I open my pocket watch and see that I've been given plenty of time for this assignment. It's 1:08 p.m., and the assignment's deadline isn't until 2:05 p.m. That means I've got almost an hour to kill.

Wait – what was my assignment again?

The cover of my pocket watch is useless, so I pull out the pages I'd torn out for my assignments. I glance up and down them and can't believe what I'm reading.

. . . this can't be right . . .

I'd chosen the assignment for 2:05 p.m., but my heart drops when I see the other *two* assignments set for the same date and place!

I'd forgotten that I chose this assignment because there were two others at this location as well.

I'd been distracted before by the delicious cotton candy, but I'm now realizing just how extremely hot it is outside! I'm sweating from the heat *and* from the pressure I'm suddenly feeling to complete all of the assignments at this location.

How could I have forgotten? Three assignments at the same location?

I take a moment to just breathe, hoping it will help me think clearly. Collecting my thoughts, I glance back down at the torn-out page. I read what the three assignments are:

- *August 3, 1904 ~ St. Louis, Missouri ~ 2:05 p.m. ~ Stop the Cone*
- *August 3, 1904 ~ St. Louis, Missouri ~ 1:30 p.m. ~ Stop the Song*
- *August 3, 1904 ~ St. Louis, Missouri ~ 1:04 p.m. ~ Stop the Cone*

My heart sinks with the last entry. The time has passed. I re-read the cryptic description of the assignment, trying to decipher what it could mean by "Stop the Cone." But as I look down on the page to re-read the description, I instantly know what it means. The image of the cotton candy cone by my feet is also within my sight. I was to stop the invention of the cotton candy cone.

My blood boils. I should be angry at myself, but my thoughts skip around, trying to find someone else I can blame for having missed the assignment. For a fleeting moment, I even wonder if I'd lost my chance – if I could actually travel to the past again to try and change the events leading to the invention of cotton candy. Those thoughts don't last very long, though, when I suddenly wonder ….

Why should the invention of cotton candy have been stopped? How could mankind's invention of it be an evil thing that I should prevent?

In the past, I'd made a conscientious decision to not even question the purpose behind the assignments. But after having eaten the cotton candy, I can't help but wonder about it. My thought is interrupted, though, when I remember the random stranger who offered to pay for my cone.

Could it have been…? No … It was probably just a coincidence.

The feeling lurks, though, and I can't just shake it.

Was it the same man I'd seen back in Lexington? But if it was, why did he buy me a cone instead of trying to kill me like he did as a redcoat?

The contradiction in the behaviors of the strangers doesn't add up – so I dismiss the thought. Looking back at my watch, I see now that it's 1:12 p.m.

I may have missed one of the additional assignments, but I can still get to the next one!

With eighteen minutes to go until the second assignment, I'm again feeling the pressure. I still have to figure out where to go and what exactly I'm supposed to do to "Stop the Song."

I glance at my pocket watch yet again to see that I have to head southeast to make it to the next assignment's destination. But other than that, I have no clue how far away it is. Frantically looking around for anything or anyone who could help me out, I see a man with maps across the street. I run over to him, only to find out that he, too, is wanting to be paid a nickel for a copy.

Great. You'd think as a Sorcerer I'd be able to make money appear or something.

I probably actually could, if I knew a spell or something to do it. But I'm in such desperation to get one that I instead start thinking of whether I could use another spell on him to make him just give me one. Luckily, before I decide to use some type of a cruel spell, I notice I don't have to do it – I see a crumpled up map just a few feet away along the sidewalk. I scramble over to pick it up.

It's crumpled, but it'll do.

When I open the map, I'm instantly filled with rage.

This place is huge!

On the right it says: "St. Louis World Fair, 1904." I remember the cotton candy vendor telling me that these were fairgrounds, and now it all makes sense. This is the world fair. This is undoubtedly where influential new products and experiences are displayed. Whatever I'm actually doing with these assignments must be important – these things could affect the whole world … somehow.

Knowing that the seconds are just ticking away and I still have no idea where I need to go on these huge fairgrounds continues to fuel my anger. These grounds are so large that it would take me half a day to get from one side to the other! I desperately wish I had my wand with me right now, as I could use it to help me fly around right now.

But would I really want to fly? Would that be smart in these circumstances?

The fact that I have two more assignments to complete at this same location has changed things. I again feel restricted to avoid using as much magic as possible. If I use magic at this one, then that may just make the next assignment move its location or time to somewhere or someplace I no longer know about – due to the reaction in people that my magic could create. Even though my father told me I could start to use magic in the human world now, I have to be cautious.

This map is daunting. To quell the anger inside of me, I just stop and breathe for a moment.

Down the street, I see a woman with a young boy reading a map as well. Running over to them, I ask the woman: "Excuse me, 'mam? Do you know where we currently are on the map? I've gotten lost."

She smiles at me and is quick to be helpful. "No problem. See, we're here – in the Pike."

I glance back at the map to see where she's pointing and see that there's a long street with different vendors and exhibits on each side called the Pike. It's at the very north end of the fairgrounds. I quickly read the descriptions all of the exhibits and locations to the east of the Pike and spot one area called the "Band Stand."

That's got to be it!

I turn to say thank you to the woman, but she's kneeled down to talk to her son now.

"Come on, Peter – we only have 10 minutes until the music begins." She takes her son's hand to begin walking away, but I interrupt her.

"Oh, well sorry again, 'mam, but I was wondering what music you were just talking about?"

"Why, I'm talking about the great Billy Murray. Have you heard of him? He's supposed to debut a new song just for this world fair, which is supposed to be just grand. It's really going to put this fair on the map."

"Thank you again, 'mam."

With that, the woman and her son dart off toward the band stand.

She has no idea how much she just helped me.

I obviously want to get to the band stand before the music starts, so I take off running in the same direction. As I do, the heat pounds down on me, and I can't help but have to stop running for a moment due to how exhausted I've become. I walk briskly through the rest of the Pike, quickly observing some of the stands as I pass by. Each stand is so unique and displays a different culture from the human world that I'm amazed by all of the different locations there must be in this world.

That would explain, I suppose, why the Book of Historiarum is so full of assignments.

Finally, I reach the end of the Pike. I can see the band stand across the courtyard, so I pick up the pace. I'm unable to actually look at my pocket watch while scurrying along at this speed – but I don't have to. I'm close enough to see that there's a tall wooden stage set up across from where I'm at. I panic when I see a middle-aged man in a black tuxedo walk onto the stage, wave, and sit down at a piano. He's obviously got to be Billy Murray. There's a large crowd assembled in the courtyard and a plaza just south of the stage, waiting in anticipation for Billy's new song to start.

I'm quickly approaching the stage, but I know I won't be able to get there before he plays. The thought that I would fail *another* assignment enrages me. It's unacceptable. I'm a Sorcerer now – I don't fail anymore assignments.

Billy begins playing the piano – with the upbeat piano melody being exactly opposite of how I feel right now, it's more than I can handle.

This song sucks – I will have no problem making an example of this assignment and stopping the song.

Billy's now singing along with the tune, but I pay no attention to it. The wooden stage is raised several feet high so that the entire crowd would be able to have a view of him playing. The band stand is located on the central plaza in front of the fairground's main entrance – Billy Murray's new song for this fair is meant to draw an audience and help make this fair an event for the ages.

Not if I have anything to do about it.

The words of the melody dance through the air, and the audience is obviously captivated.

> *"Meet me in St. Louis, Louis,*
> *Meet me at the fair.*
> *Don't tell me the lights are shining*

Any place but there. . ."

While Billy is performing on top of the stage, I walk casually to the side of it where no one else seems to be. I duck down under the floor of the wood stage so that it's just above my head. I'm about ten feet away from under the piano's legs. I know what I want to do – I just shouldn't do it.

I want to use a spell to ignite the piano into flames. But I know that would be a bad idea because everyone would see that I did it. It would accomplish exactly what I wanted to avoid in drawing attention to my magic and causing alarm throughout the fairgrounds. Rather, I decide to do the next best thing: set the stage on fire.

I have to act quickly to make sure I've still stopped the song while it's playing. So I reach out and touch the wooden stage with both hands.

"Et interius ignem."

In a flash, the stage above me ignites into a blaze. In only a couple seconds, the fire spreads throughout the entire stage. I'm surrounded by heat that is quickly spreading beyond my control and throughout the entire stage. Screams fill the area, both from the stage above me and from the large audience nearby.

To avoid being burned by the raging fire all around me, I quickly recite another spell I'd learned from the Library.

"Calorstragulum!"

But just then, a flash of light engulfs my view.

No – I don't want another vision!

In this vision, I'm perched next to a large pile of wood which is also burning just like the stage is. I look next to me and see an old man with a beard, also perched behind the pile of burning wood. He looks suspiciously like one of the Wizards I would have read about in the Great Library, but otherwise I don't know who he is. He's listening intently to something that's happening on the other side of the wood. I hear voices, but don't know what the context of the conversation is about. There are two voices arguing – both female. If I listened hard enough, I'd be able to hear what they're arguing about. But I don't want to.

I no longer want a thing to do with these flashbacks … or visions … or memories … whatever they are! They keep appearing for some unknown reason, and I don't know why. The frequency of them has picked up, and each time they happen I get the same uneasy feeling – the feeling of familiarity. And since I don't actually *remember* what's being shown to me, I'm done with them!

The vision is still before my eyes, but, again, I'm done with it. I stand up, and begin fleeing through the burning pile of wood before my eyes - hoping it's just a vision rather than being real. I've recited the spell to keep me safe from fire, anyways, so I have nothing to lose by trying to find out how real the vision is. Luckily, as I pass through the burning pile in the wood, it dissipates and disappears into nothingness. Finally, the burning stage is now back in front of me again.

Wait! The stage is falling down in flames and I'm still under it!

I rush out from under the stage toward the surrounding crowd. By now, Billy Murray has long fled, along with the rest of the audience. Responders have come to the scene and just begun to try to put out the flames. One of them sees me exit from under the wood and comes running up to me.

"Hey – are you okay?"

A look of surprise and shock that I've escaped unburned adorns the man's face. To avoid suspicion, I play along.

Coughing, I cover my mouth with my hand and faintly respond. "Yes, I got lucky. I was able to get out just before my part of the stage collapsed. What happened to the song? Did it get finished?"

"The song? Son, how could you care about a small thing like that right now – no one does. The real headline tomorrow will be how today's record heat caused the stage to light on fire. No one will remember any song."

Perfect.

Before the man can call over medical attention to me, I dart away from the stage and get lost in the audience which is still fleeing the plaza in panic. I stop on the outskirts of the plaza to catch my breath; however, the view of what I now find myself staring at instead leaves me breathless.

In front of me are several large lagoons, interlocking with brick bridges that pass over them. At the center is a large waterfall feature, and interspersed throughout each lagoon are large, sprouting water fountains. The water glistens under the sun, causing the entirety of the scene to look like an oasis in a desert of these hot fairgrounds. Small, passenger ferry boats dot the water, allowing visitors to get an up-close view of the magnificent features.

The waterfall structure in the middle is especially impressive. A concrete dome with intricate columns and detailing which stands a couple stories tall is located in the center of the largest lake. On each side of the dome, flowing out between the columns and down several tiered steps, are the waterfalls themselves with water as blue as the sky. The view of the cascading structure is a welcome sight to someone who spends most of his days studying in the Great

Library. And most welcoming is the fact that the water spraying from the water features feels *amazing* – especially since I was just under the burning stage.

I stop on one of the bridge footpaths constructed over the lagoons and enjoy feeling the mist from the fountains lightly spray me. I just heard the fire fighter say that today held a record for heat, and I believe it. But in this moment, the contrast of the heat and the light mist has made this assignment especially enjoyable.

I suppose I'm also elated by the fact that I just completed the assignment after having been worried that I'd miss it like the one involving cotton candy before. But at the thought of my assignments, I stop basking in the mist and take out my pocket watch.

1:46 p.m. - that means I only have nineteen minutes until the next one!

I remember that the next assignment is at 2:05 p.m., but I don't remember the instruction for it. I pull out the torn page again and read the description: "Stop the Cone."

That's right.

I now recall that this assignment's instruction was the same as the first assignment. Only, I'm going to complete this one.

I just have no idea at all of what I'm actually supposed to do . . . or where I'm supposed to go!

Now only having nineteen minutes until the deadline, I open the pocket watch again and just start running in the direction where the magical hand points – hoping that I'll find the destination in time.

I'm going to complete this assignment – no matter what it takes.

Chapter 8

Forestry, Fish, & Game

If not for already being lightly drenched from the water fountains, running at my quick pace would be unbearable. The sun is at its peak in the sky, and there's nothing to protect me from it. As I dart through the crowds, I can tell that I'm not the only one feeling the effect of the heat. Families search for shade, and everyone is looking for some kind of water or other cold refreshment.

I continue to pass by stands, as I did before, of displays from different parts of the human world. Mexico, Siam, Nicaragua, France, Brazil, and many more. The next one I pass by is very familiar to me from a recent assignment – Great Britain. When I remember the assignment with Newton's Apple, just the thought of it again instantly revives a despising feeling towards what happened at it.

Whatever it takes – I will complete this assignment.

I begin to wonder if my prior assignments have taken me to any of the other countries that I'm passing by. I've probably been to several of them – but I have a hard time remembering. Over the last six years, I've been on so many assignments to different parts of the human world that there's absolutely no way I can remember most of them.

A short cut!

Just as the fatigue from running in the record-setting heat starts to overwhelm me, I see a short cut through a large building with a sign saying "Forestry, Fish & Game." I've only got about ten minutes left, so I'm all for taking short cuts!

I reach the entrance of the warehouse-like building and stop running for a couple seconds.

Oh my goodness! What is that smell?

Just as soon as I smell a strong odor – I realize I think it's coming from *me*. And my clothes are damp enough for me to believe it!

Wow - I think my sweat has replaced the water that'd been drenching my clothes!

Hoping the smell of "Fish & Game" will mask how bad I smell, I open the door to the building. But I instantly stop in my tracks.

This is certainly not a small display, inside of this massively-sized warehouse. I walk cautiously into the building, both aware of my impending deadline but also surprised by the life-like displays adorning the room all around me.

Large, intimidating animals surround me. I know they're stuffed and not real, but something just makes me feel uneasy. I'm sure that these animals would make a cool display to anyone else, but to me … I don't know, I can't put my finger on it.

Giraffes, elephants, eagles, and gorillas – the list goes on of the animals which are stuffed – but, again, very life-life. And I'm sure I can't even see them all while I'm passing through at a brisk pace to reach the exit on the other side of the building. At the sight of a lion, I unexpectedly find myself stopping right in front of it and just pausing for a moment.

The lion's glare seems to be looking directly ahead right at me – or, rather, *into* me. The look in its eyes may be what caught me off guard and made me stop momentarily. I would expect a lion's gaze to be fierce and predatory. But, instead, this lion's gaze is different. I can't quite put my finger on it, and suddenly my thoughts are distracted from it.

On the ground below me, I see the glare of light reflecting from something *humongous* above me. At first I didn't notice that I'm standing in the shadow of some type of large animal hanging in the rafters above me, because it's *that* large. I can tell just from its shadow that it takes up the majority of the ceiling of this building, and that all of the exhibits below are lying in its enormous shadow.

Whatever is above me is not only massive but it's certainly intended to be the primary display in this warehouse.

I keep staring at streaks of light dancing on the floor below me being reflected off of whatever creature lurks above. My heartbeat is racing – I'm too nervous to even look above to see what it is. I instead stare straight across the room at the exit that I'm about halfway to and decide to just make a run for it.

I take off sprinting, passing by the other exhibits. I can't tell if heat exhaustion has gotten to me or something, but I seriously feel like most of the animals are watching me as I run by them. Worst of all is the sinking feeling that I get from the gigantic creature above. The light reflections on the floor seem to shift in unusual ways, making it seem like whatever is above me is *moving!*

No – it can't be. What's going on?!

I keep running down the path through the displays, sweat pouring down my face from my anxiety of what's happening – and from the immense heat. My eyes go watery from the sweat and I blink to try and clear them.

No!

When I open them again, suddenly there are tall walls of water jetting up from the floor towards the ceiling on both sides of me!

What is going on?

I didn't see a flash of light – or at least I don't think I did – so I'm pretty sure I'm not experiencing a flashback. I could be wrong, but I don't even care. Right now, I'm running for my life through this nightmare of a building from whatever is suddenly happening.

I turn and look at the wall of water to my left, and jump when I see a giant octopus and a couple of dolphins swimming next to me.

They can't be real, they can't be real. They are just displays...

I tell myself this, however inside I know that something inexplicable is happening to me. But what I *hear* just as I reach the exit door makes my stomach jump into my chest. I'm instantly so scared that I stop breathing and am unable to move at all.

"Aaaaaaccccceeeeaaaa."

It's my name and I know it. And whatever loud, large animal is behind me said it as it's moving directly toward me inside one of the large walls of water!

I close my eyes and tell myself this isn't happening – it's all a flashback. It must be.

I open my eyes, but the deafening sound of rushing jets of water behind me tells me that this experience isn't gone. This is really happening. I glance directly ahead at the exit door and decide I'm going to get out of this place. The assignment isn't even on my mind – I just want to *leave* this fair now. But before I do, I'm going to confront my fear head-on. I'm a Sorcerer now, not just some kid. I have to confront it. I take a deep breath and turn around to face the walls of water and whatever is inside of them chasing after me.

A blue whale!

"Ahhhh!" I yell out loud, seeing the world's largest animal staring straight back at me from inside the water-wall. I don't even think about my next movements. Instinctively, I burst through the exit door, shut it behind me, and just pant heavily in the sunlight on the other side of the warehouse-building. I close my eyes to catch my breath for a second, with my head resting against the exit door. I'm sure I look unusual to the crowds of people passing by on the path, but I couldn't care less right now.

That wasn't real. That wasn't real. It couldn't have been.

Realizing I only have a couple minutes until the next assignment's deadline, I pull myself together.

But...

A thought enters my mind and I can't let it go.

... if it was real, wouldn't it still be in the warehouse?

I turn back around to face the exit door, and crack it open a little. I peek inside of the large building to see what's going on.

Nothing. Absolutely nothing.

I can't believe my eyes. Everything is back in its original place on display. Numerous animals are all stuffed and standing still just as they had been when I had first entered. Hung from the ceiling rafters is a gigantic cast-model of a blue whale. It just hangs over the entirety of the floor – not moving at all, and not looking like it has ever moved.

What just happened?

I'm speechless. Nothing that I can think of can explain what just happened to me inside of this building. And between that experience, what happened to me at Lexington, and my recent flashbacks – I know that I'm not making things up. Something is happening to me, and I have no idea what it is. My initial concerns about the flashbacks are now legitimate. I'm not making things up.

Sweat pours down my cheeks from the blistering heat. I'm standing along a path that also has several stands of vendors lining each side. Many have now resorted to selling primarily water or soda due to the heat.

"Hey, Ernest, how are your sales?" I hear a short, stalky man ask from a concessionaire stand next to me.

The tall man at the stand next to him, who must be Ernest, responds: "I'm afraid not very well at all. It's this heat. My zalabias aren't selling at all."

"What's a zalabia?" The short man asks.

"You've never heard of a zalabia? Here, try one." Ernest fries something on his stand's table then hands it to the short man.

The short man seems grateful and offers an exchange. "Here, I'll give you some of my ice cream. Besides, I'm all out of paper bowls – I've been selling so much of this stuff due to the heat that I can't sell anymore. I've got ice cream, but no bowls!"

Ernest hands the short man a zalabia, and holds another outward toward him. "Here, since you're out of bowls just go ahead and plop some of that ice cream down on this zalabia. I could certainly use some in this heat!"

I stand next to these two vendors listening to their exchange, but still frantic over the approaching deadline for my assignment.

I also want some ice cream!

Ernest takes a bite, and I watch him – jealous of how delicious the ice cream must taste on this hot day. When I see that he's got chocolate ice cream, I can't take it any longer. I'm going to go ask for some.

"How's it taste" The short man asks.

"Albert, I think I just discovered something." Ernest replies in excitement, still chomping down on the ice cream and zalabia.

Wait a minute . . . is that . . . .? <u>What</u> is a zalabia?!

I never even noticed it from where I was standing several feet away. But as I've walked closer, I now see it. The zalabia is a waffle. I'm supposed to stop the invention of the ice cream cone – and I think I just failed!

Intense hatred towards Ernest and Albert overtake my emotions. The only thing I can think of now is that I want to destroy them. I've missed another assignment, and it's all their fault.

Knowing that this is the last assignment at this location and time, I decide I'm not going to hide my magic. They must pay. I charge over toward the two stands while raising my hand.

I'll make them pay.

But just before I cast a spell, a stranger bumps into me. My focus is distracted momentarily. I ignore the stranger, though, and re-focus on the two men while raising my arm again.

"Sorry, I guess you should watch where you're walking." The stranger says to me, still standing right by my side. I don't even look at him. Instead, the only thing I care about is how I failed another assignment. But, to my surprise, the stranger continues talking directly at me, despite the fact that I'm obviously ignoring him. "You better watch out, *you never know if you will hurt someone."*

The stranger's words ring in my ear. They have purpose. And worse yet, it's the exact same voice I heard earlier in the day who bought me a cotton candy cone.

In shock, I instantly jolt my head toward the stranger and begin to move my hand in his direction to shock him with my magic. For just a split second, I see that it's the *same* man who shot at me back in Lexington! But before I even have a chance to say a word to him, or use magic on him, he's thrown a black bag over my head to capture me!

"No! Leave me alone! Who are you?!" I scream while throwing random punches in all directions. I feel his arms wrap around me, pulling me in to him so that I'm under his control. Despite my efforts to flail and escape while not being able to see anything, my efforts fail. This man is in control – just as if he's been planning this. I find it odd that no one around us is calling for help at the fact that I'm being kidnapped in public, but I can't wait for someone else to come to my rescue.

The man doesn't say a word while kidnapping me, instead continuing to wrap me up with rope – as if he's aware of how dangerous my magical powers can be.

Time to show him.

I stop flailing and instead stand still, with my arms wrapped to my side. I point my hands up toward the rope and let my emotions take over. An intense desire for revenge against this stranger flows through my body like a lightning rod attracts lightning. Instantly, power zaps from my hands and burns the rope free. I must have surprised the man, as I have just a moment before he tries to again take control of me. I use this split second to shoot a bolt of power at the man from my hands and take off the black sack from my head.

The man is now laying partially maimed on the brick floor, surprised by the fact that I was able to escape from a situation which he thought he had control over. He must be surprised by my ability to use magic without a wand. I raise my hand and am about to more seriously injure the stranger, but I stop when I'm shocked to see that everyone else at the fair around us is frozen in place by some type of spell. I instantly know that I'm up against an extremely powerful Wizard, but have no idea who this older man is.

I've never seen anything like this, nor have I read about such a power in the Great Library.

This is why no one came to my rescue.

"Wait, get back here!" I suddenly exclaim when I see the stranger quickly create a *tempus initere* in the middle of the street and fall through it. I dart over to the doorway to follow him, but am too late. The man closes the *tempus initere's* doorway. I get there just in time to only see the man's face disappear into thin air as the doorway closes. Once it's shut, the crowd around me unfreezes and continues moving as if nothing had happened.

I'm left standing in the middle of the walkway in shock.

Not only was I actually being followed, but this is a very powerful Wizard.

I'm partly relieved that I haven't been making up my feelings of uneasiness about potentially being followed. But really, I just feel hopeless.

Here I am, an almighty Sorcerer now, and what can I do?

For the first time that I can ever remember, I feel powerless. Not only am I being hunted down, but I don't know who's doing it. The stranger has been at my last couple of assignments – he's obviously tracking me somehow. And having seen some of his powers, I'm left questioning my own capabilities.

What if I'm not powerful enough to beat him next time? How does he know where I'm time travelling to? What does he want?

The thought that he wants to kill me enters my mind, especially due to the fact that he shot at me in Lexington.

But, then, why didn't he kill me just now? . . . maybe he was going to – maybe he wasn't going to kidnap me, but try to render me physically powerless. . .

I keep going through question after question in my mind, but in the end I really only find myself thinking the same thing.

What can I do?

I can't stop trying to complete assignments just because I'm now finding myself having difficulty with them. Vesuvius specifically instructed me that I'm supposed to be completing assignments to help out with the war.

I suppose I could go tell my father about this, but honestly I'm too embarrassed to.

I'm a Sorcerer now just like he is – what could he do that I'm not supposed to be able to do myself?

I could retreat back to the Great Library and do research to try to find out about this man and his powers – but that's like fishing in a lake which I don't even know has any fish in it.

What good would hiding in the Great Library do for me?

My thought-process has therefore led me to one conclusion: I must keep trying to complete assignments. This man is clearly on the other side of the war which my father mentioned. And if completing assignments helps with the war, then I must try everything I can to continue to complete them.

I know I'll likely confront the stranger again – he's obviously chasing after me through time. At least now I know what he looks and sounds like.

I pull out one of the pages that I'd torn out from the *Book of Historiarum,* and randomly pick an assignment.

Maybe if my next assignment is completely random, then he won't know where to find me.

I close my eyes and move my finger up and down the page, stopping on a random assignment.

- *September 18, 904 ~ Tikal ~ 6:30 p.m. ~ Prevent the Mayan's Extinction*

I'm heading back in time almost exactly one-thousand years from where I'm currently at. This should be interesting.

I don't know where Tikal is located in the human world, but I hope it's far away from the St. Louis Word Fair of 1904. I'm done with this place.

No longer caring if the people at the fair see my magic, I create a *tempus initere* and disappear through it. What had started out as excitement about quickly completing several assignments has now been replaced with dread. Between what I experienced with the blue whale and the stranger, I'm not looking forward to the next assignment. Things just keep getting worse.

For the first time, I'm fearful at what may be waiting for me at my next point in time.

Chapter 9

The Mayans

Though I have no clue where Tikal is located, it's beautiful! The doorway has transported me to what looks like the highest peak in the city. Pyramid after pyramid line the lands of this strange civilization, and a deep river runs through the middle. There are other smaller rock structures in Tikal, too – but it's the large stone pyramids that are the accomplishment of this great empire.

My doorway opened near the peak of the tallest pyramid, and I just sit here for a minute gazing out at the unique view.

I'd probably be in trouble if anyone caught me up here.

Indeed, from my view of the valley below, I can tell that my clothing would make me stand out as an outsider in a second. I can't see a lot of detail from this high up, but I can tell that they don't wear normal clothes. It looks like some men walk around without shirts on, and instead wear large necklaces, loin-clothes and head gear – all made with bright colors or gold. I may have been to other ancient civilizations before, but this one just seems so unique and isolated compared to anything else I've seen. And the thing is – it's not a small group of people. This civilization is *huge* - both in the size of its structures and the amount of people. From the amount of people I see just in the dirt streets below, I'd guess that the entirety of this civilization is at least fifty thousand people. Even though their culture may look primitive, it's still *that* large!

But it's easily the stone pyramids I see that make me want to just pause and observe things for a moment. There are more pyramids than I care to even count, and they range in all sizes. Each one looks like a set of giant rock stairways leading up toward the heavens. Some of the pyramids are a couple stories tall whereas others, like the one I'm currently perched on, look like they are meant to transcend the clouds. Regardless of their size, though, the sheer magnitude of work that each one would require to build emphasizes that this is a society rich with history. And there must be a great lineage of rulers to lead the continued survival and growth of the empire.

I glance back down at the page to remind myself what the assignment is.

Prevent the Mayan's extinction.

What? Could it be anymore vague? How am I supposed to do that?

Looking at my pocket watch, I see that it's 6:08 p.m.

And I only have twenty-two minutes to find out <u>how</u> and <u>where</u> to prevent an entire civilization's collapse? Yeah right...

My skepticism at being able to successfully complete this assignment is as high as this pyramid. I stop and look out at the quiet, peaceful land that comprises this city and its surrounding forests. The sun is beginning to set off in the distance, and from so high up I can see it slowly fade along the horizon. Sharp currents of red and orange light shoot through the sky, creating a beautiful tapestry of colors against the forests' deep green color below. Even the grey pyramids are illuminated as if by a transcendent being. Each pyramid holds a room on top of the cap stone, just as the one I'm standing in now, which bursts full of light as the setting sun's rays hit it. From this high up, I see the capstone tower on each pyramid illuminate as the sunset's rays hit it, making the valley look as though the pyramids are illuminated beacons of light built to honor a higher being.

From being so high up, I find it odd that I can't see any other civilizations off in the distance.

If the Mayans were to become extinct, they're so isolated that no one else would know how it happened.

. . . I still don't know how it'll happen. . .

I do know one thing, though – they don't become extinct by an act of war. Rather, this place is so peaceful tonight.

I wonder how it does happen.

Knowing that the clock is ticking on my assignment, I decide I should start moving in the direction that my pocket watch is pointing. I'm not as shy to reveal my magic to this ancient civilization, and I have a lot of ground to cover in a short time – so the thought which pops into my mind makes sense.

I'm going to fly like my father taught me to do back at the Wright Brothers' assignment.

Ascendet indignation caelum.

Just thinking the spell which my father taught me immediately whisks me up into the sky above the pyramid. Flying this time is just as easy as I remember it being, due to having such an ease with commanding my magic. I fly down the side of the tall pyramid which I'd been perched on, amazed by the skill and craftsmanship displayed in the detail I observe etched into it during my descent. Intricate engravings line each stone. Though I don't know the language, I easily recognize the engravings as being hieroglyphics – I'd seen other similar things in other civilizations. And just like in those assignments, I'll be prepared with a very useful spell I'd learned in the Great Library that enables me to understand and speak other languages.

Transferendum.

I'd say that over the years, this particular spell has been one of the most helpful things I'd learned from my studies.

As I continue to descend toward the ground, I'm enthused by the great gathering of people I see accumulating toward the base of the pyramid I'd been on top of.

Something must happen during this meeting which eventually leads to their extinction.

It occurs to me that the people may have been gathered at the base after seeing me. Such an ancient civilization seeing a strangely dressed man suddenly appear at the top of their tallest monument and then fly down it must give them the impression of some sort of higher being.

Maybe I can quickly capitalize on this to prevent their extinction.

"Ohhhh," I suddenly hear many of the people in the large crowd exclaim. At the same time, others gawk: "Ahhhhh!"

When I see many of the people also point in my direction, I initially think they're impressed with my slow descent toward the crowd. But when I instantly see the people below illuminated by rays of red and orange sunlight, I know that the tower at the top of the pyramid behind me has suddenly burst with light from the sunset. Without a doubt, my timing couldn't be better – they must think that I'm some type of deity.

It should be easy to convince this civilization to do whatever I find necessary to prevent their extinction . . . I just have to figure out what that is first.

Then I spot him. The stranger standing in the middle of the crowd. He easily stands out from among the crowd the closer I get to it because his clothing is also similar to mine. It's the man who's been hunting me.

I reach my hand out to shoot a magical burst of lightning at him, but he raises his wand and jets straight up into the air. Instantly, the ancient group of Mayans is treated to a duel between a Sorcerer and who must obviously be a Wizard.

At first I react to the man flying towards me by retreating back some distance, in a defensive stance.

Wait - I'm a Sorcerer and he's merely a pitiful Wizard. I must be more powerful than he is.

With my confidence now heightened, I fly directly at full speed toward him. My cape flaps in the wind in a display worthy to instill fear in the Mayan audience below.

Light crackles from my hand, shooting power towards the stranger. But he raises his wand and deflects my power. Though I'm shocked by the ease with which he detracted my power, this doesn't stop my high speed chase towards him in the sky. He also continues to fly directly at me. At our speeds, it's no doubt that we'll collide in mid-air, and the person with the stronger powers will prevail.

The cool night air breezes through my hair, and my focus is only on stopping this threat. I exert every ounce of energy I have into shooting my powers at him. Though the sweat is pouring from my head now in exhaustion, the sacrifice is worth it. This isn't just about a war. Now it's personal.

I fly closer, my anger at the stranger turns into mockery at his weakness – I can see how frazzled the old man looks from having to defend against my powers. His arm holding his wand appears to be shaking, all while my magic seems to intensify with my disdain towards this enemy. For the first time, I feel like a Sorcerer with unrestrained abilities. When I remember how this man had shot at me and later bagged me up like an animal, I have no trouble wanting to end this threat without even learning his name.

Zap!

The man's arm, which had been defending against my bolt, suddenly gives out! I watch as my bolt of lightning now quickly maims him. This happened so unexpectedly that I just stop and hover in mid-air, watching his hurt body fall down towards the ground. I can't help but laugh uncontrollably, elated by how easily I overcame this stranger once I actually had a chance to battle him. If my power didn't kill him, then the fall surely will!

Wait!

I instantly stop and just hover in the air while watching him. Instantly, I jet down toward the ground where the stranger is at. Before he hit the ground, he awoke and caught himself!

How could that be? He must be stronger than I anticipated. I must strike again before he has a chance to compose himself!

I raise my hand to shoot the stranger again, but pause for a moment before doing so. If I miss him, then I'll easily take out several people below him on the ground.

It's worth it.

But before I even have a chance to act on my impulse, he's flying back at me with quicker speed and using his wand to strike back! I'm now the one having to defend against his attack.

I've never actually shielded myself against an attack, and I don't think I know how. I certainly don't want to have to try to figure it out right now – so I instead take off in mid-air to try and avoid his attacks. I dodge up and down the sky, trying to retaliate by shooting back at him when I have a chance. Unfortunately, I'm not having any luck hitting him.

Our dueling powers flash in the sky above the Mayans, giving them a magical display among the sunset's lights, which will surely be enshrined for the ages in many hieroglyphics. One crackle after another, the stranger and I shoot to kill.

Just as I'm sure the older stranger must be feeling exhausted, my fatigue has also started settling in. I fly back to the large pyramid and around its corner, trying to hide up against its side for a moment to catch my breath.

I can tell that the old man is still on the hunt. He approaches the other side of the pyramid which I'm now perched against. I leap over the corner of the pyramid to move to another side, and pause for a moment to see which direction he'll come from. I'm hoping that he'll fly by around the exterior of the pyramid without seeing me, as that would allow for a clear shot at him from my position right against the pyramid's stone wall. I'm now panting uncontrollably, and I hope that maybe I'll have a couple moments before the fight continues.

"Acea, I know you're there - hiding from me." My heart stops when I hear the man yell. It's not the fact that he's talking which surprises me most. Rather, it's the fact that he knows my name. "There is no need to run – I don't want to hurt you!"

Lies – all lies.

I don't believe this man – I've already seen him try to hurt me twice. I just stay still while catching my breath, hoping that my positioning will give me the advantage in this fight.

"Acea – you have no need to fear me. We can work this out."

But as the man continues to talk, his voice cuts right into me. Surprisingly, it's not what he says which is ringing in my ears. No, no. It's the sound of his voice.

I've heard his voice before.

I heard it at the World Fair, but I've also heard it somewhere else. I can't put a finger on where his voice is familiar from, but something about it seems to echo deep inside of me. My mind wanders, trying hard to find some memory of this stranger's voice. But I just can't figure it out. It's almost as if there's a wall between me and the memory of this stranger – and I can't knock it down.

Flash!!!

I see a crackle of light from the stranger's wand as he jumps from around the edge of the pyramid, and the next thing I know I'm falling several hundred feet toward the ground! I know I'm falling, but I can't control what's happening to me – light dances through the sky as if it's mid-day, much different than the sunset colors I'd just seen. While falling, I keep blinking my eyes, trying to stop the changes in my vision that I'm now experiencing. My focus shifts from what's happening in my vision to the fact that I'm about to hit the ground. I manage to just barely control my flight at the last moment. I help slow my speed but don't avoid impact with the ground. Instead, I go tumbling on it and come to a stop at the base of the pyramid.

My head aches, but I'm just happy to be alive.

That man didn't kill me. He shot me . . . but it wasn't to kill me.

I could keep questioning why I'm still alive, but the intense view in front of me has quickly distracted my thoughts. I'm now at the base of an even larger pyramid – one which is much different than the Mayan's pyramid. The magnificent structure in front of me is not like the pyramids that the Mayans made out of grey stone. Rather, this one is made of shimmering white stone. It's so pure and smooth that it glistens under the bright, noon-day sun which now blares down from above me. At the top of this pyramid is a large golden cap, which itself looks like a mini pyramid that is equally as impressive as the large pyramid itself.

I feel blood dripping down my face from having hit the ground, and think for a moment that I must be hallucinating from the amount of blood that I've lost.

When I turn to try and find the stranger's location, I jump backwards at the unexpected sight of the valley being full of giant trolls! They're about twenty-five feet tall, green, and massively built. Each one holds a large white stone and is walking in a line to another pyramid that is being built. When I see the other Mayan pyramids are gone now, though – I know what happened.

I'm having another flashback!

I shake my head uncontrollably from the anger of having another one. I desperately want these things to end!

"No! Stop! Go away!" I yell angrily.

I hear the stranger's words, but don't see him anywhere. He's not part of the vision, but I can tell that he must be standing nearby. "Don't fight it, Acea. *Feel* it. *Remember* it!"

Between the overwhelming flashback and the sound of the stranger's voice piercing through my mind, I take off running. I don't really know where I'm running to, but I just want to get away from everything. Step after step, I run – not sure if I'm running from the assignment, the stranger, or an unknown memory. I don't know why, but this flashback won't end like the others.

If I can't make the flashback leave, then I'll leave it!

While running, I extend my hand out and open a *tempus initere* to a random assignment that I remember reading.

"Tempus initere 6-28-1914, Sarajevo, Bosnia-Herzegovina, 10:56 a.m."

I can't see it in front of me due to my unwanted vision, but the doorway opens in real life and I run through it.

Chapter 10

Franz Ferdinand

I'm relieved that my vision instantly ends when I pass through the doorway in time. But in anticipation that the stranger may follow me through it, I quickly recite the spell again to shut the doorway. I turn around just in time to see the stranger's face dissipate into thin air through the last crack of the doorway before it closes. The man's expression catches me off guard. It's not one of revenge or hostility – rather, it looked for a brief moment like he was worried about me.

I don't know who this man is, but it's time for this chase through time to end.

Sure – I want to complete this assignment, but my main purpose at this one is to catch the stranger and get answers.

Who is he? Why is he hunting me down? What is this war about? How does he know where to find me in time?

I know I've selected a random assignment, but I had done so with the Mayan assignment, too. Somehow he knows where I'm travelling to in time.

Speaking of time, I check my pocket watch to see how much time I have until the assignment's deadline.

10:40 a.m. – nineteen minutes.

I'd been able to randomly remember this assignment's date and time because the description of what I was to do for this assignment stood out to me as particularly … different than other assignments. Many of the other assignments I'd been to involved inventions or wars, but this one was much different.

Drive Archduke Franz Ferdinand to the Latin Bridge.

It just seemed so simple. Drive a guy to some bridge. I think that's why this assignment stood out to me and was so easy to remember from the pages I'd torn out - how difficult could it be? It made for a perfect emergency assignment.

The thought of the stranger's constant threat against me lingers in the back of my mind, but I know I need to focus. I'm going to be extremely cautious going forward – and if I see him again, it will be our final fight.

The doorway I had come through is around the back corner of a brick building. Luckily, no one from this time had seen me arrive. I peek around the corner to the front of the building, to see if there's anything nearby that can help me drive this Archduke Franz Ferdinand guy to the bridge.

Perfect.

Just on the other side of the building are three cars. The first two have people in them, but the third is empty – making it perfect to carry out this assignment.

This will be tricky, but this is my opportunity.

I walk toward the empty vehicle, trying to convey confidence in my actions so as to not stand out as unordinary. I can feel the passengers of the other two vehicles inspect me while I approach the car. I assume my dark cape matches the uniforms of drivers, as the passengers turn back around and continue talking to each other. They don't even seem suspicious of me.

Whew.

But if I thought I was nervous about whether they'd suspect I wasn't the real driver, I become even more nervous when I glance inside of the car and see all the pedals and mechanisms there are to drive it! I'd read about cars in the Great Library, but never thought I'd actually have to drive one – because Wizards and Sorcerers don't drive cars. Humans do. And I'm not a human.

I really wish I'd paid more attention to the books that talked about how to drive them!

Though I don't know how to drive it, the vehicle in front of me looks *amazing*. It's a black vehicle with brilliant golden rims. Even though there's a cover that can go from the rear of the passenger seats over the cabin of the vehicle, it's left open. There's not a scratch on it, making me think it's been carefully prepared specifically to transport the Archduke. The rustic yet eloquent design obviously must be modern for the age that I'm currently in. However, the vehicle also looks like it'll one day make a fascinating antique due to its simplistic mechanical style. It's a simple, small gas engine – probably one of the earlier inventions of this type of car. I look for the name of the manufacture, just out of curiosity.

"Gräf & Stift," I try to pronounce to myself out loud. I've obviously never seen these words before in my life, so I'm just glad that I'd already recited the *transferendum* spell back in Tikal. I'll have no problem understanding or speaking whatever language is used here, until I recite it again.

While I stand staring in awe at seeing my very first car, three people walk up behind me. One man calls out to me. "Hey, they told me I'm supposed to drive the Archduke and his wife." The man's interrogating tone tells me I have to think fast if I'm going to find a way to instead be the driver. However, I want to also adapt to try and fit in with the style which they speak in – this is something I'd learned to pay attention to in prior assignments.

"And who might you be?" I ask back accusingly.

The man, suddenly feeling as though he's on the defensive, responds: "I'm Leopold Lojka. Have I been replaced?"

I'd noticed a proper-sounding tone from the passengers in the two other cars while admiring my vehicle, so I try to reflect that in my response. "Yes, good sir," I respond, trying to again display confidence in who I am and what I'm doing. I'm not used to having to interact much with people during the assignments, but my determination to do whatever it takes to complete this assignment makes it simple to act the part. "You have been replaced. I apologize for such short notice."

Without giving the driver a second to respond and dispute my representation, I strategically shift to talk to Franz Ferdinand and his wife immediately. The Archduke is dressed in a military uniform and his wife is dressed in an extravagant dress, so I make extra sure to treat them with dignity. "Sir Ferdinand, if I may," I say while opening the rear car door.

The driver doesn't even argue about being replaced, instead having turned around and left.

It worked.

Once Franz is settled into the vehicle, I turn and extend my hand out to his wife to help her in as well. "And, ma'am."

"Oh, thank you. And, kind gentleman, you may call me Sophie. What is your name?"

I see no purpose in lying, so I just respond astutely: "Acea Bishop."

I shut their rear door and sit behind the large circular steering wheel. I have no idea what to do to get this car started and moving. I turn around to pretend to look at one of the other two cars, but I'm really noticing that Franz and Sophie are too busy talking to one another to notice my ignorance about the vehicle.

I'm glad they're distracted because all I can do is use my sorcery-magic to start it. I don't have a specific spell that I use to get it started, but instead I focus on the vehicle and just *feel* it. This ability comes rather easy to me. With my hands on the vehicle, it feels as though it's an extension of myself – one which is easily controlled by my thoughts.

The car starts, and I instinctively place my feet on a pedal on the floor. The car jolts forward then abruptly stops, jostling all of us passengers in surprise.

"Acea, let's be careful, shall we?" Sophie reacts in a surprisingly calm tone. With how bad the jerk forward was, I'd have thought that the royalty behind me would have been infuriated. I don't even look behind me, though – so perhaps the Archduke isn't as gracious in his reaction.

"Sorry, ma'am – er, Sophie. This is a new Gräf & Stift model –

but I think I have it under control now."

The couple doesn't even listen to my response, and are instead enthralled in whatever conversation had been interrupted by my bad driving.

I use my magic to again make the engine turn on. I take a quick glance at the pedals.

Not happening.

I place my feet next to them to make it look like I'm using them, but I decide to instead resort to controlling the car with my magic.

Humans are definitely not as technically advanced....

I begin driving forward, hoping that the Latin Bridge is where Franz and Sophie are wanting me to take them.

Finally, Franz speaks. The tone of his voice is certainly befitting royalty, but I'm surprised at how willing he is to be conversational. "Acea, do you know where to take us?"

"No, sir." Again, I'm hoping it's either to the bridge, or that the bridge is on the way.

"We're going to the local hospital. You can follow General Potiorek's vehicle."

Just then, another vehicle pulls ahead of ours and proceeds driving away from the building and through the streets. The third vehicle in our motorcade pulls to the left of our vehicle – I assume in some type of protective position of our vehicle. I glance down at my pocket watch, hoping that it's pointing in the same route we're currently driving. If it's not, I know we're going to have problems. I'm following the watch's route, not General Potiorek's vehicle.

I keep one eye on the watch and one eye on the vehicle in front of us. Luckily, we're both going in the same direction – for now, at least.

"Acea thank you for filling in the last minute. Your service to our country in this dangerous time will not be ignored."

Dangerous time?!

Part of me is wondering what he's talking about, but really – I'm just wondering what I got myself into. This was supposed to be an easy assignment.

"Indeed," Sophie interrupts mockingly. "Leopold Lojka didn't seem too sad that he wouldn't be driving us today!"

Great...

Wanting to change the subject, I focus on our destination. "So, what's at the hospital?"

Franz responds, his prior authoritative tone changing to one that's more humanistic and full of hurt. "That's where the soldiers who were victims in today's earlier assassination attempt against me are being treated."

Assassination attempt!?!?

The Archduke continues: "You know, some people say that if the assassination attempt had been successful, then that would have sparked some kind of world war. I don't know whether I should be flattered by that or not, but it's incredible nonetheless. Really, though – I don't think it would have. Surely it would take more than one man's life to result in such a serious consequence. Either way, it's a good thing the assassination attempt failed – for my own sake *and* the world's!"

Now I know it. I've interjected myself into a dangerous situation. Somebody is out to assassinate the Archduke – and I'm currently driving him down the public streets of Sarajevo!

What if they try to assassinate him while in my vehicle?

What if they try to assassinate me!?

. . . What if I'm supposed to drive him to the next assassination attempt?

. . . What if the stranger is waiting for me at the location of the next assassination attempt?

The questions keep piling up in my mind, and I foresee that I'm going to have to be both bold and prepared for what lies ahead – not for the Archduke and his wife, but for myself. However, at least now I know to look out for the stranger.

The mountain of questions in my mind quickly leave, though, when I'm confronted with having to make a bold decision: the pocket watch is telling me to turn right and the rest of the motorcade is continuing to drive straight.

I do it. I'm not nervous for what the Archduke and his wife are thinking; rather, I'm nervous for what may be waiting for me as I round the corner towards the bridge.

The right wheels squeal as I jolt the steering wheel to the right.

"Acea, where are we going!" The Archduke's inquiry isn't really a question, it's more of an order for me to turn back around.

I don't even say a word to them.

"Driver, turn us around this instant!" Sophie yells at us.

Too late. As soon as I round the corner to the north end of a bridge, there's a herd of people both alarmed but waiting. They look surprised, as if they had not yet expected the Archduke's vehicle to be unguarded and so easily within their grasp. I instantly know that I led the Archduke and his wife to another assassination attempt, but I don't have a moment to pay attention to whether or not it's successful – or what it's importance in preventing evil is.

He's there. Waiting for me. Lurking among the crowd. Waiting for the perfect moment to surprise me. But this time, I have the upper hand. I see him. Somehow, I *felt* that he would be here and during the drive a part of me was ready for this to happen. I'm not running away this time. The threat ends here.

As the herd of people angrily approach the car to Franz and Sophie, I slip out the backside. I don't think the stranger is aware yet that I've seen him. I duck and dodge throughout the crowd of people surrounding the vehicle and make my way in stealth towards where the stranger was waiting at the back of the crowd in the street. Rather than confronting him head-on, I decide to maneuver around the crowd and come at him from the back. My ability to move quickly and unharmed through the crowd is surprising – they're all so focused on the Archduke that I wonder how evil my passenger had been.

There. The stranger stands ten feet ahead with his back facing me. He doesn't even see me, instead paying attention to the crowd, trying to find me.

I've got you.

I raise my hand toward the stranger to pulse lightning in his direction. Feelings of hate and anger take over me. I know that this threat will be finished with one swift ....

What is happening!?

Let me go!

My heart beats a thousand beats per second. I can't move!

Every muscle in my body is fighting to move, but it's like the air around me is restricting any movement at all. It's just as if the stranger cast some type of freezing spell on me! The hate and anger builds up even more inside me, giving me confidence that my Sorcerer abilities will eventually prevail – if only I continue to fight back. My eye-balls move to look at my frozen, out-stretched hand.

Do it. I can do it.

All I need is to shoot just one bolt at the stranger ahead of me, and I know this will all end.

Do it!

Every ounce of energy and focus builds up to my hand. I can feel the magic intensifying in my fingertips, about to explode out to strike the stranger. But instantly, my hand is forced upwards into the sky, and the stranger spins to look directly at me.

Just as at the world fair, everything and everyone around has been brought to a pausing halt. The only things that exist at this moment in time are the stranger and myself.

No!

I have to find a way. With my only weapon being aimed upwards and the rest of my body unable to move, I'm defenseless. And worse yet, I also have no ability to harm the man since I'm completely frozen in place!

He walks toward me, his hair still frazzled from our last encounter at the Mayan civilization. He doesn't say a word as he paces slowly right at me. Rather, he's inspecting me – as if this is the first real time he's actually been able to *see* me.

As he walks closer and closer, sweat and tears somehow find a way to seep out from my body despite me being unable to move. I don't want things to end like this. I will not end like many of the Wizards I'd read about in books at the Great Library. I will prevail, I just don't know how. The likelihood of death from this unknown man increases exponentially with every threatening step he takes toward me.

I fight with every ounce of energy and magic I have to free myself, but it's useless. Eventually, the old man stops right in front of me. He continues to inspect me for just one moment before leaning over so that his face is right in front of mine.

His eyebrows rise, in a look of pity towards his prey. I'm so exhausted from my continued internal struggle that I want to faint, but I work hard to overcome it for my own survival.

The stranger says just one thing to me before he raises his hand and casts a spell causing me to pass out: "This ends now."

Chapter II

The Stranger

"Wake up, Acea," the stranger says in a tone that I can't quite decipher.

I awake gasping for breath – since I did not expect to still be alive. I try to move, but I can't. My movements are still magically being restrained, but this time I'm lying on a wood table instead of standing on the streets of Sarajevo.

Can I talk?

I try to move my mouth, and it works!

I'm about to recite a spell to harm the stranger, but he instantly whips around and shuts my mouth with his hand. "No," he says in disappointment. "No more magic."

I grunt loudly, and he releases my jaw. "Well, then release me!"

The man examines me before responding: "Can I trust you?"

I pause for a moment and just stare in anger at the old man standing beside me. Now, I am the one inspecting *him.*

Why hasn't he killed me yet?

We stare at each other for a moment, and I think about how I want to lie, be released, and then make him cry for mercy. However,

I decide that there are too many questions I want answered before I decide what the man's fate will be. Besides, he's obviously learned a form of magic that I don't yet have the ability to overcome. If I want released, and thus have any chance of defending myself from him, I have to play by the stranger's rules … for now.

I just nod, notifying the man that I won't harm him yet. The man eyes me suspiciously before responding. "How do I know?"

"If you're going to hurt me, just get it over with already." I say, partially testing to see his intentions.

"Acea, why would you ever think I would *hurt* you?" The man asks, surprisingly. With our conversation, the man's forgotten that I'm still being restrained by his magic. But, really, I can't even believe his question.

"What? Why do I think you would hurt me? Are you kidding?" I ask accusingly. "First you shot at me back in Lexington. You tried to capture me at the world fair. Next, you tried to hurt me in Tikal. And now you're restraining me and saying this is all going to end."

The man looks right at me, and I can tell that he's trying hard to see things from my perspective before deciding how to respond.

"I bought you cotton candy, though." The man says, strangely trying to make some type of joke.

Without any further provocation, my entire body is let loose – free to move. As soon as I feel unbound, I instantly move my hands up to the stranger, though I'm not sure if it's out of an instinct to defend myself or to hurt him.

However, the man doesn't see my posture. Rather, he's obviously decided to trust me since he turns away from me. Before I even have a chance to react and use a spell in his moment of vulnerability, he speaks. For some reason, his question strikes deep within me and rings in the air for several moments: "Acea, don't you know who I am?"

Over and over, I search my mind trying to decipher who this old man is. From the way he phrased it, the man is expecting me to know who he is. As curious as this seems to me, I just have no clue. Several seconds go by where I just stare at the old man, trying hard to recall anything that could give me an answer to his question. But the man eventually interprets the silent moments as a 'no.'

"Well, then," he says, obviously having been hurt by the fact that I don't know who he is. "I suspect you've long surpassed the grasp of the oath. It's been so long that you've naturally changed. I waited too long to act."

I can't tell if the old man is actually talking to me, or if he's coming to a realization of something out loud to himself.

Regardless, I have no idea what he's talking about, and I intend to get to the bottom of who this man is and what he means.

"What are you talking about? What oath?"

The man turns back and looks at me, an expression of both hurt and sympathy overcoming him.

Surprisingly, he comes even closer to where I'm now sitting on the side of the table. He kneels down so that his eyes are directly in line with mine, looking right into me.

"No, it can't be. All hope is not lost."

Trying to avoid the discomfort I feel in his stare, I look aside and ask him again. "What do you mean? Who are you? What oath are you talking about?"

Out of the corner of my eye, I see that the man's stare has not diverted from me, so I turn back to look at him again. His look of hurt has only intensified, to the point that a tear has fallen down one of his cheeks.

I'm about to ask him again who he is, but my breath is cut short at the unbelievable words which ring in the air. "Do you not recognize your father when he is before you? You are my son, Acea, and I am here to bring you home."

"No!" I yell. The man goes to embrace me, tears now streaming down his face, but I rebuke his touch. I get off the table to distance myself from this lunatic. "You are not my father!"

"Son, I have waited *so* long to bring you home."

I shake my head in disbelief that this is happening. And actually, I'm so confused about *what* and *why* this is happening, that I figure this must be some type of trick by the other side of the war which Vesuvius had mentioned. They want me to join them – they know the magnitude of my powers.

It must be a trick. Just a minute ago, this man had been trying to kill me – and now he says he's my father?

"You're not my father," I say sternly. "I'm leaving."

I walk over to the door of the room that we're in and open it to leave. But I stop. What I see out a window to my left completely surprises me. I let go of the doorknob and walk over to the window. Everything outside of this room is grey and flickering like it's half there. I know this place – we're in Lemuria.

"How can this be?" I ask in shock. "Only I have the doorway here."

"I'm here because I never left." The man's words come out as a plea for me to believe them, but it's all still too shocking to me to make sense. "I never left . . ." I hear his words through his tears, as if it's a secret he's been wanting to divulge for a very long time.

"Acea, please – before you leave – at least hear me out."

This man obviously has a story to tell, and I don't know why – but I just feel like I should at least hear what he has to say. At the very least, I figure that hearing his story may help end his threat against me. I don't move – I don't even look at the man – I just continue standing and staring out at the grey streets and buildings of Lemuria.

The man interprets the fact that I don't leave as permission to continue. "It started the day he took you away from me. The day Vesuvius took my *son* away from me."

I defensively jolt my stare at the man's direction. Out of instinct I rebuke the thought that this man would talk about my father like that.

He can tell I'm not happy, but continues in a desperate plea: "Acea, I know this may all come as a surprise to you. But before you judge, hear me out." He doesn't give me a moment to react, and instead just carries on saying what he's waited so long to say. "I can't explain everything right now, but you took an oath of *dominium* to become Vesuvius's son. You did this to free me and your mother, Vivian, from a debt which we owed to Vesuvius. You also did it to save your friend, Emma's life. You saved our lives, Acea. You saved me. Because of the oath, you'll have no memory of this – but you took the oath right down there on the street you see out the window below. Your mother and Emma left to go back to build an army against Vesuvius's kingdom, but I stayed here. I couldn't leave – if I left, then I'd never be able to come back to you."

I look back at the street which the old man just mentioned, and a flickering light from a room in a building across the street catches my eye for the first time. It's much different than the rest of the the greyness of Lemuria – it's a single light which has been left on in a room that shines through its window.

I know the building it flickers in – that's my trophy room.

"For the last six years I've watched over you. I've followed you to many points in time, protecting you when needed. I've been waiting for the right time when I could approach you and help bring you back home. I almost approached you at the beginning, but it was obvious the oath was too strongly imbedded in you. I had hoped it would loosen over time, so I waited. I waited years and years, hoping I would know the right time. And I watched you grow, Acea."

The man gets up and stands beside me. He places his hand on my cheek. I instantly want to dart back away from him, but I don't. The man's touch gives me a strong feeling of warmth which radiates deep inside of me. It's unusual, but I know I've felt it before. I don't know when – but the feeling is like a distant memory of something good I once experienced. I close my eyes, momentarily enjoying the feeling inside of me. Images of a large tree, a stone circular table, and an ancient-looking, motherly woman flash in my mind when I embrace the feeling. These images don't make any sense to me, though, which actually frightens me. I know there's something about my past that I don't remember beyond six years ago. I can feel that these images flashing in my mind all occurred more than six years ago – the exact timeframe this man is talking about.

Could it be?

"I watched you grow into a man. I'm proud of you, son."

The words echo in the air, and I take a moment to dwell on them. I don't make any movements or say any words – instead finding my heart being seduced by this man's story.

"But then, one day I saw you wearing a Sorcerer's black cape." The man swallows, revealing his fear of the consequence of a mistake he's made. "I knew you had become a …." He trails off, not wanting to say it out loud. He swallows again, but continues. "I feared that I had waited too long. I had to act fast."

"By trying to kill me?" I ask, unsure of whether I'm asking out of skepticism or disbelief for the man's strategy.

"I wasn't trying to *kill* you, Acea. Son – I was trying to *save* you, hoping that my actions would spur on memories of your past."

It's not the man's explanation for his actions, though, which hits me the hardest – it's the fact he called me *son*. My heart pounds like the engine of all life at the thought that what this man says could be true. I want so badly to believe it, but I just feel like there's something holding me back from accepting this unbelievable and unexpected tale. I know what Vesuvius would say to all of this – he would say this is a strategy to get the most powerful Sorcerer on the Wizards' side before the war. I decide to test this perspective by mentioning it to the man.

"But the war…" I begin, before being interrupted, as if the subject I raised has opened the door to something else the man had been waiting to share with me.

"Yes, the war! The time is almost here. Vesuvius wants nothing more than to finally take over the Wizard world – Terra Fabula. Acea, it's time to come back to us. It's time to stop changing the events of the human world's history. I don't know why Vesuvius is having you do it, but it's leading to disastrous consequences in their world. I don't know how he thinks that will help him take over Terra Fabula, but things are developing quickly now. We must leave."

The man takes my hand and turns to leave through the room's door. But I don't move. He looks back in surprise by the fact he'd incorrectly assumed I had decided to join him. The same expression of hurt he'd displayed before has now returned at the thought that his son may not be joining him.

"I can't," I say. The crack in my voice tells the man that I want to believe him, but that I can't just switch sides so easily.

I'm a Sorcerer. I've taken the Oath of Sorcery. All I've ever known is that Vesuvius is my father. And now this old man tells me something completely unexpected. My feelings may be persuaded, but I have to use my head.

"I need proof."

A tear returns to the man's eye, as if his worst fear is being realized. I'm surprised at how his response *feels* like proof enough of someone who wouldn't be lying to me. "Acea – son, I am William Bishop. I am your father. Your mother is Vivian Bishop. You feel it. You know it."

William and Vivian.

The sound of these names also brings tears to my eyes. I don't know why I'm crying, but I can sense that the man – William – is telling me something I've known for a long time. It's as if the final puzzle piece to a mystery has been revealed.

William sees my reaction and again places his hand on my cheek. In a consoling tone, he gives me advice that sounds as if it's coming from a father: "But, like I said – I think I waited too long before acting. It's not me who needs to convince you – *you* need to convince *yourself.*"

"But how?...." I ask, revealing my desire for something more to convince me to make the gigantic leap of faith to disown Vesuvius and change sides in this war. Despite my internal belief that what William is telling me is true, what scares me is that I still have *no* memory of anything past six years ago. It's all just a vague, but overpowering feeling.

"Acea, travel ten years into the future to see yourself. That's all the proof you'll need."

I nod my head in reluctant agreement – knowing that doing so would completely go against one of the three time travel rules I agreed to before taking the Oath of Sorcery. But I know I must. I just feel like I should do whatever is necessary to find out what my past may be. And if discovering my past requires visiting my future, then that's where I'm headed next.

"Where should I open it to?"

"Friday Harbor, San Juan Island, Washington." He says, cracking a calm, confident smile now that I've decided to follow his advice.

I raise my hand and open a *tempus initere* to my side, ten years into the future. I don't even have to think it; just *feeling* it is enough for this spell. The doorway in time splits open in a flash of light, which crackles through this otherwise grey room.

I take a step toward the doorway but stop when I hear William speak behind me. "Acea, this is where I leave Lemuria. If your future is proof enough, I'll be in our Kingdom. You'll know what I mean. But no matter what, know this: Your mother and I love you to no end. I'm so proud of you, son."

The words stir inside me, and echo softly in my ear as if I've heard this man say them before. I look back at the piercing, bright light shining through the doorway and step inside. For the first time, I'm not travelling through time trying to change something. Rather, I'm travelling through time for it to change me.

Chapter 12

Friday Harbor, Washington

The source of the piercing bright light through the doorway is revealed as the shining reflection of the setting sun along the calm ocean in the distance. With the light receding behind snow-peaked mountains along the horizon, the serenity of this place settles all around me. Snow falls lightly, creating a muffling effect that absorbs all sound. It's the type of snow which doesn't leave any type of cold sting; instead, it feels as though it's a blanket wrapping this silent, serene winter scene in warmth.

I've appeared on a hill overlooking the setting sun around this island. With the last remaining daylight disappearing, a single light stands out from within a wooden cabin only a short distance away in a grove of trees. I walk through the woods toward the cabin. Though I should be drawn in by the fact it's the only source of the light I see, I instead am walking towards it for a different reason.

Something about this cabin, and the feeling I get from it, is . . . familiar.

It's the same feeling I had just moments ago when William touched my cheek.

I recall how I experienced images in my mind of a large tree, a stone circular table, and an ancient-looking, motherly woman when

William touched me. All of these things gave me this same familiar feeling.

It's a feeling I want so bad...

Whatever it means, this cabin is also giving me the same feeling of ... I can't quite explain it yet, but I desire it – strongly.

Whatever it is, the cabin is where I need to go.

Though the peacefulness of the snowy woods is comforting, the coldness begins to set in with each step I take. There's just enough snow on the ground to form tracks for me to find my way back to the doorway. And that means there's enough snow to finally make me shiver.

I pull my cape around my shoulders and tie it closed at my chest. The wind whistles through the trees, making me wish I'd been better prepared for the weather.

Wait a second...

At the thought of wishing my cape was warmer, something unexpectedly magical happens. It actually becomes warmer – as if it was shielding me from the harsh sting of the snow accumulating on me.

I didn't need to know an actual spell...

I don't know whether to be impressed or frightened by the fact that I didn't even know the full extent of my powers. But either way, I'm relieved. Now I can focus on the approaching cabin.

I slowly approach the front of the cabin, careful to not make any type of sound to alert whoever may be inside. But as I approach, more than just the glowing light inside comes into focus from the front window. Through the darkness of the surrounding woods, I see light – but they're soft, colorful lights draped around a tree standing at the cabin's front window. Golden strands of tinsel also adorn the tree, and other things are hanging from it as well.

I've read about this holiday before in the Great Library.

I stop outside in the snow, just taking in the unique feeling I get from staring at the sight in front of me. Not a single sound is heard, other than the soft pattering of snow all around me. Then suddenly, a sound is heard from inside.

Wait... that's ...

I focus on what it is I hear and realize, it's not a sound I hear – it's the soft chorus of a few voices singing. I'm too far away to be able to make out what's being sung, but it's beautiful. Instinctively, I'm drawn in to wanting to see who would be making such beautiful music. It's so warm and welcoming that I want to be a part of it.

From my position about ten feet away from the front window,

the decorated tree obstructs my view inside of the house. So I carefully walk closer to the window, trying hard to peek inside without being seen. Between the melody of the music, the glow of the tree, and the feeling being radiated from this cabin, I have to see inside. Nothing else exists in the world – in all of *time* – right now except the few voices I hear singing inside.

I step slowly up to the wooden windowsill and glance inside from one side of it. I peek inquisitively past the tree and can see just beyond it.

At the moment I glance inside, the singing stops. Instead, the echoing sounds of two laughing children fill the air of the tiny room which lies beyond the tree. I see a slim, blonde woman about a foot taller than me standing up in the room, holding one of the children – a boy about three years old. She's holding him on her hip, swaying around the room holding one of his hands in hers while she dances with him. His laughing rings out loud and permeates deep inside of me.

What am I seeing?

When the woman sways and turns toward the window I'm peeking through, I quickly duck down so as not to be seen. But she doesn't even look in my direction – instead focusing only on the boy in her arms. I see her face long enough, though, to notice that she's in her early thirties. And she is *beautiful.*

In the background, I see another child fly up into the air and then fall into the hands of a man lying on the ground. He's obviously playing with the child, who is laughing hysterically at being thrown into the air and caught. I can't quite see the man, but this child is a girl. She looks to be the exact same age as the boy who was dancing with his mom.

Suddenly, the man on the ground raises to his feet, picks the girl up in his arms and begins dancing along with the woman and boy. They all begin singing again, this time a much more joyful song which provides the melody to their lively dancing.

The faces of the family blur through their fast movements in the background of the illuminated tree. I stand and watch longingly. The feeling emanating from these four dancing figures draws me in and I can't help but tear up while watching them. Tears stream from my eyes as I stand and feel the love in this tiny cabin in the snowy woods.

I want this. I want this so badly. I want to feel this type of love from a family. I don't want to be so full of hate and anger all the time. I want to have parents who want me like these parents want their children. I want parents who love me like they do.

Why can't I remember anything? Why, why, why?

Tears fall like tiny shards of redemption from my cheeks, but in the blink of an eye it all suddenly halts when the family stops dancing.

My heart stops. For the first time, the man's face comes into view. I should have guessed it before, but nothing about this scene even made me think it's possible. The man is me.

"Emma, dear," I hear my future-self say to the beautiful woman, "gather around with the children. I want to tell them about the first Christmas Eve I remember."

I absolutely cannot believe what's happening in front of me.

The woman sits down in the room on the floor in a circle with one child in her lap and the other at her side. "Kyler, Eden, pay attention. This is an important story your father wants to tell you."

I see my future-self sit down in the circle with the rest of the family. My future-self is facing the window I'm peeking through, so I duck down a little to avoid being seen, but still listening closely to what's going on inside. "Kids, I want you to know how much I love you. On this Christmas Eve, we celebrate family. *Nothing* else in this world matters more to me than the fact that we are a family. And the story I'm going to tell you tonight is about how we became a family. It's about the very first Christmas Eve I can remember."

I see my future-self glance up from staring at the family and look directly at me through the window. Our eyes meet.

Flash!

A kaleidoscope of emotions and memories instantly fill my mind as if a wall has been knocked down that had been blocking who I really am. Memory after memory rushes into my mind, and I remember everything. I remember my mother tucking me into my bed, and falling asleep staring at my constellation-adorned ceiling.

This cabin was my mother's house...

I remember awaking on the brick floor of the Animal Kingdom's throne room. I remember all of the friends – and enemies – I made while going through each of the Animal Kingdom's rooms. And I remember the man who cast the spell over the Kingdom.

I choke at the thought of what I've been doing, and the vile man who I'd sworn my loyalty to these past six years. Vesuvius.

What have I done?

I hear the echo of my parents whispering "I love you into my ears" for the split second that we had been a family before they disappeared to Lemuria. I remember that feeling of completeness and of love. I remember the first time I'd felt it when I touched the Family Tree, and I remember Isis - the mother of the Founding Family – explaining to me that it was the feeling of a loving family.

And in front of me is that loving family – *my* family. *My* children. And my wife.

It all makes sense now – almost like the answer to a riddle that was right in front of me the entire time.

I have to fight against Vesuvius and his army. I have to win so that I can create a world where this type of love can exist. I want to fight so that I can create a world in which I can raise my children and family safely. I want to create this future. The oath of *dominium* has ended.

Chapter 13

The Discovery

I take one last glance through the window at my future-self, searing the image of the family into my being. My future self looks at me and slightly nods, as if to say I must go do what is necessary to make this event happen one day – as if he remembers what I just experienced.

Along the snowy path back to the *tempus initere* at the top of the hill, questions and thoughts flood my mind.

My father – William – was correct. That means he waited for me, watching over and protecting me for six years.

My mom . . . and Emma . . . I hope they're alright. But that means my mother hasn't seen William for six years.

As much as I've been trapped for the last six years, I know that everyone I hold dear to me has also experienced much sacrifice. The feeling that my parents would do anything – *anything* – to protect me burns in my mind. This is exactly what I must do for my two future children as well. I must do whatever it takes to ensure that Vesuvius does not take over Terra Fabula. I must make sure that there is a safe world for my children to be raised in.

But if I just saw this even happen in the future, does that mean it is carved in stone? Does that mean it'll happen no matter what I do, or is it something which can still change depending on my actions today?

These difficult questions about my family, friends, and future permeate me. Luckily, they also distract me from the immensely cold, snowy winds that blow during my walk back to the top of the hill.

I finally reach the top. When I glance back at the cabin one last time and see how far away it is, it hits me just how exhausted I am from the trudge through inches of snow. But, unfortunately, that's not the only realization I have.

I should have flown up the hill instead. Darn it – that would have been much easier! I'll just have to remember I can fly the <u>*next*</u> *time that I have to climb a hill.*

I turn back to the *tempus initere* and touch my hand to the flickering shimmer of light comprising the doorway. Reappearing in my father's room in Lemuria, I just stop and inspect the loneliness of my father's bedroom now that he's gone – and now that I know he wasn't lying to me.

Six years.

The room is barren – so much so that I wonder how he kept his sanity while living here alone in the greyness and isolation of Lemuria. I think about the moments I'd had in my trophy room –

how they were brief, and sometimes just for passing moments. If my father was really watching for me for six years so that he could keep me safe, he would have had to be on constant watch for these fleeting moments. *That's* dedication; *that's* love.

I leave the room and shut its door, hoping that this is the last time *anyone* ever has to live in this place.

Out on the street between my father's building and my room across the way, I stop and just stare. I stare at the street and see the scene where the events between my family and Vesuvius happened years ago. While I stare, I can see the forms of the events almost materialize in a grey haze, as if the memories are entombed in this place. That memory is tangible. I remember standing right here, with Emma screaming in horror, as I made the decision to take the oath of *dominium*. When I listen close, I can't quite tell if it's the wind or not, but I seem to faintly hear what sounds like Emma screaming "No!"

I was so young then.

For a fleeting moment, the thought crosses my mind that if I'm no longer Vesuvius's son, then I should be joining the black forms swirling up high over Lemuria. Haven't I broken an oath, and thus should be imprisoned here like my parents were?

But just as the question enters my mind, I dismiss it. I know I haven't broken an oath, I've *overcome* it. And moreover, the oath was never to another Wizard. Vesuvius is far from the dignified, honorable person which a Wizard is. Rather, he's just the opposite.

I continue into my trophy room, and quickly touch the doorway back into the Great Library.

I want to never return to Lemuria. If I could, I would destroy its very existence.

The sight of being back in the Great Library is no more welcome to me than the thought of Lemuria. Though I used to think of this as my home, it's now evidence of my imprisonment by Vesuvius for these last six years.

Vesuvius.

I associate that name, now, with pure evilness. Darkness.

Vesuvius.

How could someone become like him?

The more and more and more I repeat his name in my mind, the more I dwell on who Vesuvius *actually is*. Frankly, I don't know much about the man I used to call father for these last six years. If I was still clouded in the vail of anger which shrouds a Sorcerer, I would say that I don't care who he is – I'd want him dead so that his intolerable threat was ended. But, surprisingly, I feel the complete opposite. Now that I have greater perspective of things – now that I remember that I'd previously been good before choosing evil – I can't help but feel sympathy for him. Maybe it's my wizarding teaching, even though that was very brief, but I have overwhelming feelings of compassion and pity for someone who lives in such a lowly state.

Then, out of nowhere, something Vesuvius said to me when I saw him last enters my mind. He mentioned it just briefly, but it stands out to me as important – so important that a methodical, low drumbeat seems to pulse as soon as I remember what he told me. The drum beats so slow that I even wonder for a moment if it's my heartbeat. I know it's not, though, when I realize that the sound is coming from a different part of the library – as if to beckon me to it.

I pass rows of books, most of which I've scoured during my studies.

I've seen every inch of this place – there's nothing here I don't know about . . . right?

The last drum beat sounds with an extra emphasis when I arrive and stare at where the sound seems to have been coming from. The wooden stand at the upper part of the room with all of the tapestry-doorways surrounding it. This room also stands out to me because of the last main event which I experienced in it – bowing before Cadeyrn to take the oath to become a Sorcerer.

What is it about this stand that's so important?

I inspect it for a moment, trying to decipher why I would have been drawn to it when thinking about that brief thing Vesuvius had told me. I know what he told me was important, but what is it about this wooden stand that relates to …

"Ah-ha!" I exclaim in excitement to myself.

On the underbelly of the stand's surface, is a small switch – so small that anyone who wasn't looking for it probably wouldn't ever find it.

My heart begins beating like the drumbeat sound that led me to it – I'm excited! Before it was burned, the book that contained the oaths, covenants, and spells of the Order of the Nine used to sit on this stand. No one would ever have moved it, so no one would have expected there'd be a hidden switch on it!

I have absolutely no idea what to expect when I flip it. I should be nervous, but I'm not. Something brought me to it. Without even thinking, I flip the switch and then quickly take a step back.

To my left, the creaking of metal mechanisms moving inside of the brick wall startles me. I turn and look where they're coming from, but it's what the mechanism reveals that is so treasured – so meant for no one but sorcerers to ever find – that I feel as though I just discovered treasure. And more importantly, it leaves me with the feeling that, somehow, I've discovered what will help us Wizards have an edge on the war against Vesuvius. I've found what Vesuvius briefly mentioned to me. I've found the secret area of this library that's been used only by Sorcerers.

Chapter 14

Memories

To my left, a section of bookshelves between two tapestry painting-doorways have been mechanically moved to reveal a hidden enclave.

Not surprising that it's right next to the tapestry leading to Vesuvius's Kingdom. Too bad the tapestry is still blacked out.

As I approach the opened enclave, I can't help but be distracted by the fact that the Kingdom is still blacked out. I know that I'll have to eventually travel to Vesuvius's Kingdom to defeat him, but the fact that he was coy about revealing what his Kingdom is now like is very disturbing.

I even became a Sorcerer and Vesuvius refused to divulge anything about it.

The wooden bookshelves which had concealed the Sorcerer's enclave have now moved aside. The enclave is comprised of a brick area curved back about five feet deep, standing about as tall as I am and is roughly six feet wide. It's nothing more than a little hidden brick room, but I know that what's been stored in here matters more than how it looks.

This curved brick covey is damp, and just feels musty – like it's been entombed without anyone touching it for a very long time. Inside, are a couple of small, simple wooden tables with some trinkets and manuscripts being stored on top. Undoubtedly, these trinkets have been stored as some type of relic that may have held value to the Sorcerer's Order – but which has faded over time. As I glance at all of the things that have been hap-hazardly stored inside of this small area, I can't help but feel the same pity as I felt before for Vesuvius.

I think it's sad how certain Wizards have lost their way and end up hiding in darkness, calculating some unfortunate and unearned doom for the good which Wizards stand for. Whatever value these relics and papers may have held to their masters were just that – a temporary means for them to think they'd stumbled upon a dark power that could help them carry out whatever form of revenge they sought. Sadly, it's really only taken a few Sorcerers to undo the Order – Vesuvius and his teacher, Cadeyrn. And unfortunately, they've got the upper hand – at least momentarily.

One book sits alone on a stand at the very back of the enclave. It stands out from the rest not only in that it sits alone, but because it'd been left open, as if it's still being written in. I walk back to it, and pick it up – careful to keep it open to the page it's on. I carry it out to the main room surrounded by the tapestries so that it's not hidden in the dark. This way, I can read and study it more carefully. I place it on the wooden stand in the middle of the room that held the hidden switch to the enclave.

Nothing. The pages it's open to don't have a single word written on them. Figuring that the pages before these must have something written on them, I flip through the prior pages. But still, nothing.

Huh? This is obviously the book I'm meant to find, but there's nothing written in here. How can that be?

What is this book anyways?

I flip it shut, no longer caring if I leave it open to any certain page. The cover and binding is old. Indeed, it feels as though it's about to fall apart. It's not just a form of leather, but feels more like it's been constructed out of an actual animal skin. Whatever this book is – and where it came from – it's definitely much older than the Book of Names from my father's Kingdom *and* the Book of *Historiarum* that Vesuvius had given me. And, frankly, I didn't even think it was possible for a book older than those two books to possibly still exist. But, somehow, this book has made it through the ages. Even the pages are just as delicate as the binding, almost as if any page-turn could be the last for each page before it disintegrates into thin air.

The title is barely even legible, as it's faded with time. But, I think I can still make out the ancient cursive writing on the front. I read it out loud:

Vesuvius: Memoriae

Flash!

Instantly, the room around me disappears and I'm standing in the middle of a giant space that is only white. The book stand still exists in front of me, but everything else around me no longer exists – like I'm standing in the middle of a blank, white page. I now know that whatever *memoriae* means – it's some type of spell.

Being amazed at what's suddenly happened, I'm left trying to discern what I should do. I open the book to see if there's something hidden inside which may shed light on this unexpected turn of events.

"There's words!" I exclaim in both relief and shock.

The same pages that had previously been blank are now filled with words. It's an ancient language – one that I recognize is the same mythogenese language I'd learned about years ago. I still don't have a clue about what these words say, as I'd never gotten around to learning this ancient language. I had always relied on the *transferendum* spell to help me understand other language, but that spell doesn't work on this book. Mythogenese must be so old that it surpasses when that spell was discovered.

With no other alternative, I decide to try to at least read the book out loud. Starting on the first page, I give it my best effort to pronounce these unusual words. And the very instant that I do, something magical begins happening. It's so unexpected, and so unlike anything else I've ever experienced, that I can't help but be amazed by the beauty of what is happening all around me. With every word I say, the black ink on the page raises and dances off into the white abyss surrounding me. Each strand of the letters enlarge all around me and form figures – as if the words I recite are actually *coming alive!*

I finish the words on both pages in front of me, and stand back to watch the magical images which I now stand in the middle of. Undoubtedly, the *memoriae* spell brings memories to life. And seeing as this book was entitled "*Vesuvius: Memoriae,*" I know who's memories I'm now watching.

The black figures have now sharpened to become a cinema of actual, colorful events all around me – as if I'm standing in the middle of a memory.

In front of me are a line of desks in the middle of a marble room. At the front is an old man who must be the teacher for the class of students in front of him. I recognize the type of majestic room I'm in – I've seen several of them in the Capitol.

"Alright class, today we'll be learning another spell involving senses. Can anyone remember the spell we learned yesterday?" The old teacher asks.

The students in the class look no older than six years old, filled with both boys and girls. One proper girl in the front quickly raises her hand, eager to show off her whit at remembering things. The teacher just looks at the girl and nods, which is all the girl needs before anxiously blurting out her knowledge. "It was the *vident in tenebris* spell."

"Very good. And I'm sure all the other students remember that as well. Right, class?" The old teacher smirks as if cracking a joke to himself. "And does anyone remember what that spell allows us to do?"

Again, the same girl in the front row jets her hand up in anticipation that the teacher would ask that follow up question. "Go ahead," the teacher instructs to the girl.

"The *vident in tenebris* spell allows Wizards to see in darkness, as if making the darkness light for their eyes. But to everyone else, they still see the dark."

Two boys near the back of the class catch my attention. They sit right next to each other and tell secrets in each other's ears while the girl gives her answers. I'm not the only one who is distracted by these two boys, as the teacher obviously notices them as well.

"Well, now – we have some boys in the back who think there's something funny they would like to share. Tell me, what's so funny?"

Both of the boys blush in embarrassment, and neither volunteers to respond – hoping the teacher will just brush past this moment. They're not so lucky, though.

"Well then, we shall use this as a learning experience, then. Yesterday's spell was about sight. Today's spell will be about speech. Everyone repeat after me: *verum.*"

All in unison, the class of young children repeat the spell.

The teacher continues: "It's such a simple spell, but one of extreme usefulness. You see, now I have used my power on you to make you tell the truth. Go ahead and try to repeat it – doing so will not reverse the spell for you. Rather, I have cast the spell on you and it won't be reversed until *I* repeat it."

The two boys in the back of the class are in trouble. They may be young, but they know what just happened.

"Now, I know you two are twins, but I'll ask you both again to answer my question. What was it that you thought was so funny?"

The boys both look at each other. Despite being twins, they're also obviously very close friends, as neither of them want to rat the other out. But they're not so lucky.

"Very well, then. You may be twins, but I'll put the responsibility on the older one – for the older sibling has the mantle of being the example on his shoulders. Whichever one of you two boys is older, please stand and humor the rest of this class."

The boy on the right side looks sadly at his brother, knowing what he must do. He slowly rises and says out loud. Being under the spell, he's forced to tell the truth: "My brother said that he doesn't understand why Vivian knows so much about spells. It's not like she can use them because she's not a wizard – she's just an Oracle." Sheepishly, the boy sits back down and looks at his brother as if sorry he had to tell on him. The brother doesn't look back, though. Instead he sits at his desk, staring down at the floor like he knows what he said was out of line.

"Thank you, William," the teacher says. I can tell he's fully aware that what he thought may have been a situation which would be a funny lesson has now turned into a difficult one. He keenly uses this as a teaching moment. "And, Vesuvius, is that really how you feel?"

I'm amazed at the perspective I have standing as an unseen

observer among the students – staring at Vesuvius while he's such a young age. This boy would grow up to be the most evil Sorcerer, and ex-Wizard, ever in the history of Terra Fabula. And here he sits as a young boy.

Was he born evil, or did be become it over time? What is this young boy thinking as he sits here, being called out on a derogatory comment he made?

Luckily, today's lesson has left Vesuvius under a spell which forces him to answer truthfully. And knowing that what he's about to say will be the truth answers the questions I'd just been wondering.

"No," Vesuvius says sincerely, "that is not how I feel. I don't know why I made such a stupid joke." He looks up from staring at his desk and speaks directly to Vivian. "I'm sorry if I hurt your feelings, Vivian."

I'm floored by the fact that such a young boy apologized for his remark without even being instructed to. Though Vesuvius had made the joke, it's probably one that half the boys in the class would have been thinking at their young age. But what stands out to me is just how genuinely sorry he was – not just because he was caught, but because he didn't really feel that way.

Vesuvius was good once!

Another thing stands out to me as well – just how close my

father and his brother were. They were obviously close friends while they were young. And, they're also twins!

The colorful images around me begin to fade back into black figures and retreat back onto the page in front of me. As they do, I hear the teacher's voice fade while saying: "Thank you, Vesuvius. I knew you didn't really feel that way. Now, tomorrow, class, we'll be learning a spell about our sense of smell. Try not to eat before you come to class – if you let it out, the whole class will know it was you!"

With that, I'm now standing in the middle of the white room again. I stare down at the book, in shock of the magical spell which I've witnessed and the extremely useful insight it's given me into who Vesuvius was.

But what made him into what he is?

I flip to the next page, and begin reading the words on it aloud – hoping it'll reveal the answer.

Chapter 15

The Meeting In The Courtyard

Once again, the words dance off into the space all around me. When the figures come into focus, this time I find myself in the middle of a grassy field. The field sits in the middle of tall buildings, just as if it's a courtyard meant to be accessed only by those people from the surrounding buildings. I can tell instantly from the architecture that we're still in the Capitol. My guess is that this is some type of field within the school I'd seen William and Vesuvius in before.

"William!" I see Vesuvius call out from one side of the field. I've appeared closer to where Vesuvius is standing, and William is located on the far end of the field away from us. From the look of it, I'd say the brothers are around eight-or-so years old. "Get ready to release it!" Vesuvius lines up with his wand in hand, pointed directly down the field where William is standing.

"Are you sure?" William calls back. "Aren't you sick of it hitting you in the gut yet?" Vesuvius laughs to himself, knowing that his brother's just giving him a hard time.

Vesuvius calls back playfully: "You know, some of us have to work at being a Wizard. I can't just rely on my good looks!"

"Ok, then – here it comes!"

Just as William yells back, I see a bright red ball fly through the air. I know exactly what's going on. They're practicing using their wands with a tumbling ball.

Ugh, not one of those.

Right now is one of the rare moments where I probably wish that I didn't have a complete memory of everything from six years ago. Just the sight of seeing a tumbling ball zip through the air is enough to remind me of how horrible I was at this game. Ironically, Vesuvius appears to be just as bad.

He tries hard to aim his wand right at the ball, but it's obvious from when he releases it that he still needs a lot of practice. The wand darts by the ball about five feet to the left of it, leaving the tumbling ball crashing into Vesuvius's stomach and knocking him down into the grass. Apparently this isn't the first time that Vesuvius has been hit by it. And from the looks of how much more he needs to learn to control his wand, this won't be the last time.

William comes running up to his brother, and extends a hand to help him up. While doing so, Vesuvius jokes. "So, is this payback or something for me calling your girlfriend ditsy?"

"Hey!" William exclaims back. "She's not ditsy … and

Vivian's not my girlfriend! She's just ... a ... friend."

Vesuvius now stands back on his feet, brushing off the grass from his shirt and pants.

While putting his arm around Vesuvius's shoulders to embrace his brother as they walk back to the school, William continues: "Besides, you wanted to play this again. You're crazy, this is supposed to be recess and you're treating it like it's a chance for extra credit or something. Just relax, Vesuvius and have some fun."

William raises his other arm not hanging around Vesuvius and casts a spell in front of them. The spell is just some type of magical firework which explodes into bright colors and then floats away into the air. "Have fun, man." William says gleefully. "We're Wizards in the lineage of the Order. We're special – just enjoy things."

Vesuvius stops in his tracks, as if what William just said to him hit some type of a serious nerve. He slips out of William's embrace and William continues to take a couple more steps forward before realizing that Vesuvius is stopped behind him. In this brief instance, before William turns around to notice Vesuvius, I see something. It's just a fleeting look, but I see Vesuvius shoot a glance over to someone on the right side of the courtyard. It's a hidden moment which only I witness, telling me that Vesuvius is hiding something from William.

When William turns around, he asks naively: "What?"

Vesuvius just smiles, continuing his cover-up. "Oh, I think I left a book over in the grass. You go ahead. I may be late to class, so just save me a seat."

Without thinking anything of it, William just shrugs then runs off to one of the tall buildings nearby. Vesuvius, however, turns and looks at the opposite end of the courtyard.

There he is.

On the other side of the field, is a man. To anyone else, he wouldn't stand out. But I'd recognize that mischievous look anywhere. It's Cadeyrn.

Vesuvius walks coyly over to the man, trying not to bring any attention to the encounter. I also follow him, watching intently to see what's happening. For a moment, I wonder if the scene I'm observing will end here – but it doesn't. Rather, there's more to this memory.

My view follows behind Vesuvius as he approaches Cadeyrn, and I'm close enough to hear what they say.

"I've been practicing like you told me I should," Vesuvius says, as if he's seeking the approval of this devious man.

Cadeyrn shrugs. "Good. But from what I saw, I think you

should keep practicing." With a sharp change in tone, Cadeyrn quickly moves on to a topic which he obviously cares more about. "Did you bring it? The one from your father's kingdom?"

Vesuvius reaches into his pocket and pulls out a paper. "Yes, but you promised. I give you my portion *after* you give me the rest of it."

Cadeyrn chuckles to himself. "Yes, yes. No problem at all." He also pulls out a piece of paper and hands it to Vesuvius.

"But how can I know whether I trust you?" Vesuvius asks. He may only be about eight years old, but he seems to know what he wants.

Again, Cadeyrn chuckles. "Because, kid, we're going there *together*."

Vesuvius hands over his piece of paper, and Cadeyrn grasps it like it's gold.

"Finally, all these years later. The spell to Lemuria is complete!" Cadeyrn exclaims. When he realizes just how loud he spoke, Cadeyrn quiets and shoots glances around the courtyard to see if anyone heard him.

"I told you, Cadeyrn. It's not Lemuria I want to go to. I want to visit the human world."

"Oh, you will…" Cadeyrn assures the naïve kid.

And with that sentence, the images disappear and retreat back into the book. Once again, I'm left staring, astonished by what I just witnessed.

Vesuvius was such a young age when the abhorrent perspective of sorcery was unknowing planted in him.

Part of me feels bad for Vesuvius. He was so young when Cadeyrn plucked him out of the lineage of heirs to the Order – did Vesuvius even have a chance? For whatever reason, Vesuvius has a strong desire to visit the human world. And who can blame the kid? If I'd been him, my imagination would be off the charts with what the human world would be like. And Cadeyrn is preying on this to facilitate his own end-game.

I turn the page, anxious to see what transpires next in these unfortunate memories of Vesuvius's past.

When I repeat the words on the page, the scene around me materializes into a large audience.

I'm standing in the walk-way of an old theatre, with rows of seated audience members all around me. This looks nothing like anywhere in Terra Fabula that I've seen before, so I have no idea exactly where this is.

The audience laughs at what's on the large stage in front. I examine the audience, looking for where Vesuvius is sitting.

I know he's in here somewhere…

I jump when I hear my name spoken from the stage.

Do they see me? No … it's not possible…

"I've brought you a visitor, Miss Mary Meredith, Mr. *Asa* Trenchard, our American cousin."

Whew!

I relax for a second when I realize that it's just the name of a character in the play up on the stage.

Hey! That means I'm not the only person named Acea! … I wonder if it's spelled the same…

I brush my questions aside, though, to continue examining around for where my uncle could be.

Out of the corner of my eye, I see movement up in the balcony to my right. Right next to the stage, is a small box-room with four people seated watching the play. Behind them is a butler leaving the door out of the box. Among them is one man I *definitely* recognize from being in elementary school years ago. It's the President, Abraham Lincoln.

My heart begins racing in anticipation of what I'm about to witness. But at the same time, I'm completely confused.

I'm in the human world? Vesuvius's memory is in the human world? Wait … that must mean he's on an assignment.

My eyes light up with what this means. Out of fear of what I just realized, I can't help but yell out loud to try to stop what's about to happen. Unfortunately, no one can hear me.

"The butler left the door open!"

Vesuvius was the butler! No!!!

I run from being down by the stage over to a side door, somehow thinking – hoping – that I'll be able to interrupt Vesuvius from successfully completing the assignment. I'm just under the Presidential box in the balcony above, though, when I hear the frightful sound of a gunshot. The shooter jumps down from the balcony onto the stage right next to me and yells "*Sic semper tyrannis!*" before running off.

For a moment, the audience is captivated by the turn of events, obviously not knowing whether this is all part of the play or not. But with the scream from the first lady, the audience erupts in fear and worry – both for themselves and their President. Quickly, everyone rushes to the doors leading outside.

Then I see him slip out the back among the rest of the crowd. Vesuvius has gotten away with his assignment and must be on his way to the doorway to leave this time period.

I have to follow him – there must be a reason this assignment, out of all of them, stands out enough to be in the book of memories.

I take off running, luckily able to pass through the crowd of worried people with ease since I'm nothing more than a ghost to this memory. I rush outside of the Ford Theatre and into the courtyard where everyone has assembled, scrambling for any sight of him. I remember what he's wearing, but that doesn't help. He was actually wearing clothes that fit in with this time period – something I never did. Interestingly enough, he wasn't wearing a black cape, which tells me that he must not yet be a Sorcerer.

The crowd in the courtyard outside is dense, but I move fast enough through it that I'm able to catch up to where Vesuvius is at. He's also moving quickly, trying to get as far away from the scene as possible to wherever his doorway back through time is located.

But something unexpected happens. While he moves through the crowd, he accidentally bumps into the back of a girl. The bag which she'd been holding falls and splashes into a puddle below. This must take Vesuvius by surprise as he stops and picks it up to help the girl. I move closer to observe what exactly is happening in this strange turn of events.

Vesuvius picks up the bag and brushes it off before handing it to the girl. From the looks of it, I'd estimate that Vesuvius is fifteen or sixteen years old. I can't really see the girl, but I'd guess that she's also about the same age.

"I apologize, Miss. I really should be more careful," Vesuvius says in a genuinely apologetic tone while handing the bag back to the girl. When he looks up at her, though, he pauses the very moment his glance meets her eyes. A nervous smile adorns his face, and I can tell he's at a loss for words.

"Oh, thank you," the girl responds. Her tone also tells me that she's caught off guard and nervous to talk to Vesuvius.

It takes him a moment to say something else, but finally he breaks the silence which filled the air as these two young teens' eyes did all the talking. "I ... well, I never expected ... it's just that, excuse me for saying this, but you're the most beautiful woman I've ever met."

Wow – that was bold. Way to go, uncle ... I guess ...

Part of me is curious about this memory – it's completely unexpected. But the other part of me is also curious because I've never really flirted with a girl before, so I wonder if this is the type of thing a guy is supposed to tell a girl.

I keep watching, enthralled with what's happening next. In the middle of the surrounding chaos, Vesuvius managed to find love at first sight.

The girl's voice is cheerful and surprised, while accepting of the compliment that she just received. "Why thank you, sir. Might I ask your name?"

Vesuvius, bows to one knee momentarily in a sign of respect which he must think fits this time period. He holds out his hand, as if waiting for the girl to out-stretch hers into it. She does! Vesuvius is quick to hold her hand in his and then kisses it. Looking back at the girl, he then says: "My lovely, if I tell you my name, promise me one thing in return?"

The girl chuckles in delight, still with her outstretched hand being held by Vesuvius. "And that is?" She asks gleefully.

"That we shall see each other again."

The girl chuckles again before straightening her tone to sound like she's doing Vesuvius a favor. Her answer, though, says she's the one who fate has shined down upon. "I would like that – I would wish to see you often."

"Then often it shall be," Vesuvius quickly retorts. "My name is Vesuvius." He again kisses the girl's hand before asking: "And yours?"

The girl turns so that I can see her face now. My heart drops. I don't need to hear her answer. I know who it is. I just didn't know she was really a human rather than being from Terra Fabula.

"My name is Circe."

Chapter 16

The Dinner Party

As this memory fades back onto the page, the last thing which seems to disappear are Circe's green, piercing eyes. She may have been a young, beautiful girl that seemed the complete opposite of the Circe I'd met before, but those eyes … I know those eyes.

How did she turn from this happy girl to the witch I'd met before?

As if I'm reading a novel that's a real page-turner, I quickly flip to the next page of this book of memories – eager to find out the next chapter of this saga.

Just as before, the words come to life all around. This time, I find myself standing next to a grand dinner table in an extraordinary dining hall that appears fit for royalty. The ceiling of the room is tall, and hanging from it is a long chandelier located right over the middle of the dining table. My eyes are fixated on a serving platter containing a wide variety of food that look *delicious.*

Just then, I realize – I'm hungry! How could I not be while staring at this meal fit for a king. I want to reach out to scarf much of it down, but it's no use. As I learned from the last memory, I'm merely just a ghost that's unable to actually touch or change anything of substance in the memories. I'm just an observer.

They even have dragon fruit?! Oh man.... This memory better be quick – I want to go find something to eat now!

My attention is turned to the doors of this hall, which swing open. In walks Vesuvius and two adults who I assume are his parents – my grandparents! Just as they make their way to the table and sit at it, William also walks in. He's not alone, though. Rather, he's holding the hand of girl – my mother, Vivian.

Wow, I had no idea that my parents knew each other so long and must have fallen in love at such a young age!

I'd guess that William and Vesuvius are about a year older than when I saw them last, making them probably about seventeen years old or so.

But it's Vesuvius's body language that stand out to me most while the family, and Vivian, sit around the lavish dinner table. Immediately once William and Vivian walked through the door, Vesuvius went from interested in talking with his parents to looking like he's reluctantly having to attend something he doesn't feel comfortable at. He becomes more introverted – like his brother has something that he's jealous of.

As everyone eats appetizers from the dinner platter, they make small talk about their day and what's been going on at school lately.

I can tell from the way the adults – my grandparents – are talking politely and properly that this must be an unusual thing for Vivian to be invited to dinner.

All of a sudden, the family's cordial conversation is interrupted by three young waiters entering into the hall with plates containing the main course.

Oh man . . . if I thought I was hungry before, I'm even hungrier now!

Wait a minute! I know these men!

It took me a minute to recognize them, but I know the three waiters! Liam, Spike, and . . .

"Thank you, Phoenix," I hear my grandfather say to the waiter who serves him.

My heart sinks, remembering the undeserved and fatal ending which Phoenix met at the fangs of King Khachatur. He didn't deserve it – it was a sacrifice for the better of the war, but it was still undeserved nonetheless.

I should be angry at Khachatur, and I should be wondering where he's been lurking all these years while I've been in the Great Library. But I don't. Instead, I stare at Vesuvius. I must not forget that this is all *his* fault. Though I may have seen his younger, more innocent past, that doesn't change what he's turned into. And something about this memory is imperative to that transition.

It's wonderful to cast my eyes upon my old friends – the three waiters – but they abruptly leave once the family is served. Then the real conversation begins.

"It's so wonderful to have you with us this evening, Vivian," my grandmother says genuinely with a smile. She really does appear to have been a kind-hearted, welcoming person.

"Thank you for having me," Vivian replies with charm. "I've been looking forward to this dinner party all week. It's not very often that someone's invited to a dinner party with a Wizard from the Order."

"It's not, is it?" My grandfather remarks like the thought never occurred to him, but still being inviting toward having a guest at his table.

"You know, mom and dad," William says, "one day when I'm ruler over this glorious Kingdom, I'll have lots of dinner parties. I'll invite people from *all* over – inventors, politicians, other Wizards…"

"Is that so?" My grandmother interrupts, chuckling. "And your wife – will she be fine with this?" She doesn't seem to allude that it'll be Vivian, but the lighthearted question begs for Vivian to chime in.

"Oh really?" Vivian says, laughing.

"Hey, it was just an idea." William responds. "I . . . I kind of like having everyone together. I like having you here with my family."

A moment of silence overtakes the group, and Vesuvius's quietness stands out awkwardly.

"What about you, Vesuvius?" His mother asks. "How is school going for you?"

Vesuvius looks up from keeping to himself, and glances around the table while eating a roll – almost as if he's wondering whether it's his place to even be a part of the conversation. What's unusual is that I don't get the sense at all that Vesuvius is evil or has any type of evil plan yet. He still seems more introverted like he was when he was the young boy in the class – but only now his best friend, William, has found someone else to give his attention to. Vesuvius now just seems . . . lonely.

"It's going well, thank you for asking mother." Vesuvius just simply responds, as if he doesn't expect anyone else to really care about the details of his life. But the thing is, I can tell that everyone in the family actually *does* care about Vesuvius. There's a disconnect going on between him and the family – but it's not exactly apparent what the reason for it is.

"Oh come on, son, tell us more. What types of things have you been learning lately?" My grandfather asks him.

Vesuvius just looks awkwardly at his plate, like he's not sure exactly what to say yet. Like there's something he wants to say, but he just isn't sure whether it's appropriate to.

William chimes in, trying to help bolster his brother. "Our teacher says that Vesuvius is far ahead of the rest of the class. He seems to have a unique connection with magic. It's almost as if everyone else has to learn it, but he just feels it instinctively instead. Isn't that right, Vesuvius?"

Vesuvius smiles, appreciative of the compliment. But before he can say anything else, his mother interrupts with the question that brings the whole awkwardness of the situation into light.

"And what about girls, Vesuvius – have you met any that you like?"

Vesuvius smiles to himself, but is reluctant to share anything.

Again, William interjects to try to help brag about his brother. "Yeah, Vesuvius – spill it!"

William looks at Vivian, who glares at him to not say too much. She quietly remarks: "William, I think maybe he'll say something when he's ready…"

"Oh, so there is someone?" My grandmother asks both inquisitively and out of hope.

William ignores Vivian's caution and continues. "Go ahead, brother – tell them about Circe."

"Oh, Circe's her name?" Their father remarks. "That's a nice name. I don't think I've ever heard of a Circe, though – which Kingdom is she from?"

Vesuvius sighs when realizing that this is the moment when his secret must come out. He immediately changes from being introverted to being forthright in his response, as if he's both a well-raised, obedient son – and also someone who wants to stick up for the girl he likes.

"She's not from a Kingdom," he says in a flat tone.

A moment of silence rings in the air, as if everyone – including William and Vivian – are digesting what was said and trying to figure out what it means.

"Not from a Kingdom?" Their father asks. "Like, she's an orphan or something?"

"No, father. She's not a Wizard. She's from the human world."

Looks of shock overcome everyone. They all put down their forks and sit with mouths wide open, as if learning that a myth was actually real. Their father seems to be the most knowledgeable about the subject, though, so eventually he breaks the silence.

"The human world? Son, that's impossible. The pathway there was broken and hid many years ago. My predecessors in the Order ensured it."

Vesuvius's tone in response is quite interesting. He perks up and speaks as if he's a scientist or explorer who discovered something hidden without realizing the potential risks of the discovery. "You're right, father. It was! It wasn't easy, but we were able to piece it back together…"

"We?" His father interrogates while cutting Vesuvius off mid-sentence.

"Yes, it's a man I met that has a different perspective on … well, everything."

"And what's this man's name?" His father continues.

"Oh, him? His name is Cadeyrn."

Before Vesuvius can say anything else, William interrupts: "Vesuvius, I warned you about that man. Something about him just seems not right."

"That's because it's not. I know of this man, Cadeyrn. I have heard about him from others. He cannot be trusted, and whatever it is he's up to is no good. Vesuvius, you are not to talk to him again – let alone go to the human world again."

"But father! That's where Circe is…."

"And that's where she belongs. And you belong in Terra Fabula. Besides, you know the rules, you and your brother both are to marry women from within Terra Fabula. That is the only way that the Order survives. You both are heirs to the Order, and your children will ensure that this Order – which preserves all that is good in this world – will continue."

"But father ..." Vesuvius says again.

"Vesuvius, I will have no more of it. It is forbidden for you to travel there again, or to talk with Circe and Cadeyrn anymore. Besides, Circe is human. She biologically cannot bear wizard children, and thus there is nothing else to discuss."

My grandfather's strict, authoritative instruction hangs in the air, leaving Vesuvius tearing up. The internal conflict he's feeling is displayed on his face. Finally, he wipes away his tears and nods his head. "Yes, father." He looks down momentarily, turning again into the introverted boy I'd seen back at his desk when he was six years old. With this change in demeanor, I know he's lying.

He's going to see her again.

Even though I *know* he sees her again, this is the moment when Vesuvius changes. He changes from someone who was exploring the human world out of curiosity of the unknown and interest in a girl – to someone who is now going to willingly violate a rule imposed on him by his parents. This is the moment when Vesuvius's emotions for Circe trump his desire to listen to his parents. And the thing is, I can't really blame him. If I were him, I'd probably be planning to do the same thing – see the girl I like again.

Yes, but even though I'd probably still see her, I definitely wouldn't end up being the same evil person he becomes.

I know Vesuvius's past is tragic, but that's still doesn't excuse everything he ends up doing. I'm sure there's more to his past which explains how he went from this turning point to the night that he cast the spell over the Animal Kingdom. But I've had enough.

Luckily, this memory begins fading. I perk up, though, at the last image I see of the scene before the memory retreats back onto the page. The image is of an extremely proper person, dressed in a tuxedo that strangely resembles a penguin, and having an accent, stepping into the room. "Head Master Wizard, if I may interrupt you for a moment…"

Mr. Butterfields!

The thought that my father's butler and waiters were also servants for my grandfather is actually heartwarming. And it was great to see them – even just momentarily!

With the atmosphere around me being completely blank white again, I decide I've pretty much seen enough. I have no desire to continue flipping through individual memories of Vesuvius. So instead, I flip to the last page in this book. When I start reading it, though, this memory is shockingly different than every other memory.

Chapter 17

The Last Memory

I know this place!

All around me materializes a familiar, circular stone room built with ancient stones and having a circular table in the middle.

This is the house of gold I met the Founding Family in!

And sure enough – there's the mother, Isis, sitting at the far end of the table. She's writing in a book with an ancient feather quill – looking down at it. But there's no one else in this house.

Where's Vesuvius? How can this be his memory if the Founding Family lived so long ago?

I search my mind trying to think about what this could do with Vesuvius, but nothing comes to mind. The feeling I have while standing at the entry of the house watching Isis concentrate on her writing is very puzzling.

I don't see Vesuvius – or anyone else – at all.

. . . What am I doing here?

What happens next is so unexpected that my heart skips a beat. Surely, I'm missing something.

"It's alright, Acea, come have a seat."

I look around in shock, seeing if this memory involves myself at another time having gone to time travel to visit her. Nothing – there's no one here but me and Isis.

Isis pauses for a moment, looks up from her book, and smiles warmly while looking right at me. "Yes, Acea – I see you. Come have a seat."

I'm extremely nervous from the unexpected experience happening to me, so I just sit on the chair right in front of me.

Isis chuckles, while pulling out the throne-seat right next to her. "Oh come closer. Let me have a good look at you. It's been so long since I've seen you last."

As I get up and walk closer to the mother of the Founding Family, I can't help but recall the circumstances under which I had seen her last. Really – not much has changed other than our age. I've obviously gotten older, and I can tell that she's gotten much older as well. As I get closer to her, I see from the amount of wrinkles now on her face that, for her, it's been much longer than six years since when we met last.

"Oh, my boy," Isis says as I sit next to her, facing her caring smile. "Did you find your mother then?"

Instantly, I want to pour open my heart and tell her everything that's happened to me since we met last. Something about the love which radiates from this woman is beyond words, and I can tell that she would happily listen to every word I have to say. But I use my best judgment. Isis is not in the condition to be able to talk very long. Though she fights to show strength, I can tell this is a struggle for her.

She lifts her hand, and feels my cheek for a brief moment, while I shake my head. "Yes, I did. Thank you Isis, you have no idea how much you helped reunite my family."

I pause for a moment, still confused about what is going on and why this is a memory in Vesuvius's book. "Isis, forgive me for asking, but what is happening? How can we be talking?"

The tone of Isis's voice may be more faint, but it's still the loving mother I met long ago. "Oh, Acea – don't concern yourself with technicalities. Magic is just the means to an end, not the end itself. Once you learn to master it, you realize that you don't really need spells or any of that. It just becomes a part of you."

"Yeah, but - I thought this was a book of Vesuvius's memories?"

"Oh it is!" She perks up, smiling as if she's happy to share an accomplishment. "You must have skipped several of his memories and jumped right to the end!"

"Yes…" I admit, but still not knowing where Isis is going with this. "But, where's Vesuvius then?"

"Oh, young man. This isn't a memory. Think of this more like the 'About the Author' page at the end." Again, her smile permeates the air.

"You! You wrote this book?!" I have so many questions, but all I can really do is just be shocked.

"Indeed, I did."

"But why was it in the hidden chamber with the other items belonging to the Sorcerers?"

"Well, I knew you'd find it there. Oh, come now – I've known about that hidden stash for so long. It was my son, Cadeyrn, who started it. He thought he could hide things from me." She stops and chuckles again, this time more to herself. "But believe me, every mother knows about the things that her kids think they're hiding from her."

"But … but …" I trail off, still in shock with many questions filling my mind. "But how did you know Vesuvius's memories?"

"Acea, you're not the only one who can travel through time." Her response is obvious to me, but I just didn't think about it.

"But then, why did you do it? Why did you spend so much effort to travel through time and find the memories to include in it?"

"Well, I started the Order of the Nine, didn't I? The least I could do is help win the war against the Sorcerer that's so close to ending it." The tone in her voice almost cracks. I'm not sure if it's from her old age, but I don't suspect it. There's something she's not saying out loud – but I can sense it. Just as any mother would – she feels responsible for what Vesuvius became. She knows that it was her own son, Cadeyrn, who trained and facilitated Vesuvius's descent into evil. She feels responsible for her son's actions and the consequences that followed. Isis continues: "And after I met you last, and having heard you talk about Vesuvius, I had to look into it. It's taken a lot of time, but I'm just now finishing the book."

She puts down the quill and closes the cover, running her palm over the engraved title: "*Vesuvius: Memoriae.*"

I don't mean to belabor Isis with question after question, but I have to ask one more. "But why, Isis? Why did you write it for me to find?"

"Oh, this book has taken much of my life to complete. I would battle Vesuvius myself if I could – but I'm much to frail now. And I'm afraid I don't have much time left before … before I finally get to see my husband again in the life after."

Her eyes light up, as if to quell a worry I might have. "Oh, but don't worry, Acea – the Order lives on. My sons are healthy and all is as it should be for now."

Isis turns away from talking directly at me and faces the center of the old table while continuing to talk. "But the real answer to your question is that I wrote the book so that you would understand how a man can become so evil. Not just Vesuvius. One day Vesuvius will be long gone. No, no, Acea – these lessons are for you."

I instantly recall all of those years reading – studying – in the Great Library. All of those stories I'd read only interested me because of the lessons I would learn about the mistakes each wizard made that would eventually lead to their downfall. And now, Isis has written a book to teach me the most important lesson of all: how not to become evil.

Isis interrupts my thoughts, though: "But in the meantime, you have to understand who Vesuvius is in order to defeat not just what he is, but what he stands for. He stands for hate, selfishness, and revenge. Let me show you."

She waves her hand at the center of the table and a sparkling of light occurs. It's unlike any type of magic I'd seen before, and I'm impressed with the simple, natural amount of effort it took for her to do it.

"What is this?" I ask in astonishment.

"These are the memories that you skipped over," Isis says in a calm form of mockery, as if she's lovingly giving me a hard time for jumping to the end of a book.

The next several moments amaze me. As Isis talks, the middle of the table becomes a magical movie screen raised above the table, reenacting whatever Isis describes. But it's not like a movie is being played and she's narrating it. Rather, it's as if she can recreate visualizations of the memories at will as she talks – as if the pictures in her mind are projected for me to see.

"As you would guess, Acea, Vesuvius lied to his parents at that dinner party. He had every intention of seeing Circe again. And he did. Why shouldn't he? You would, I'm guessing. I probably would, too, if I were him – such a young, determined, and gifted young man in such desperate desire to find love from somewhere other than his own family.

And so he did. Vesuvius travelled back to Circe. Oh, and how they fell in love quickly. They were two young kids who didn't care about anything else in the world, or in time, other than each other."

As Isis explains the relationship between these two, scenes of Vesuvius and Circe laughing and spending time together shine over the table in front of us. I'm amazed how Vesuvius and Circe are absolutely *nothing* like how they currently are. They're excited, eager to discover things together, wanting nothing more than to just be together, and don't have any ill-motives or evil plans at all. They're just, well ... in love.

But these happy scenes fade, though, as the tone in Isis's voice darkens. "Your father caught on. One day, he followed Vesuvius into the human world and saw the two together. He confronted Vesuvius and reminded him about ..."

"Right, right – I know." I interrupt eagerly. "He told Vesuvius about how their parents had told him not to go to the human world and see Circe."

"No, Acea, that's not it at all. William was happy for his brother that he had found love. William had found love himself with Vivian, and was thrilled that Vesuvius had also finally found it, too. He'd seen the change in Vesuvius's demeanor for the year or so prior and knew that it was all on account of Circe. No – William actually reminded Vesuvius of *why* his parents said that it could never work out between a Wizard from Terra Fabula and a human from the human world – because they are unable to have children together."

"But, Isis, how do we know that a Wizard and a human can't have a child together."

Isis just laughs in her old age. "Well now, that's a longer story from Terra Fabula's history for a much different time."

When she composes herself, Isis continues on: "For years, Vesuvius continued to see Circe. As time went on, he visited her more and more. He'd begun to spend so much time in the human world that he started disregarding his own duties and schooling in Terra Fabula. And during this whole time, the reality of the fact that they would be unable to bear any children never really hit him.

Vesuvius ended up marrying Circe in secret in a ceremony in the human world. No one but your father knew, who swore he would keep it secret from their parents. Vesuvius and Circe were quite young when they married, but it didn't matter – nothing mattered to them but their own love for each other. Rich, poor, Wizard, human – none of it mattered."

Isis again chuckles to herself when recalling one specific memory that she displays over the table. "In fact, William once joked that he thought Circe was actually a wizard because of how in love with her Vesuvius was – William said that Circe must have cast a spell over Vesuvius, as that's the only way anyone could love someone so much."

Isis's tone again darkens, though. "It took some time after they got married, but eventually Circe wanted a child. She said she loved her husband so much that she wanted to have a little Vesuvius around for when he went back to Terra Fabula. By then, nothing was a secret between them – she knew how Vesuvius had to live his life between two worlds, and she wanted a child to raise while he was away.

And out of all the times I'd travelled thru time to observe Vesuvius, I'd never seen him so completely overcome with sadness when he revealed to his wife how they would be physically unable to have a child. He wanted nothing more than to give her the one thing she wanted, but the power to do so was outside of his ability.

Vesuvius retreated back into the Great Library, scouring every book for some way to harness his magic to have a child. He became obsessed with finding a way – so much so that I even observed how Vesuvius began to slowly descend into madness. Cadeyrn saw his chance to influence Vesuvius and casually introduced him to sorcery. Though Vesuvius was not initially devoted to it, a part of him was intrigued by the alternative perspective which it introduced. But because it didn't have the answer he was looking for – the ability to help him bear a child with his wife - he didn't latch onto it … at least, not yet. Nevertheless, Vesuvius still invited Cadeyrn's lessons.

Then one day, Vesuvius had an idea. He wasn't sure if it would work, but it was the only thing he could think of."

"What was it?" I ask eagerly.

Isis smiles at how interested I am in the story, before continuing: "Vesuvius decided to bring Circe through to Terra Fabula. And not only that, but he decided that having Circe drink from the spring that gave life to all of wizardry may help her become a Wizard, and thus be able to have a child with him."

"Yeah, but – how did he know where to find it?"

"Who do you think showed him it?" Isis replies.

I don't even need her to say who it was, though.

Cadeyrn.

"Well," I continue asking, "why wouldn't that work? You and your husband had people drink from it, and they all became wizards … to varying degrees."

"That's exactly what Vesuvius thought. How was he to know?"

"Know what?" I ask, sitting forward eagerly on the seat while hanging on every word that Isis tells of this amazingly true story. I'm no longer watching the video still being displayed over the table, but instead fixated on Isis as she continues.

"Circe was more than willing to come to Terra Fabula. She was thrilled at the idea of never having to be alone in the human world while her husband split his time here. She was excited to not only see this place, but to start a more permanent life with Vesuvius here – she'd live anywhere that she had to, just to be with him more. But that wasn't the part of Vesuvius's plan which failed."

Isis glances over at a part of the room that is walled off by stone, looking just like any other wall inside of this ancient dwelling. But I know what she's looking at. I remember that area being a secret doorway to a hidden passageway behind it. And that passageway was the only path leading to the spring that gave life to all wizardry.

"The moment that Circe drank from the spring is when *everything* changed. Everything for Circe and everything for Vesuvius. And before this moment, sorcery was just an alternative, lesser perspective. But after, the war between wizardry and sorcery began."

"What happened?" I again interrupt.

Isis's glance turns to the scenes still being depicted in front of us above the table, so I turn to look at them too. I see the moment where Circe cups her hand and drinks from the spring. The change is almost instantaneous. Her skin turns from being pink and rosy to being pale - sickly. Her eyes turn even more green and fierce looking. Her beautiful hair rots and darkens. And her teeth that had come into contact with the water instantly become rotten and cracked. In viewing her sudden transformation, I am amazed that she even lived - as I can tell from her crying screams that the transformation was painful.

"But it didn't just change her appearance," Isis explains. "Vesuvius was in love with more than just her looks. He loved who she *was* – but that changed instantly as well. It was if drinking the spring-water removed Circe's soul. She went from being a cheerful, carefree girl to being a soulless, animalistic ... witch. Circe had gained powers, but in doing so she lost who she was. For some reason, the spring-water is like poison to people from the human world – and this was unknown until that moment.

Vesuvius was livid. His plan had failed. He continued to be with Circe, but more as someone who loved the past memory of her instead of who she presently was. And as I'm sure you're aware, they were still unable to have children.

In his jealousy over what your father had, a normal relationship with his wife, Vesuvius became vile. Hoping that the joy of having a child would somehow bring his real wife back to him, Vesuvius never gave up his quest for a spell to allow his wife to bear a child. Such efforts were futile – it would forever be impossible.

His envy consumed him – fueling his actions and demeanor, and ultimately becoming the basis of the evil Sorcerer he ultimately became. You see, the expanded scope of emotions that sorcery seeks to embrace comes with consequences. And Vesuvius was now descending into evil as a consequence of just a handful of those emotions – hate, envy, and revenge. Ironically, rather than finding a way to make Circe like she was before, Vesuvius ended up becoming more like her. Vesuvius even renounced his Wizard heritage, including his right to jointly rule their families' Kingdom with your father. He said numerous times that he wished he was instead born a human. He wrongly faults wizardry for his own actions. He's caused many people hurt and loss beyond words – right up until things happened with your father's Kingdom when Vesuvius found out you were to be born."

"Wait a minute ..." I say to myself, as if the final brushstroke on a painting has been laid. "You said he hates wizardry and wishes he was born a human?"

"Yes..." Isis responds, as though she's not entirely sure of what about the incredible story stood out to me.

"Isis – it all makes sense."

I hear the hesitancy in her voice – as though she's not sure what to say because she's not sure what I've just realized.

"You've told me about the past, which is important. I needed to know who Vesuvius is before I defeat him. His story is tragic, without a doubt. But anyone can say that they've had difficult circumstances that they've had to deal with. This is why I'll have no problem killing Vesuvius – he's allowed what's happened to him to cause pain and suffering for everyone in Terra Fabula."

"Yes, but…" Isis says, still unsure of where I'm going with this.

"And that's just the thing," I continue, talking over Isis. "Look at it from Vesuvius's point of view. He hates wizards – he hates Terra Fabula. He loves the human world. He told me once that he sees Terra Fabula and the human world as one glass being half empty and half full. When he told me this, I thought he meant the human world was the half-empty part. It's not – it's the half full part."

I think that Isis is picking up on what I'm saying, as she gives an expression of both worry and like a lightbulb illuminated in her mind.

I continue talking, though – probably saying what Isis now understands. "Vesuvius used to give me assignments, and I thought he was going to make the human world fall. He's not. He wants to take over the human world. He doesn't want to take over Terra Fabula – he wants to destroy it!

He told me he's trying to find a way to bridge the two worlds without Lemuria. Isis – Vesuvius is going to literally, physically *merge* the two worlds so that Terra Fabula is destroyed! And he's been giving me assignments in the human world which will make the humans less advanced, and more evil. Just like when the humans were in the dark age – he's been doing this so that humans are easier to conquer! If humans are evil, then they will surely recognize him – such a powerful, evil Sorcerer – as their leader!

Isis – we have to stop him … NOW!"

Chapter 18

The Wand

"And you *will* stop him." The tone in Isis's voice is both confident and empowering. But rather than instructing me to leave, or having this part of the *memoriae* book end, she turns to the portion of the wall containing the hidden doorway to the spring. "But, might I trouble you to first take an old lady on a walk to the spring?"

My urgency is through the roof – I want to run to my father's Kingdom and tell him everything I've realized about Vesuvius's plan. I want to tell him how we've all been wrong the whole time – how Vesuvius isn't planning to take over Terra Fabula. But what do I know compared to the mother of the Order of the Nine and of all wizardry? Surely I owe her a walk if that's all she requests. And by how frail she looks, this really might be among her last requests.

Like a gentleman, I stand up and extend my elbow out for her to grab onto. She smirks and holds on while slowly lifting herself out of her throne-chair. We walk slowly over toward the wall and I'm amazed how the stones in the wall just effortlessly peel away, as if a curtain is being rolled back announcing the presence of their queen. Though the path into the mountain had been dark for me before, there's somehow light illuminating down it - just as if it was turning on for its owner. We walk into the passageway, and my memories of being here before flood my mind.

I remember how this was the first place I met Cadeyrn. I remember how he sniffed out my invisible presence as if he had learned the spell to heighten his sense of smell that was mentioned in one of Vesuvius's memories. But I also remember the moments where I'd seen the shadows of my parents, and how they led me to the spring.

"This is a strange mountain," Isis says, as if reading my mind. But despite all the things I'd been remembering about this passageway, I'd forgotten just how deep into the mountain the path takes us until now. Isis's tone is eerily one of reflection and trying to reveal to me a hidden message. "I've seen a great many things along this path – things which I can't quite explain..."

I want to blurt out question after question to learn as much from this old mother's lake of knowledge, but I instead exercise restraint as a sign of respect.

Isis's reflection continues: "Sometimes I'd wondered if it was a mistake for my husband and myself to discover the spring – with all of the hurt that has transpired from its discovery. Other times I've felt that we were compelled to find it. And, Acea – there has been much beauty and good in the world that has come from the spring and wizardry. For example, the Order. I know that ages upon ages of Wizards in the Order will rule over Terra Fabula – good, moral Wizards who undoubtedly will make Terra Fabula a better place for all within it.

…But lately, I've been seeing something, er rather – *someone* else down here. It's made me think that I'm being compelled to my next great adventure."

"You mean? …" I trail off.

"That's right. I've been seeing the shadow of my deceased husband, Aki."

"Wow," I find myself saying out-loud in amazement. "But he's passed away. How can that be?"

"How, indeed," Isis says without a true answer. "Like I said, there's something strange about this mountain."

"And your children, have they seen him yet?"

"Oh, them? Acea, they moved out a long time ago. They're all grown up and carrying on the lines of the Order. It's just me and this old mountain these days – and the shadow of my husband to keep me hoping."

"Hoping for what?" I realize I may be overstepping my bounds by asking a question that perhaps Isis doesn't want to verbalize the answer to.

"Hoping that I'll see him again in the great ever-after."

I want to tell Isis about how I'd seen the shadows of my parents when I was in this passageway before, but I decide not to. Telling her about it may be a way to shift focus away from the hope she has and to myself instead. And that just doesn't feel like the right thing to do in this late hour of Isis's life. Besides, the next thing I know, we're at the ledge of the cliff where the wood and leather-bound ladder lead down to the spring.

This is going to be tricky getting Isis down this thing!

But when I turn to help her down the ladder, I'm surprised – she's not there! I turn around in shock and look down the passageway we'd just walked down.

"Are you coming, or what?" I hear the old lady's voice taunt from below.

She's already at the bottom of the cliff!

I should be surprised that she'd gotten down the bottom by herself, but then I remember that she has magical powers too!

I bet she took the walk down the passageway slowly with me just because she enjoyed the company – she didn't have to walk at all.

"So, do you need help or something?" Isis again teases, chuckling in humor to herself.

"Oh, very funny you old lady!" I yell back.

Without even realizing that I, too, could fly down the cliff, I just turn around instinctively and begin climbing down the ladder. When I reach the bottom, Isis actually calls me out on this.

"You know, Acea – don't be afraid to use your magic. It's not something to ever be ashamed of. Like I said, sometimes I wonder if the spring wanted me and Aki to find it – as if our bloodline was chosen."

Feeling slightly embarrassed that I didn't fly down the cliff like Isis just did, I make a lame excuse for why I didn't. "It's just that … I lost my wand, and even though I don't need it to use my magic – ever since I lost it, it just hasn't been the same."

"I know," Isis says in her warm, motherly tone, just as if she could read my mind. "Why do you think we're here at the spring?"

"Huh?" I ask, my interest suddenly perking up.

Isis's prior playfully mocking tone returns as she speaks, while turning to the spring directly ahead of us. "Every time, Acea. Every time you visit, you need a new wand. I tell you, kids these days…"

And all this time I thought I was doing her a favor by coming on this walk. She really was doing me a favor instead!

From her long sleeve, Isis pulls out a wand. Its simplicity matches what I would expect from how far back in time I am right now – as if the wand was simply broken off of a tree limb.

"The thing about a wand, Acea," Isis begins to explain, "is that its power doesn't come from what it looks like – but instead from the person who holds it."

She hands the wand to me. But as I grab it, I'm disheartened – I don't really feel anything. My prior wands had reminded me of a lightning rod, extracting the power from me. But this one just feels like I'm holding a … well, stick.

"Oh, it may look like a stick, but it's more than that. Do you remember when you visited me last?"

"Yes, what about it?"

"Do you remember how just before you left, you took Aki's place as one of the nine Wizards in the Order?"

"Yes, that's right!" Actually, until just now I had completely forgotten about that.

"Well, you never took his wand – until now."

I look down in amazement at what I'm holding. "You mean…."

"That's right, Acea. This is the first wand to ever have existed. And now, it is yours."

"But I don't feel anything from holding…"

"Oh, no – of course you don't. This wand doesn't just harness power from the Wizard holding it – instead it *draws* it out. For the right Wizard, this little wand can magnify the Wizard's inner powers more than any other wand can. And to prevent just anyone from using it, Aki cast a spell on it to sync it to just himself."

"And you're giving it to me?"

"Yes, of course I am. You'll need its untapped abilities to draw every ounce of strength from you to defeat Vesuvius. He is *that* evil and *that* powerful."

"But if it's synced to just Aki, then how am I going to be able to use it?"

Isis turns and looks at the spring and the small puddle of water in the pool of rocks under it. "That's why we're here."

It hits me. I know what I'm supposed to do, and Isis doesn't even have to say it. I remember how my wand was broken the first time I met Isis, and how it became fixed when dipped into the spring water.

With the wand in my hand, I dip it into the puddle at the pool atop the raised platform of rocks that the spring drips onto. Instantly, the wand zips alive. A strong, intense sensation emerges from the bottom of my hand – almost as if the wand is not only syncing with me, but as if it's becoming an extension of my hand. This feeling slowly grows throughout my entire body, making me feel more alive and connected to my magical abilities than I ever have. But it's not as though it's *giving* me powers, but instead as if it's unmasking the powers already within me. This wand is unlike any other wand I've ever had!

When the syncing is completed, I turn back to thank Isis and describe just how amazing the feeling is – but she's gone!

I glance all around me by the spring, but I know it's useless. She's gone to join her husband in the next great adventure.

Suddenly the dim lighting of the cavern begins to recede. The image of the spring, and all the rocks around me dance back onto the page of Vesuvius's *memoriae* book on the stand in front of me.

But I'm left both breathless and empowered by the last thing I see before the scene is gone: I see the ghostly-apparition of Aki and Isis holding hands smiling in the cavern, looking younger than when I even first met them. As the mountain is sucked back onto the page, I hear the faint sound of two carefree voices exclaim: "Good luck!"

But luck isn't going to be enough. Once the memory has ended, I'm left standing in the middle of the tapestry-doorway room of the

Great Library, with my back to the doorways while staring at the book. And something is wrong. Very wrong. I can't move.

Chapter 19

The Battle

"You lied," says a scolding, vindictive voice from behind me.

I would turn to look him head on, but I can't move. It's as though the same spell that my father used on me back in Sarajevo is being used against me again. I know that I'm normally strong enough to repel the spell, and especially with my new wand, but this time it was cast on me by surprise. Just as if I was stabbed in the back by a coward.

It's Cadeyrn.

"No need to say a word. There's no way to explain or excuse what you've done. I saw the conversation between you and my mother, Isis," Cadeyrn snarls while moving into my eyesight from behind me. His back now faces some of the tapestries to the Kingdoms, and he's several feet away – as if he wants to ensure he keeps a safe distance from me. He must recognize how I'm incredibly more powerful than him – this would explain why he cast the spell on me while my defenses were down. His wand is raised pointing at me while holding me captive. "You took the Oath of Sorcery and you broke it. Now I will break you!"

As if being electrocuted from all of the air around me, the entirety of my body suddenly burns with pain.

Ahhhh!

I want to yell out, but I can't – I can't move at all! The intensity of the pain magnifies to an unimaginable degree, and I know I'll surely die like a fish that's being cooked in a pan – left to sizzle in the agonizing electrical shock overwhelming my entire body. The fact that I can't yell or move at all is unbearable. My heart races as if it's going to explode in my chest. My feet and hands feel like they're engulfed in flames. All I want is for this overwhelming, unstoppable pain to end – whatever it takes.

This is it. This is the end.

I begin to close my eyes, but not voluntarily. I'm still being held suspended in motion, so the fact they're beginning to close is from my body starting to break down. And I'm sure this is why they're closing when I feel tears of blood stream down my cheeks from my body starting to physically die. The only thing I can do is hope that the pain will end if I just drift off into death.

But all of a sudden my entire body drops to the floor like a bag of sand dropped from a window. My head hits the ground, but I don't feel the pain from it – I can't feel anything but fire radiating from each of my nerves. Now that I've inexplicably been released from Cadeyrn's hold, I want to scream out loud from the pain. But I can't, I'm much too exhausted and paralyzed from the throbbing ache that is still overwhelming me. Instead, I just lay on the ground on my side, in disbelief of what I'm now able to observe from my half-cracked open eyes.

I should have died. Cadeyrn should have killed me like the coward he is by catching me off guard. And he almost did. But from what I'm now watching, I know what happened.

My father told me he'd be in his Kingdom waiting for me. And he was. He must have seen what Cadeyrn was doing from his Kingdom's doorway to the library, and caught Cadeyrn by surprise himself. When Cadeyrn turned to strike at my father, he released his grip on me, sending me crashing to the ground. And now, the two are dueling in front of my sight while I lay paralyzed in pain and physical exhaustion – still on the brink of death.

"Cadeyrn, this ends once and for all!" William shouts while shooting a bright flash of blue light at him. Cadeyrn deflects the bolt and jets to his left before returning the shot. But my father is fast enough to evade the blast and fires directly back at him. "First my brother and now my son - no more!"

The duel intensifies with repeated flashes of light emerging quickly, one after another, as they fight. They're both successful at avoiding being hit from each other's shots.

"This never would have happened if you just joined me as your brother did! You could have stopped all of this!" Cadeyrn's shrewd voice rings through the sound of magical bursts.

My father never even responds to Cadeyrn's ignorant attempt to blame him. Instead, his fighting intensifies. But for each time that my father picks up speed, Cadeyrn's efforts also intensify. Eventually, the rapid-fire of the flashes fill the room so much and so quickly that I'm unable to follow who is winning in the glare of all the bright light. But when the flashes of light quickly recede, I'm no longer distracted by the overwhelming physical pain I'm still experiencing. Rather, the pain I feel now is purely emotional.

"No!" I squeal out in terror.

My father squirms on the floor, writhing in pain at the end of a bolt of Cadeyrn's magic.

At the sound of my weak response, Cadeyrn turns and looks at me – sharing the same evil grin I've seen Vesuvius adorn several times before. "So, here it is. Another pitiful line of the Order ends!"

"No it doesn't!" An earnest, energetic voice surprisingly interrupts. It's a woman's voice – one I haven't heard in over six years.

Emma!

With his attention fixated on killing me and my father, Cadeyrn never even saw her coming. Emma swiftly maneuvers through the tapestry leading to the Temple of Artemis. Emma jumps around the room acrobatically, shooting bolts of energy at Cadeyrn from all angles.

Wow – Emma!

I knew that she was a Wizard and an heir to the Order, but she'd just barely found this out when I saw her last. Now, she's not just a Wizard, but a warrior!

Emma's been busy these last six years!

With Cadeyrn distracted by Emma's threat, he releases my father from his grasp. It takes my father a moment to regain his strength but eventually he stands and begins retaliating. Cadeyrn doesn't stand a chance but puts up a formidable fight to try to avoid being cornered by the two Wizards' attacks. One by one he blocks each of the Wizards' bolts; however, he's unable to actually shoot anything back at them. The two-on-one fight is too much for him. I try to raise to my feet to end this battle even quicker, but it's no use. Though I'm conscious, my body is not reactive. I'm still paralyzed.

However, my efforts are unneeded. In the blink of an eye, Cadeyrn isn't just cornered, he's bound in bolts from each side of his body – one from Emma and the other from William.

Just as a coward would, he attempts to barter for his freedom with his two captors. "I … I can help you! If you free me then I'll tell you everything you need to know about Vesuvius's plans."

Impulsively, I squeal from the ground a couple feet away: "No! Don't do it!"

My father looks at me, as if what I say is all he needs to here. I see Emma a couple of feet away, wink at me – like she agrees with me. With the wink, she flashes a smile at me – telling me that she recognizes she's finally seeing me for the first time in over six years.

It's my father that speaks to Cadeyrn: "There's no way to explain or excuse what you've done." My father says, echoing the unforgiving line Cadeyrn told me just moments ago. His words tell me that my father was watching for my return back to the library. With that line, my father is quick to end Cadeyrn's life. With one final zap, Cadeyrn's lifeless body falls to the floor. My father walks over and stands above it while Emma runs over to me. I see Emma approach where I'm lying, but I hear my father's words in the background speaking to Cadeyrn's lifeless body: "That's for my family."

"Acea!" Emma cries out in both joy of seeing me and fear of seeing my physical condition. "I should have gotten here sooner – I'm sorry."

I see her face over me, cradling my head on her lap. I want to say so much to her – about how impressed I am with how she's grown up and become a Wizard, and about what I saw in Friday Harbor. But for a moment, it feels good to just be held by her – even if I really can't feel much of my body.

With my head in her lap facing up at her, I tirelessly crack a brief smile to let her know I'm happy to finally see her.

She brushes a part of my hair behind my ear while caressing my cheek. "Acea, I was so worried. All these years. I never thought I'd get to see you again…"

Her voice trails off but is interrupted by my father quickly approaching to see what my state is. "This isn't good. There's only one person who can help right now. Emma, I'm sorry but my son needs his rest."

William's hand lightly touches my forehead and I hear him whisper *"Somnum,"* instantly sending me into a deep sleep.

Chapter 20

The Uniform

My eyesight is momentarily blurred when my eyes slowly open. I see the outline of a woman.

"Emma?" I ask, not sure yet of where I am.

"Try again," a warm female voice says while running her hand through my hair. I'd know that voice anywhere.

"Mom!" I exclaim, while raising my body up off of a cot. "Mom, I missed you so much!"

By now my eyesight has returned and I see her warm smile. "Oh Acea, I missed you *so* much. All of those years …"

I see my mom glance up at my dad, who is standing to my side. This moment. This very moment we've worked so hard for – all of those years. Now, finally we're …

"Whoopie!" It worked! I hear an old, energetic man exclaim, completely oblivious to the moment he just interrupted.

It's Shaman!

The old Shaman continues: "You see? I told you my *rememdium* potion would do the trick! Now, which one of you doubted me again? Was it you, Vivian?"

My parents chuckle at Shaman's absent-mindedness, allowing our reunion to be interrupted.

"No, it wasn't me," my mother says. "It was Rzezna."

Rzezna comes into sight from behind my cot. Instantly, she's defensive, as if she doesn't want to have to deliver on a bet she just lost out to. "Now listen here. That was nothing but luck, Shaman! Why, you even mixed up your potions and turned him invisible first!"

All of us laugh before I look around and realize who's missing. I'm lying on a cot in the middle of the Temple of Artemis, surrounded by my parents, Shaman, and Rzezna – but Emma's missing.

I go to ask my parents where she's at, but my mom can pretty much read my thoughts. "Don't worry, she wasn't sure when you would awake. She's down with her troops, preparing them for the impending war."

"War!" I instantly remember how important it is for me to tell my parents about what I learned Vesuvius's plan *really* is. "Mom, dad. You're wrong."

"Typical teenager," Rzezna interrupts. I'd forgotten just how nosey and busy of a person she is. With how fast she continues talking, I don't even have a chance to continue telling about

Vesuvius's plan. As Rzezna just blurts on and on about something, my parents stand by my side, trying not to laugh at how unusual of a personality she is. "Typical teenager," Rzezna repeats. "Alright, stand up now. Yep, that's it. See, you're just fine now with Shaman's potion."

"Rzezna, I need to ..." I try to sneak in a line to cut her off, but it's no use.

"Wow, you've grown Acea. I mean, that's what I'd expect since it's been, what – six years? I don't know what took you so long to come back, but – well, now that I think about it, I'd actually say you're a bit on the small side for your age. You're what, eighteen?"

She pauses for a moment to await my response, completely naive to how everyone else around her is baffled but amused by her rambling nonsense. I go to confirm that I'm eighteen, but she doesn't even let me say anything.

"Yep, you've got to be eighteen. Anyways, I suppose we'll need to make you a new uniform. There's *no way* you can walk around down there looking like you do – I mean, really, do you still think you're a Sorcerer or something? Lose the cape, kiddo."

"Hey, I'm not a kid anymore! Now, we need to ..."

"Oh, nonsense!" She interrupts. "Now turn around so that I can get your measurements."

Luckily, there's a few moments of silence from Rzezna while she measures me – enough for me to talk seriously to my parents. "Like I was saying – Mom, dad, you're wrong about Vesuvius. He's not looking to take over Terra Fabula!"

Just as I finish my sentence, I see Rzezna step to the side and work furiously with her wands to sew something magically out of thin air. I'd seen this before when I met her, and though I'm just as in awe as I was then by this use of magic – I try to focus instead on what I'm telling my parents.

My parents exchange looks of concern to one another before looking back at me.

"Acea, this is extremely important, tell us everything you know," my father says.

I sit back down on the cot, and my mom instinctively holds my hand. I'm not sure if she does it to comfort me or if she's just embracing the moment that we are all finally having together – but it doesn't matter. I'm embracing the moment just as much, only I have to prioritize conveying my message.

I tell them everything I learned from my conversation with Isis. They already knew the history between Vesuvius and Circe, and how Circe lost her soul when trying to find a way to bear a child with her husband. But the information I tell them about Vesuvius really wanting to take over the human world, and how he wants to directly merge the path between it and Terra Fabula, is new to them.

My mother is the first one to speak after I tell them everything. "It makes sense, William."

"It does," he agrees, obviously still contemplating what it means. "But the question is what do we do about it – if anything."

"What do you mean, if anything?" Shaman chimes in. I get the feeling that this isn't really a conversation which he should be a part of – rather he was here just to help heal me. But the obviousness of the question makes him react out loud.

Vivian understands the way her husband is thinking. "It's not that easy, Shaman. If Vesuvius's plot is to take over the human world, then why should the rest of Terra Fabula fight a war that isn't against us? Why sacrifice so much for the human's war?"

"Because they don't know it's coming!" I say. "Mother, you haven't met the humans. They're good people. They're just like us, but without the magical abilities. They have *no* idea the degree of evil that's coming to overtake them."

My father is listening to the exchange between all of us, as if he's still deciding which course of action should be taken. Though he's been absent from Terra Fabula for a very, very long time, it's obvious that he's still seen as the head of the decision making. He is, after all, the oldest living Wizard, which would make him the Head Wizard in the Order … if the Order still exists.

I get up from the table and speak defensively. "Well, with or without you, I'm going to defeat Vesuvius. I can't allow him to exist in *any* world – human or wizard."

"Now, hold on, son." My father's voice is reassuring. "Let's not act in haste. I agree, Vesuvius needs to be defeated. But does it necessitate war, and all of its accompanying sacrifice?"

"You don't understand, father. His plan involves *destroying* Terra Fabula. He wants one world – the human world. And he wants to be the ruler of it."

"Then you're correct." My father finally admits. "I've never heard of any power strong enough to actually *merge* the two worlds. But if what you say could even possibly be true, then you're right. And I could see my brother wanting to destroy Terra Fabula. We have to act. And we have to act now. Vivian, please tell me that we have enough support from other wizards to go to war."

"Oh, we don't just have enough support," My mother says smiling. "We have an army."

"Now, hold on everybody!" Rzezna interjects. My parents and I all roll our eyes before looking at her. "No one is going out to the field looking like *that* – and certainly not Acea!"

Before I even know it, Rzezna scrambles over to me. She unclasps my cape, lifts my shirt off, and throws a new shirt over my shoulders.

"What is this?" I ask, knowing that Rzezna's done it again. She's made me a uniform.

"Oh, don't be so naive, kiddo. You know I'm the best seamstress in all of Terra Fabula."

I run my hand over the shirt, excited to see the full symbol of the Order of the Nine embossed on the front. However, the last uniform she made me was blue – the color representing my father's Kingdom in the Olympics. *This* uniform, though, is a beautiful, rich golden color. "It's gold…" I begin asking.

Rzezna's her usual self and anticipates my question. "Well of course it is! Don't you know?"

"He doesn't…" my mother cautions. Interestingly, Rzezna pauses, as if to give it a moment to see if my mom will continue talking. In the brief moment of silence, I find it interesting how Rzezna must recognize her place before my mom. This leaves me wondering just what my mother has been up to the last six years, and what her rank is among the army she mentioned.

With my mother saying nothing more, Rzezna runs over and quickly grabs a hand from myself and my mother. She looks at my father and just says "We'll meet you outside."

"No!" I exclaim quickly, but it's too late.

The next thing I know, Rzezna has transported all of us outside on the ledge of the Temple of Artemis.

Cringing, I turn to Rzezna to scold her. "Rzezna – tell me you remember that I told you *never* to do that again!"

But I stop from saying anything else. There's a strong reflection of light coming from the field to my side down below. Distracted by what could be making the glow, I turn my head and am amazed. On the field below – which was where the Olympics had taken place years before – is a *large* group of people. And they all are wearing the same gold uniform that I am. They stand in well-formed lines. I'm not even going to guess how many people there are, but it's well into the thousands.

Rzezna can't help but say something out loud while I just stand in awe staring at the large group standing in order below. "Once you left, they abandoned the different colors for each Kingdom. Now, they all wear the same color – the color representing the house where the Order began."

"The House of Gold," I say in amazement.

My mother stands next to me. Speaking eloquently and nobly, she explains: "This is what you began, Acea."

"Is it the Safari Army?" I ask excitedly.

With a tone of respect toward what I'd started at such a young age in the Animal Kingdom, she responds: "It started out as that. Now, all but two Kingdoms have joined – Vesuvius's and Khufu's. What you're looking at now is The Army of the Seven Kingdoms. And they are ready to go to war."

Chapter 21

The Army

The sight of the army on the field below is impressive. And honestly, just seeing it almost brings me to tears at the thought that the little, but determined, group we started in the Safari room has somehow grown into the multitude of warriors below. I never really gave any thought as to what the other Kingdoms had been doing the last six years, but now it's obvious that they've been assembling and training for this day.

We have a chance at defeating Vesuvius and his army!

The Army of the Seven Kingdoms below is obviously well trained. Everyone stands unified in order on the field, as if awaiting an impending command from my mother on the above hill. At least, it's obvious to me that my mother must be the commander or leader of it.

The army is also certainly diverse, with there being all shapes and types of people – and many different kinds of creatures are in it too, like centaurs, dwarfs, some trolls, minotaurs, and a whole bunch of other creatures that I have no idea what they're called. But even though it's comprised of such a diverse group, there's no doubt that this army is well trained, orderly, and unified in their cause. Unfortunately, the next sound I hear is not as welcoming as the sight of this army ready to fight Vesuvius.

"And there he is, ladies and gentlemen – your Wizard has returned!" The boisterous voice comes from an announcer who I'm not too thrilled to find out has somehow kept his job over these past six years. It's Pelops, and he's still just as annoying as before. Undoubtedly, he's standing somewhere on the field below, using his wand as a microphone as he had done during the Olympics years ago.

I stand still at the top of the hillside, hoping that he's really talking about my father who is now also standing at my side. He *should* be talking about my father and not me, after all – my father is the Head Wizard!

But he's not. Pelops continues, sucking up to the Army about my return - as if somehow it'll make the troops like *him* more. "Oh, Acea – step forward and waive to your troops!"

I do as he says. If there's one thing that is needed, it's ensuring that the army knows I stand with them, even if it means hiding my disdain for Pelops at the moment. It's just that … I'd like to have introduced myself to the Army without the assistance of Pelops. I'm sure it's only a matter of time until he finds a way to make some underhanded, back-biting comment in his usual sarcastic, flamboyant tone.

"And we certainly hope that Acea's been practicing his magic in the time since we've seen him last, don't we everyone?"

... and there it is...making fun of how bad I did at the Olympics...

I glance up at my parents, who also don't seem too amused by Pelops's remarks, but are holding back as if in recognition that this is my moment and not theirs. And after looking at my parents, I know exactly what I'll do.

I'm no longer the boy I was six years ago. I've grown so much in looks, confidence, and power since the moments where I was embarrassed on these same fields during the Olympics. And now it's time to show Pelops that I *have* been practicing my magic. This will be my first true use of the wand given to me by Isis, and just as she advised – I won't be hesitant to display my magical abilities.

With Pelops's voice still echoing throughout the stadium's field while he talks on and on about the Army, I instantly cut off his microphone feed with a flick of my wrist. This tells the army not only that I'll command respect from Pelops, but that my magic is more powerful than his.

Instantly, I rise up into the sky about ten feet from where I'm standing – just enough to show off my ability but not too much to make the troops think I'm being egotistical. While up in the air, I see where Pelops has been standing at the front of the army on the field below facing up at us. I decide to use this opportunity to take command.

I glide down the hill slowly, in awe of just how many troops draped in gold now comprise the army that was started so humbly by the safari animals to take down Nero. I turn around and see that my father and mother have also begun walking down the hill behind me. Unlike myself, they're probably walking because my mother isn't a wizard and therefore can't fly. I smirk to myself when I see that they're holding hands. It occurs to me that I've never actually seen them casually be unified and conversing *together*. The excitement of seeing my parents reunited motivates and excited me – finally, we've taken a step towards overcoming Vesuvius's evil grasp! We've already won many battles to get to this point!

I land on the ground next to where Pelops stands on the field. As I walk up to him, I can see that the years have not been kind to him. He's covered up his aging wrinkles with plenty of make-up to try and preserve his youth. This guy is all about appearances.

But, again, I decide I'm going to try to take the high road and command respect through my actions *and* words. I walk up to him and put my hand on his shoulder. "Thank you, Pelops, for that wonderful introduction. I apologize for cutting you off, it's just that we don't have a moment to spare."

With my hand on his shoulder, I'm surprised to feel him subtly shaking. I'm caught off guard when I see a genuine look in his eyes – he's nervous. I can sense that he's worried that he'd overstepped his place by cracking the joke at me before. And for the first time, I honestly think I've misjudged his character. After all, it *has* been several years since I saw him last.

The microphones are off, so only I can hear what he says to me – confirming that Pelops is no longer totally the shallow figure I once thought he was. "Acea, welcome back. We're all relieved to see you alive." He says in a nervous tone. But it's the look in his eye that tells me he's being genuine.

"Thank you, Pelops," I hear my mother say commandingly as she approaches from behind us. "You may be relieved of your duties for now and return home. We appreciate your welcoming."

"Thank you, 'mam, but if it's ok with you I'd like to stay and fight." Pelops surprising responds.

Wow, he really has changed.

"Certainly – as you wish." My mother permits.

With Pelops retreating back into the army's ranks, my mother turns and tells me quietly in my ear. "Pelops is just one example of how the citizens of Terra Fabula have grown these last six years. They've become unified after realizing how dire the circumstances are."

"Are they ready for war?" I ask seriously, knowing that we are on the eve of it.

"As ready as they ever will be. Don't underestimate the Army of the Seven Kingdoms. They've been well trained and know they're fighting for their survival."

"But, mom – there aren't Seven Kingdoms," I respond. "No one survived Gaelen's Kingdom when Circe destroyed it."

"Sure I did!" Emma's welcome voice exclaims as she walks up to us from among the lines of troops.

"You're right!" I exclaim in excitement while running up to hug her. She's just as eager to see me and runs to hug me back. "I forgot, you're Gaelen's heir!"

"That's right. I may be the only one from Gaelen's Kingdom, but I still count." As I put my arms around her, I can't help but feel how good it is to be hugging Emma. It's been so long since I've not only actually seen or spoken with a friend, but this is really the first time I've seen Emma since I saw our future. "Oh, it's so good to see you back on your feet, Acea!" She says softly into my ear during the hug.

"Hey, hand him over!" A gruff voice interjects.

"Yeah, don't you know that if it weren't for us, you'd still be a bird anyways, Emma?" A sophisticated voice joins in.

Wait a minute . . . I know those voices. Spike and Liam!

Before letting go of the hug with Emma to turn and finally see my other dear friends, I whisper back into Emma's ear: "There's *so* much I want to tell you. Another time, though. . ."

Emma winks at me while she lets go and moves aside, as if telling me she knows she's not the only one who wants to say hi. Spike and Liam also run over and hug me. It's funny how even though I've seen them as men before, I still think of them as the small dragon-looking armadillo lizard, and a goliath frog.

"Hey you guys!" I exclaim in joy while barely being able to withstand their over-eager, running hugs.

"Oh man," Spike says, "we didn't think you'd survive."

Liam agrees and chimes in: "Oh my, how you've grown. You must be starving, we'll have to cook you up something later this evening."

"That sounds wonderful," I say to make them feel good – but I know that we won't have time later. I know war is coming today, the army just doesn't know it yet. I'm about to actually tell Spike and Liam about how I'd seen them back in time when they were young waiters serving my father, but our conversation is interrupted by a hug that grabs me from behind.

"Acea!" I'm surprised by the grasp of the hug, but I recognize the energetic tone of voice. I just don't recognize the actual voice. I turn around and am thrilled to see who it is.

"Hip-Hop!" I exclaim. "You look so old, I barely even recognized you!"

Behind Hip-Hop is the group of people I recognize as the original Safari Army. Hip-Hop, his mom High-Hop, Stix and her husband Longneck, and Hard-Horn, as well as many others. My heart melts at the sight of these friends, and I run to hug each of them as well. But while saying hi to each of them, something stands out to me.

"Wait," I say, backing away from the group's hugs for a moment. "But you guys aren't wizards – are you part of the army?"

I can certainly tell from their golden uniforms that they're dressed to be in the army, but it doesn't make sense to me that they'd actually be part of it without being able to fight with magic.

"Of course we're in it!" Stix exclaims in disbelief. "Did you think we'd let some group of wizards take over the army we started?"

"Yeah, watch this Acea!" Hip-Hop unsheathes a sword

attached to his belt and shows off an impressive sword-swing maneuver. "My mom made me learn how to fight with a sword – it was the only way she'd let me join the army."

High-Hop walks over to her son, who is now almost as tall as her! She lowers her son's sword down and says to me: "It's true. What you see around you are all of the men, women, and youth who are able to fight in any way possible. We need everyone that we can get to fight in the war."

I glance at the prior members of the Safari Army, and can't help but think about how I have one other trick up my sleeve for later with them during the fight against Vesuvius. But my idea quickly dissolves upon hearing someone speak from behind me.

"And as you saw, they're well trained. My men have trained the other Kingdoms." I turn around to see who's voice it is that interrupts my conversation with the Safari Army. I'm genuinely happy, and a little surprised, to see that it's Berossus.

I'm surprised to see Berossus - a part of me always wondered if he would stand behind his agreement to join the fight. Trying to sound sincere, I respond: "Berossus! I'm relieved to see that you've honored your oath to fight against ..."

But before I can finish, Berossus interjects: "Acea, please no longer doubt my loyalty to the fight. Years ago I saw it as your battle, but now I know it is *our war.*"

I smirk, relieved that it's no longer my job to convince people of the gravity of the situation. I can tell that things have happened in the past six years to the other citizens of Terra Fabula to further convince them of the need to unite. At the thought of this unity, a pinch of pain happens on my chest in the location the poem to Lemuria had been engraved – reminding me of the painstaking effort I'd gone to years ago to convince these Kingdoms to unite. And now, here they are carrying on that effort.

Berossus continues: "I've had the best of my Kingdom train these citizens for the past several years – and I'm proud to call them warriors and to be ready to fight besides them, whether with magic or steel."

Berossus is also not a wizard – at least, not that I know. He also raises his sword in front of his face before bringing it to his side and bowing in front of me. Soon he is joined by the prior Safari Army members around him. Slowly, the symbolic gesture of being ready to fight and being loyal to the cause spreads throughout the entire field full of warriors. I look around and can't help but lose my breath at the sight in front of me. Row after row of men, women, youth, and other mythical creatures – everyone is kneeling before me.

Who I am? I'm just a son who wanted to reunite my family. Everyone in front of me is also a father, wife, son, or daughter of some kind. They don't need to be fighting for me – they have their own families to be fighting for.

Vesuvius is not just trying to take over the human world, he's trying to destroy all of Terra Fabula in the process. But in seeking to do so, it's not just wizardry that he'll kill off – it's all of these families. *That's* what he's really fighting against – not wizardry, but the lives and families of all of these citizens. And now we're coming for him.

I can't hold it in any longer. I have to tell the army that the fight begins now. I look at Berossus, then I turn and look at the group of Safari Army members. Next I turn and look at Emma before looking at my parents – still holding hands at the front of the army. I close my eyes and just rise into the air about ten feet – just high enough for the entirety of the army spread across the field to see me. Holding my wand up like a microphone, I divulge the urgency of the war to everyone.

"Thank you all for welcoming me back. I am sorry that I wasn't here the last several years to prepare you for the war. But while I was away, I learned something. Evil is nothing compared to love. Vesuvius and everything he stands for is evil! But here, in front of me – from one end of this stadium to the other – is unity, love, and strength. And I am honored to fight with every one of you!"

Cheers ring from the army below, and I'm humbled by the fact that they've welcomed me back with open arms. I try to fight back the tears, though, and be strong. Whether I want it or not – they see me as their leader. And it is time for me to lead them into war.

I turn and point to Vesuvius's large volcano that looms over the land.

"You see his volcano, spewing ash and lava like it were sick? You see that one piece of Terra Fabula? We have forced Vesuvius to run and hide into that corner of the world. He does not rule over your Kingdoms, he does not rule over your homes, and he does *not* rule over you! You stand for freedom and all that is good in this world, and he wants to take every ounce of that from you! He can't have it!"

More cheers ring out from the crowd below, but I don't wait for them to die down before continuing.

"I am proud to call you the Army of the Seven Kingdoms, but after we win this war there will only be one Kingdom! And you will have built it! It is because of each of you that one day our children and grandchildren will be told the story of how the Seven Kingdoms were united. It is because of you that they will be told how evil was removed from this land. And is it because of you that they will be alive.

We cannot wait a moment longer. The war is here! The war is now! This is our land and we will not wait to defend ourselves. Instead we will march to take what is ours. For it is *now* that the war begins – fight with me!"

The army erupts into shouts and cheering, and I'm relieved that they all agree with me to begin the fight now.

But out of the corner of my eye, towards the far back of the army, something stands out to me. Whereas the rest of the army is waving their swords and wands around in excitement, there's a small group that does not seem as eager. Without trying to give my intentions away, I casually fly around above the army, cheering along with them. I cautiously fly over to the part of the army that isn't as eager, to peer down and try to determine which Kingdom they're from – or anything that could tell me why they haven't totally joined in along with the rest of the army.

Then I see her. I'd know that look anywhere. For the last six years, it'd been in the back of my mind – while I'd interacted with Vesuvius, I always wondered what type of devilish wrongdoings she was engaged in.

Belle Gunness.

The woman I'd learned was Mama Eagle isn't alone, though.

And I only have a moment to spot the group before they catch on to the fact I'm spying on them. Next to Belle Gunness is a man who I've never seen before. But I don't even need to have seen him in his human form to know who he is. I'd know that stare anywhere – the one which says he loathes the very fact that I'm alive. It's King Khachatur. Vesuvius's two henchmen are in a group, and it becomes very obvious to me that the other members are warrior-wizards from Khufu's Kingdom. The moment they all spot me staring at them, they grab hands and then – *flash* – they disappear back to Vesuvius's Kingdom.

The disturbing thing is that they were all wearing golden uniforms. I don't have the heart to spill it to the rest of the army, and certainly not my mother – but they've been spied on. And now Vesuvius knows we're coming for him.

I fly back to the front of the army next to where my mother, father, and Emma are standing. I begin to tell them that we must act now, but the devastating events that suddenly occur next say it instead.

The ground begins shaking violently. The army's cheers instantly turn into chaotic screams from the surprise attack. The sounds of falling and cracking stone echo throughout the stadium. I turn to see that the Temple of Artemis at the top of the hill behind me has begun to break and crumble. When I turn back around to look at the army on the field in front of me, I see the Mausoleum at Halicarnassus on the top of the other side of the stadium's hill crack along its magnificent stone structure.

I know what's happening. Vesuvius has been told that we're coming. He's begun to merge Terra Fabula into the human world.

The war begins now.

Chapter 22

Earthquakes

It's obvious that all of the members of the army are afraid to remain standing on fields that have slowly begun to split apart.

"We have to go *now* to Vesuvius's Kingdom." My mother yells through the sounds of all the chaos around us.

My father nods in agreement.

"But how?" I yell back. "I thought that only Wizards in the Order can fly. And I doubt we have enough wizards like Rzezna to help transport everyone over there."

"Right," Emma yells. I turn to see her smiling. "And some of us Wizards don't like flying in the first place." I'm amazed at how calm she appears in the middle of this violent, intense scene unfolding around us. The fact that her remark alludes to her being able to fly makes me wonder if a new Order has been established while I was gone. If the names in the Book of Names were also heirs of the Order of the Nine, then it's possible. But I just don't have time to think more about it right now. Emma continues: "That's why I've called for backup – I've got this covered. They should be here just about now."

"Who?" I yell back. "I thought everyone who could fight was already here."

Just then, a shadow descends upon me and Emma. Next, the entire stadium is covered in shadows. I look up and am relieved and impressed by Emma's plan.

"Dragons!" I yell out in excitement.

Hundreds of dragons descend upon the army, causing them to uproar with a renewed sense of hope. One by one, the dragons land on the field, allowing multiple members to scurry on top of each one.

The dragon that descends right above Emma and I is a glorious, deep shade of purple.

I'd know that color anywhere. . .

"Hey, Lucy!" I exclaim right as she lands next to us. The corners of Lucy's mouth cracks into what I interpret to be a smile. Luckily, she recognizes me after all these years. I put my hand on the scales along her neck – it feels good to be with another friend.

I couldn't be any more thrilled by the turn of events. Thanks to Emma, what had been moments of panic have now turned into a uniting turn of events. Hope can be the difference between victory and defeat, and our army certainly has hope again.

"Climb on!" Emma yells at me while mounting the magnificent

creature Lucy has become.

I stop and stare for just a moment at just how incredibly *large* she is now. She's certainly not an infant anymore! I remember that she was almost twenty feet long when I saw her last – and she was only one year old then! Now, she's much longer – I'd guess at least twice that size.

As I run up and hop on her back, I see Lucy give me a welcome stare. What amazes me most is that everything I'd read about dragons told me that they become less willing to take instruction. And here I'm climbing on top a huge one, yet the look in her eye tells me she's not wild.

As I hop on behind Emma, I have to learn more about these dragons. "You've been training her, haven't you?"

Before answering me, I can tell that Emma's eager to get into the sky. The rumbling of the ground has caused some of it to start to create crevices and fall away. Dragon after dragon darts up into the sky, saving the warriors in the army. Emma glances to her left to nod at my mother, who has just mounted a different dragon alongside my father. From the looks of it, I can tell that this is far from the first time my mother has ridden her orange-colored dragon.

"All of you," I say in amazement while looking around at all of the dragons leaping into the sky. "Everyone's been training with the dragons." It's such a simple realization, but one that I'd never really thought about.

"You got it, Acea." Emma says, but I can tell her thoughts are more distracted to getting us off the ground. "Let's go, girl!" She instructs while patting her hand down on Lucy.

It's been years since I've last ridden a dragon, and I really don't even need to be riding one now. But the feelings of taking off and caressing through the wind on Lucy's back are things that I will never forget. It's a treat to get to be a passenger on such an amazing creature fit to rule the skies. And this time is a little different – I can subtly tell that Lucy is showing off a bit for me. She must be excited to have me back, as the speed and steep angle at which she ascends into the sky are unlike any of the prior times I'd ridden her.

"You know," Emma jokes once we're in the air, "you're lucky I'm letting you ride *my* dragon." Her emphasis on it being her dragon is obviously to give me a hard time.

"*Your* dragon?" I say back mockingly.

"You bet, you left her behind when you decided you'd rather be evil." Emma's joking continues to be more harsh, but probably well deserved. She knows I didn't *want* to be a Sorcerer, and if there's one person who could actually make light of what I did –

it'd probably be her.

I'm about to crack a joke back about how she also got caught by Vesuvius. However, the travesty which comes into view makes everyone – all of the warriors on the multitude of dragons adorning the sky next to us - fall silent.

We're all so high up in the sky now that all of the Kingdoms can be seen throughout the land of Terra Fabula. The violent earthquakes have spread throughout the land and intensified so much that the moving landscapes look almost like a ripple in water. And the devastating effects these quakes have on each of the Seven Wonders is heartbreaking.

The Lighthouse of Alexandria crashes into the sea, splitting apart upon impact with the water, and being sunk into the depths of the waves. The Colossus of Rhodes is no different. The magnificently tall statute snaps at the knees – a part of it falling onto the quaking shore that it once stood over, and the other part being lost into the sea.

The Mausoleum at Halicarnassus is swiftly destroyed by tidal waves of land being thrown at it from the violent earthquakes. On the other side of the stadium's hills, I see the Temple of Artemis meet the same fate – only the foundation and fragments of its column are remaining.

I'm horrified and left speechless when I look across the land and see the last of the Hanging Gardens be swallowed by the desert sands – as if Vesuvius's earthquakes were a palm squashing the very memory of the lush garden Kingdom that is now only a memory. No trace of that Kingdom exists any longer, with every green leaf now being entombed under the sand.

The dome which housed the Statute of Zeus that I once rallied the Kingdoms in – is gone. What was once a magnificent statute in honor of that Kingdom's Wizard is now cracking and turning to dust.

Miraculously, the last of the Seven Ancient Wonders is somehow still standing. Across the sea to the south I see the distant peak of the Great Pyramid. Somehow, whether by architectural ingenuity or by Vesuvius's grace, the pyramid still stands. However, it's no longer the shimmering, white pyramid I'd seen when I came to Terra Fabula. Rather, the rumbling ground and forceful quaking has caused the outside layer of smooth stone to fall away, leaving the outside looking just as I'd seen it in my textbooks growing up.

To say that all of the warriors of the army just witnessed devastation beyond words is an understatement. The utter shock befalling everyone isn't just about the lost Wonders. We know that if the great structures couldn't withstand the earthquakes, then there's almost no way any of the other citizens in Terra Fabula survived.

The travesty of the destruction of Terra Fabula is overwhelming. I glance at the men, women, and youth who adorn the sky flying toward the very evil which just destroyed their families. I'm taken aback by the sacrifice of these warriors. If I thought the sacrifice I'd gone through to reunite my family was difficult, it's nothing compared to what these warriors have just experienced. Though I'm humbled by their sacrifice, I'm also emboldened and encouraged by it.

We can win this war.

I tighten my grip around Emma's waist while she holds onto Lucy. She notices this, and breaks the solemn silence from the shock of what we just witnessed. "What is it, Acea?"

"We can win." I say, verbalizing my realization.

I see Emma wipe a tear aside from her cheek, and chuckle in doubt. "Yeah? Why do you say that?"

"Because we now have nothing to lose."

The thought lingers in the air, as if saying anything else would make it less true. The sun hangs in the mid-day sky, reflecting off the sea underneath of our army of dragons. We fly together toward the immense volcano spewing ash and lava ahead.

As we get closer, I know that we are entering uncharted territory. Not even myself – having studied under Vesuvius – knows what lays ahead.

"You know what?" Emma asks. The intimidated sound of her voice tells me she also knows we're all flying into the unknown.

"What's that?"

"None of us ever knew what to call his volcano. And after years of watching it cast Terra Fabula in its gigantic shadow – we gave it a name."

My interest perks up. "Oh yeah, what's the name?"

"Mt. Vesuvius."

Fitting.

I tighten my hold around Emma's waist once more, telling her I agree with the name. It fits every aspect of the wretched, evil-looking volcano.

Mt. Vesuvius is the perfect name for Vesuvius's Kingdom. And it's where this war will end.

Chapter 23

The Forest

The air as we approach Vesuvius's Kingdom smells like death. It's the type of suffocating death that wants to ensnare you in its grasp and pull you down into it.

Though the volcano towers over this part of Terra Fabula, it's not the only thing in Vesuvius's Kingdom. Along the coastline between the sea of water and sea of molten lava and rock – is a strip of dense forest. It wasn't here the last time I'd visited Vesuvius's Kingdom, leading me to believe that this is somehow the "additional security" that Vesuvius told me he added since I had visited.

And it must be. As the army of dragons reach the coastline, everyone is perplexed. Nothing. There's no movement and no one in sight. This is why I believe the forest is the added security – whatever Vesuvius has planned for us is hidden by the dense foliage. It has to be – he knew we were coming.

All of the dragons land along the coast – not wanting to take the risk of flying over a forest that may hide unknown surprises. When the dragons land, many of the warriors cautiously dismount them, and others still remain on the back of the dragons.

Emma and I are no different. Lucy lands on the sandy shore of the coastline, peering suspiciously into the trees. Still nothing. I wink at Emma, trying to be silent about my plans in case we're being spied on. I then hop off Lucy and lead the portion of the army that is ready and willing to investigate this peculiar scene. We certainly didn't expect to find Mt. Vesuvius and the base of it silent. But it's not the type of silence which would make us think it's been abandoned – no, it's the eerie type of silence making everyone careful of our next move.

There's probably at least several hundred warriors on the shore, waiting for me to take charge. The other half of the army remained on their dragons. My parents walk up to the front of the army next to me.

"What do you think, Vivian?" My father asks.

My mother turns and looks at me, and in a commanding tone remarks: "It's certainly not what we expected. Acea, you've been here before, haven't you?"

I can only guess that my mother assumes this from the years I spent with Vesuvius. "Yes, but that was six years ago. A lot has changed since then."

"Like what?" Asks my mom, trying to investigate what's

happening from what I may know.

"Well, for starters the forest is new. Vesuvius said he added additional security. The only way a strip of green forest could exist at the base of Mt. Vesuvius is if he wanted it here for a reason. So I'm guessing that whatever the new security is, it's being hidden by the trees."

"Yes, I would agree…" My father interjects before being cut short.

There it is.

A deep rumbling interrupts our conversation and surprises all of the warriors behind us.

It happens again. But this time, it's long enough for me to tell that whatever is happening is *not* an earthquake. In fact, it's not even the earth moving. It's the sound of something large – *extremely large* – pounding on the ground.

"What could that be?" My mother asks aloud, though I know it's what the entire army is also thinking.

Everyone has paused and is now staring directly into the trees, anxious for whatever gigantic thing just made that …

Thump!

At first, I think it's my heartbeat thumping, but the repeated shakes of the ground that quickly follow tell me something *much* larger is making the sounds.

Thump, pound!

Roar!!!

The deafening sound fills the air from behind the trees, sending shivers through my spine at what large beast is hiding in the in the forest.

"... that's a ..." I can barely even concentrate to finish my sentence. And I don't even have time to!

Suddenly, the pounding sound grows from one constant sound to a multitude of repeated rumblings on the ground. From the growing intensity of the shaking ground it's obvious that it's getting closer!

I hear the trees in the forest about fifty feet in front of us crash to the ground as the intense rumblings get closer. I know what's running at us, but I don't think I'll actually believe it until I see it.

Several of the warriors have run back to their dragons, hopping on right before the dragons take flight to try to be safe in the air. My parents and Emma are among those in the army who are taking to the sky again on their dragons. But many of the warriors have remained on the ground, drawing their wands, shields, or swords ready to fight against the army of beasts stomping toward our direction.

"Ready!" I yell out loud to lead the troops. "Here they come!!!"

The front line of trees crash to the ground, revealing the monstrous front line of Vesuvius's army.

Dinosaurs!

Chapter 24

Dinosaurs

The twelve year old inside of me who used to spend recess reading about dinosaurs is *seriously* geeking out right now. But the part of me that's the leader of the army wants nothing more than to take on Vesuvius. And if an army of dinosaurs is what stands between me and Vesuvius, then bring it on – even if the odds are not favorable.

"Run!" I hear several of the troops in our army yell out.

As soon as the trees break away and crash to the ground, a hoard of carnivorous raptors jump out from behind the protection of the trees and onto several of our troops. About twenty warriors are the unfortunate victims of the raptors' attack, and shriek in horror before meeting their end. I run to help, but arrive just in time to see several of them impaled by the raptors' famous claws. That extra claw is sharper than even an eagle's talon, and much more fatal – as several of my troops just found out.

"Raptors!" I exclaim, accidentally letting out my alarm before realizing it's probably not the best move as the leader of the army. I quickly follow with the first strategy I can think of. "Wizards, to the front! Attack!"

Many warriors run to the front, yielding their wands and pointing them at the raptors. Impressively, without me even needing to advise of them strategies or spells to use, many of the wizards shoot at the raptors while the others keep focused on the forest in anticipation of other attacks.

The raptors put up good fights, taking down a handful of other warriors before being defeated. I run over to one raptor corpse to take a look at what we're up against.

Undoubtedly, this is not the velociraptor which is more popular in name. And actually, I wish it was. That's because velociraptors are actually quite small. From what I remember reading, they were only about the size of a large turkey. Instead, the dead raptor I'm examining is certainly much larger than that. This tells me it's likely a utahraptor, less famous in name but much more dangerous due to it being human-sized.

I squat down and look into its lifeless, but still open, eye. Something about it just seems more humanistic than I would have anticipated for such a violent animal.

He didn't...

The thought permeates my mind. I have nothing to base it on except my own gut feeling, but it just makes too much sense.

Vesuvius has turned some of his army's warriors into dinosaurs!

It must be – he'd cruelly transformed an entire Kingdom into animals before, just out of jealously for his brother having a baby. If he felt it was the way to win the war, then I have no doubt he'd turn part of his army into the most vicious and dangerous creatures that have ever existed.

Thump, thump!

The repeated deep pounding that continues to originate from the forest tells me that this war is long from over. That herd of utahraptors was just the beginning – meant to thin out our numbers. And something *much* larger in size *and* in quantity is still coming our way.

Fortunately, there's a break in action. Now that we know at least what type of threat we're up against, I decide to use this brief moment to reassemble.

I turn and signal to the sky for my parents and Emma to fly down to me from their dragons. I turn and look for leaders of different ranks on foot and signal them to huddle up to me as well. I have no clue if they see me as their strategic leader, but I don't really care. I have an idea, and we're short on time based upon the approaching sounds from the forest.

As soon as the group of twenty or so leaders gather around, I divulge my idea – yelling as loudly and as quickly as I can amid the constant roars and rumbles coming from the forest. "Ok, those up high on dragons, as soon as the dinosaurs come through the forest, have your dragons shoot fire at them. Those wizards on land – break into groups of fifty or so and have each group focus on different dinosaurs. Remember there's a wide array of spells, and each wizard knows his or her strengths. We can take them down. With use of magic, we can be just as fast and deadly as these ancient beasts. Dinosaurs went extinct once, let's make it happen again!"

Just before the group breaks up, Berossus steps forward. "Sir, what about those of us who … aren't wizards?"

In confidence, I look at him and smile. "I have a different idea for them. Follow me."

The group of leaders had been meeting at the front of the army, closest to the tree-line. When it disassembles they all retreat back to their brigades. But those leaders of troops who aren't wizards instead follow me. I run to the very rear of the army, right at the sands of the shoreline. Those leaders stand next to me as I yell out: "Anyone who is not a wizard, retreat back to me!"

About half of the army falls back in response, and I'm instantly captivated by the troops' courage to fight despite not having the advantage of magic. The expressions of these warriors are wide-ranging. Some of them are confident and unmoved by the fighting that's about to occur. Others, honestly, just look terrified by having just witnessed several of their fellow warriors be suddenly killed by the raptors. They look to me with the hope that I'll offer them some type of upper hand to a threat they had no clue they'd be facing. Luckily, I think I've got what they need.

Whether they look prepared to fight or not, the troops fall in order around me at the shoreline and listen eagerly to my instruction.

The stomping sounds from the forest magnify, telling us all that we're at the doorstep of war. So I waste no time in divulging my plan: "I suspect Vesuvius has turned at least several of his troops to dinosaurs." Rumblings circulate from the troops in disapproval of such an evil strategy. "Well, he's not the only one who can do that."

Looks of surprise now come over these warriors as they see where I'm going. "Many of you spent years as animals – your inner animal hasn't died. In fact, you're more of a threat as an animal as his newly-transformed dinosaurs are. You *know* your animal instincts and the strengths that come from them. *That* is an advantage which Vesuvius isn't expecting. Let's use his own medicine against him – he made you captive as animals for centuries, and now he'll regret it.

We haven't a moment to waste. Who wants me to transform them? It's completely up to you."

Certain troops are eager and instantly raise their hands. Others are obviously reluctant, and I can't blame them. If my inner animal was an ant or butterfly, I certainly would not want to be changed. So, I leave it up to them.

I walk among the orderly ranks, using my new, more powerful wand to change those with raised hands into animals in a snap of my wrist. I do this quickly, but am amazed by the wide variety of animals that are now also members of the army. And many of them I never even saw in the Animal Kingdom – telling me that there was much more in the zoo rooms than I'd even discovered.

Among the newly changed troops are: alligators and crocodiles, elephants, snakes, zebras, hyenas, many different species of primates and bears, wolves, badgers, cougars, and a wide range of other animals that could easily be a threat against any creature. I stop at the end of the group, and smirk.

"Hey guys," I say to my old friends that made up the Safari Army.

"Us, too," Hard-Horn's deep voice instructs.

I wink at the group and am grateful to have found such a loyal herd of fighters. With a quick flick of the wrist, I turn them all into animals. I hope desperately that we'll all come out of this alive at the end, able to tell tales of another victory – but I know that's an unrealistic hope.

"Get back to your spots!" I yell, feeling pressed for time.

We can no longer ignore the overwhelming earthquake-like rumblings from the approaching dinosaur army. Everyone marches back to their prior positions among the rest of their brigade, hoping to make it there before the next wave of dinosaurs comes crashing through the tree-line.

One of the gorillas running by asks: "When do you want us to attack?"

"Trust your animal instinct!" I yell back, knowing an animal's instinct for survival is among the strongest weapons it'll have.

Suddenly, the tree-line erupts into an explosion of timbers, so much larger than what had happened when the raptors came crashing through. It's as if the entire front of the forest has erupted like Mt. Vesuvius.

"Now!" I shout, pointing my wand at the waves of violent predators running at us. Through the shards of timbers I see a wide range of predators charging our army.

More raptors – this time both the utahraptor and the velociraptor – come flying right at us. Herds of vicious allosauruses charge through, intimidating everyone with its large size and versatile movements. And pachycephalosaurses – known for its helmet-like hard head – dart onto the beach.

Angry, reckless triceratops stampede through as well, with their heads down ready to impale with their horns. But the triceratops are just one of several types of horned dinosaurs. If not for having studied everything about dinosaurs as a kid, I'd probably have no clue what their names are. But I do – and I'm practically standing in shock watching a childhood dream frightfully turning into an adult nightmare.

The name of the diabloceratops says it all – but the pictures I'd grown up staring at is nowhere near the correct depiction of these beasts. They have horns protruding from their face on each side, like spears. But two large red dots adorn their skull, as if they're war paintings meant to intimidate its enemy. And from the horrified reactions of my army, it's working.

The styracosaurus is among the most intimidating and deadly of all horned dinosaurs. It's skull doesn't just have a handful of horns. Rather, it's like a giant headdress with horns spearing out in all directions, and one large horn on its nose – ready to kill from any direction. Just the image of the styracosauruses running at the army through the haze of the exploded forest is enough to induce fear into the strongest warrior.

The stegosaurus is the last species which immediately stands out to me before I shake awake from my awe-induced trance. When I see a large stegosaurus run through a group of fighting wizards and stab one with its spikey tail, I realize the real predators haven't even shown up yet . . . and I know they will.

Where are they? Bring it on, Vesuvius! Bring on the spinosauruses and tyrannosaurus rex!

The dragons respond from the sky, filling the sandy beach with waves of fire, separating the running dinosaurs from our lines of troops.

Good job – just as planned!

But the advantage of flying dragons is quickly overcome by massive swarms of flying dinosaurs. I glance up to see several different types of dinosaurs – probably pterodactyls, pteranodons, petinosauruses, archaeopteryx and many more - attacking the dragons head-on. The dragons, and wizards riding on them, seem to be easily overcoming the flying dinosaurs. But with the sheer innumerable amount of those dinosaurs in the sky, I know the dragons will be distracted for a while. The entire sky is blackened by the swarms and fighting going on above.

When the line of fire on the beach dies out, the waves of the two armies on each side crash together in rage.

The front line of wizards all lash out immediately with a diverse range of spells. Many of them flash light, causing bright bursts of light to reflect down on the war from the shadows being created by the war in the sky above. Though many troops are killed off by the deadly attacks of the wide range of carnivores, the wizards' magic is able to overcome many dinosaurs. Clearly, if able to successfully be cast at the charging dinosaurs, the wizards have the stronger weapon.

And I'm no different, I shoot repeatedly and quickly at any dinosaur which dares to charge my way. My lightning bolts take down several species, but the sheer *amount* of dinosaurs is breathtaking. The wizards may have the greater weapon, but we are outnumbered by about three-to-one. And one swing of a dinosaur tail or claw can take out a handful of troops.

Peripherally, I see those non wizard warriors who probably didn't have much hope with their swords are now able to leap and attack from all angles as animals. This is effective, but certain animals obviously fight better than others. And it takes a whole herd of the small animals to bring down one larger dinosaur – and even then the herd sustains some casualties.

I jolt around to strike at a charging styracosaurus, but my heart drops when I see a familiar man lying on the ground lifeless behind it.

Pelops!

"No!" I yell out, reacting in anger at the charging dino. Pelops may have given me a hard time, but the fact that he changed over time into a man with redeeming qualities is the type of thing I admire. I take down the styracosaurus that killed him with a flick of a wrist, and then turn around to attack a velociraptor striking at …

"Rzezna!" I yell – but it's too late. I'm the last thing she stares at before the light fades from her eyes.

Tears overtake me and I rapidly shoot at any moving creature while I make my way to her. By the time I reach her, it's too late.

I crouch down and reach out to her small body while using the wand in my other hand to fend off dinosaurs. "I'm so sorry," I cry out, tears streaming down my eyes uncontrollably.

Amid the swirling chaos, I stand up and glance all around. The smell of death and ash is opaque – and it's not even from the gigantic volcano which we're fighting at the base of. Through the blurry vision of my tears, the only warriors who stand out to me are those who I know – fighting tirelessly for their lives.

In anger, I look up at the sky and dart straight up into the war being fought high above. I want nothing more than to be with those

I love – my parents and Emma. An enormous *boom* claps down, echoing throughout the Kingdom, from the intense speed that I travel to be with them.

Flying in the sky, I shoot large bolts towards the group of flying dinosaurs, taking out as many as I can to help free up the dragons for use on the ground. When I watch these dead dinosaurs fall down into the sea below, I'm horrified at the sight of how many dead dragons are also floating in the water.

Mom, dad, Emma!

I furiously fly around in the sky, looking for any sight of them. I spot Lucy's purple scales nearby and breathe in relief for a moment – until I see that many of her scales have turned red from blood. I just hope it's not all Lucy's own blood.

"Emma!" I yell out and fly over to her.

Emma notices me and smirks, but is suddenly distracted by an approaching pteradon. Before she even has a chance to shoot at it, I kill it just by wincing at it – just like I did with Newton's apple.

"I'm so relieved…" I begin before she interrupts.

"Me too." She says before striking at a pterodactyl behind me. "Acea – we can't win. We're fighting a losing war. We're outnumbered."

"I know …" I trail off. My thoughts change, though, to the

reason I came up here. I'm about to ask where my mom and dad are, but Emma can interpret my change of expression.

"Don't worry – I've kept close by. They were just over there." She says, pointing in the sky. But it's behind where she points that stands out most to me. The towering, imposing side of Mt. Vesuvius. I know that if there's a hope of winning this war, it's wherever Vesuvius is lurking on that volcano. So far, I haven't had any sight of him – which isn't surprising. He's much more likely to be using the war between armies as a way to buy himself more time to accomplish his real goal – merging Terra Fabula into the human world.

Emma and I fly quickly over to the orange dragon that my parents are flying on, killing as many dinosaurs as possible on the way to them.

We finally catch up, and I nod to them to follow me back down to the beach. The battle in the sky won't be won, so it's the last place I want them staying.

On our way down to the shoreline, Emma, my father, and I all use our heightened positions to shoot at dinosaurs on the corner of the beach where we're about to land – to momentarily clear it from threats so that we have a couple minutes to talk.

As soon as we touch down, though, another line of attack from

Vesuvius comes charging through the forest.

"Watch out!" Many of the wizards cry out as they see a herd of gigantic armadillo-like dinosaurs come crashing through to the front line. They're known as armored dinosaurs. Their impenetrable exoskeleton bones shield the other dinosaurs from much of the bolts of lightning being shot by the wizards. From the looks of it, there are several different species – ankylosaurs, edmontonia, and euoplocephalus – but they're all equally effective at quelling the onslaught of spells directed at the tree-line.

My mother is the first to notice this strategy. "They're protecting the forest from shots – something much bigger is going to be here soon!" She yells out to us.

And actually, these armored dinosaurs are not only a great defensive front line, but they are also keen attackers! Rows of sharp spikes protrude from the ankylosaurs' tail, and all three species have spikes adorning their hard exoskeletons - making it almost impossible for any of our troops to jump or climb over them. And any time a warrior gets close to one, the dinosaur swings its massive bowling-ball like tail to instantly knock them out. A handful of our troops learn this the hard way.

I want nothing more than to stand and strategize with my parents and Emma. But we're all distracted by this new threat and realize we have to breach the line of these dinosaurs so the ground troops are not left at a severe disadvantage with the next wave of attacks.

Emma storms off, casting an impressive array of spells at an allosaur before taking on an euoplocephalus. I only have a moment to watch her in action before my parents yell to me.

"We have to breach that line, Acea!" With that, my father also takes command of his wand and shoots at several dinosaurs. My mom wields her sword with deadly accuracy to protect my father while he shoots off into the distance. I run off toward Emma, hoping we can form a formidable threat together just as my parents do.

Rather than jumping over an ankylosaur, I leap and fly through the air, landing on the neck of one. It cries out in anger, but I lean down and grab a spike protruding on each side of its head, making me able to now steer it by pulling on the horns. In anger, it darts ahead, trying to shake me off. I yank on the spike on one side, steering it into a group of inattentive dinosaurs.

"You got it, Acea!" Emma exclaims while she shoots at a pack of velociraptors who try to jump up at me.

"Woohoo!" I yell out in excitement when my ankylosaur violently stomps on a group of small dinosaurs. Its rows of spikes slash through the sides of several unsuspecting utahraptors, instantly taking them out.

When other troops see how I started a breach in the line of exoskeleton dinosaurs, they join in the effort to take down the defensive wall along with me. I see Spike and Liam – who both did not want to be transformed into animals – roll underneath of a distracted ankylosaur and stab its underbelly with their swords.

"Watch out!" I shout at them, hoping they hear my warning before being squished.

I don't know if they heard me, but luckily, they were fast enough to escape from underneath of their victim before it falls to the ground.

Whew!

Suddenly, everyone – even the dinosaurs – stop on the beach at the deafening sounds that blare from the forest. Even the look in the dinosaurs' eyes tell me they're terrified. And they should be. The deep rhythmic sounds of the stomps approaching the beach mean one thing: the king of all dinosaurs has arrived.

My heart stops at the sight.

"Tyrannosaurus rex!" Someone yells from behind me. This yell breaks the moment of silence from when everyone cast their eyes in disbelief at the king lizard's arrival.

It's eyes pierce down to the ground from its towering height, just as if it's deciding who it should consume first. When it opens its jaw and roars out loud, the intense echoing shakes everything around me. We are prey, and this beast is at the top of the food chain.

It darts out onto the beach, and the fighting among both armies resumes. A handful of brave wizards flock to the T-Rex, but a swift snap of its jaw consumes two of them. The wizards' spells can't even break through this monstrous creature, as each shot must only feel like a needle prick. A group of animals jump onto the tail of the predator, only to be shaken off like a fly being swatted.

"Watch out!" Screams another warrior from further down the shoreline. "There's more!"

No – it can't be!

From out of the woods storms *two* more king lizards, and that's not even the worst of it!

The tyrannosaurus rex is commonly thought of as being the most vicious dinosaur, but it's not. There is another dinosaur even more predatory. It's taller *and* longer than the T-Rex. It has a sail-shaped fin abutting from its spine, and unlike the T-Rex, it has longer arms that provide another weapon.

"Watch out for the spinosaurus!" I yell to a group of troops running from a T-Rex who didn't realize they were running right into the path of the other carnivore.

Once I observe the new threat, I steer the ankylosaur towards it. I'm the leader so it's my job to try to take it down. The spinosaurus is quick enough to dodge the spikes and tail of my ankylosaur.

Emma sees this and flies over to where I'm located. She knocks out my ankylosaur and hovers next to me. "Let's do this!" She says, staring up at the spinosaur. "It's nothing compared to a couple of wizards, right? Besides, we're in the Order."

I know that Emma's joking to try to give us courage, but she's actually right. No more riding dinosaurs or just zapping them one at a time. I'm wielding the most powerful wand ever. This shouldn't even be a contest.

Holding hands to move in sync, we dodge around the swinging tail of the spinosaur and maneuver underneath of its flailing torso. Instinctively, we know this is the creature's biggest blind spot.

We only have a moment to react to our favorable position, so I hold my wand up and unleash the first spell that comes to mind.

Zap!

The dinosaur freezes in place – it's the same spell that my father used on in Sarajevo to capture me. And it works, at least for a moment.

The shocked dinosaur is fighting with all of its strength to overcome the hold of the spell, as its eyes show the internal struggle. Emma uses this brief moment to jump up into the air and unleash a spell on its neck that effectively decapitates it.

When she lands, we high-five each other. Remembering my parents are now on the same beach with the tyrannosaurus rex rampaging on it, I look furiously around hoping they're still alive.

But right as I find them still fighting in the same position as before, a new threat emerges! Rapturous and intimidating hollers like an army's battle-cry emanate from the forest. I turn and see an army of about one-hundred or so wizards erupt from the forest, shooting lightning at us while our fighting was focused on the dinosaurs!

"Acea!" Emma shouts in surprise. Her voice is more of a plea.

She doesn't need to say anything else. I know we're fighting an uphill battle. Though we started with thousands of troops, the numbers have been drastically scaled back to no more than several hundred. And now we have dinosaurs – including the T-Rex – *and* wizards to combat.

But when fire rains down from the sky, many of our troops cheer in excitement at the welcome sight of reinforcements!

"Emma! The dragons are back!" I say, pointing upwards.

Lucy jets by overhead, obviously showing off in front of her co-pilots. She's one of the many remaining dragons that overcame the army of flying dinosaurs. Now, they spew fire on the foes below – directing the flares at the dinosaurs. The opposing wizards undoubtedly can avoid being engulfed in flames with use of the *calorstragulum* spell. I hear several wizards from my army recite the spell verbally before pummeling into the fire to take the dinosaurs and opposing army head-on from a surprising position.

Great strategy!

Emma and I momentarily join in the cheers of the upper-hand given to us by the dragons. With a renewed sense of hope, all of us belabored warriors focus again on what we hope is the final stage of the war.

Standing next to each other, we wield our wands and direct them toward the forest at a handful of Vesuvius's wizards. But Emma stops, frozen in her tracks. And I see why.

Peering at us from the shade of the trees are two old enemies. She's undoubtedly frozen in fear by the one on the ground, but I see the other one as well – perched on a tree branch. They watch the entire war take place from a safe spot, as if commanding the different stages of the attacks from their favorable vantage points.

King Khachatur and Mama Eagle.

Chapter 25

Old Enemies

These foul enemies are no longer in their human form. King Khachatur stands as the human sized, hairy black tarantula he was when I'd run into him long ago in the Terrarium room. Just the site of the gigantic arachnid is petrifying, as he lurks there in the shade of the trees watching the battle unfold with his large beady eyes.

And Mama Eagle is no different – a human sized predator. Though I'd defeated her years ago by cutting off her razor-sharp talon, I know her to now be the calculating, mischievous Belle Gunness that stabbed King Nebuchadnezzar in the back. She didn't even want the dignity of taking him on face-to-face. She fights dirty, and she fights to win. I am sure she is the brains behind the battle while Vesuvius is unfolding his greater plan elsewhere.

I'm not sure if they see that Emma and I have spotted them, which means we have just a moment to strike. The war rages on among wizards and dinosaurs next to where we stand on the beach by the fallen carcass of the spinosaurus. But the only thing that matters to us right now is our old enemies standing shaded at the tree-line.

"Do you think we could attack them from here?" I ask while staring at them. I know that at least I could reach them with my magic from here, but I'm not sure it's a good idea. And Emma's on the same page as me.

"We could, but that wouldn't be the best strategy." She says, saying out loud what I'd also been thinking. "If we don't take them out with our first shot, then they'd have time to run and hide back into the forest. No … if we want to end this once and for all with them, we'll have to get closer."

"But if we get any closer, then we'll be standing in the middle of the open beach." I say. "How can we get closer without them seeing … wait! I have an idea!"

Again, Emma can pretty much read my mind. "The invisibility spell!" Before I even can say anything in agreement, she whispers "*Absconditus*" and disappears before my eyes.

"*Absconditus!*" I also recite. "Wait, Emma – where are you? I can't see you now!"

"I'm right here," she says in a reassuring voice. We may be unable to see each other, but she must have kept track of where I am. I jump when I feel something touch my hand. "Calm down, silly – it's just me."

A girl is holding my hand!

Luckily, I'm invisible, so she can't see how completely nervous and freaking out I am right now. I try to play it cool, though, and focus on the mission.

"Oh hey – there you are … so, are you ready?" I ask, hoping my nervous can't be deciphered in my voice.

"So, what's the plan Great Wizard?" Emma's taunting wouldn't be funny from anyone else, but I can't help but be charmed by her ability to not get too serious despite the circumstances and all of the death surrounding us right now.

"The way I see it, if we're on the ground they could just see the sand move. So, our best chance is to glide through the air right at them, and then strike them quickly. We should probably split up who takes on who. Which one do you want?"

Instantly, I sense Emma's shaking through her hand, making me wonder if she grabbed my hand out of desire or looking for a source of strength. I decide to use this as a chance to try to impress her by calming her down.

"Hey, it's okay," I reassure, "remember we're Great Wizards now, right? You didn't even know you were a Wizard back in the Animal Kingdom – and now look at you, the heir of Gaelen himself!"

"Ha ha," I hear Emma chuckle. "Yeah – just look at me!"

I burst out laughing when I realize my speech failed miserably – we're invisible!

A moment of silence hangs in the air as I can tell we're both standing hand-in-hand, fixated on the two enemies lurking down the beach.

Emma's the one to break the silence by being decisive: "King Khachatur is mine. He has to be. You take out Mama Eagle."

I'm proud of Emma for taking on her long-time fear of the gigantic spider. We absolutely have to each take on our enemy at the same time otherwise one will get away. But my plan is to take out Mama Eagle quickly and then help out Emma.

We can't hang out any longer – we have to strike – since the longer we wait the more wizards around us are taken out. But honestly, in case things go horribly wrong for Emma or myself, this could be the last time I talk to her. I *have* to tell her what I saw on Friday Harbor.

"Emma …" I trail off, slightly hesitant.

"Yeah, Acea?"

"I just wanted to tell you something important while I still have a chance to."

She doesn't say anything, and I can tell that she's thinking the same thing – there's a real chance that these one-on-one battles go wrong for at least one of us.

"It's just that – that I traveled to the future, ten years from now."

I feel her hand slightly squeeze mine, as if she's anticipating where this is going.

"And, I saw you."

Still with our hands clasped, I feel her turn and look at me, right in front of me. We can't see each other, but I know she's visualizing staring right at me.

"… and I saw me, too. We were married and living in Friday Harbor, Washington – where I'm from. And we have two kids, twins actually – named Kyler and Eden."

No way!

It instantly hits me, the man I'd met back with the Seven Ancient Wonders was named Kyler, and so is my son! They're the same person - I sent my son back in time to help me out, once he's an adult!

As if my heart wasn't already racing from divulging these things to Emma, my mind is now racing just as fast thinking about everything involving time travel and my son, Kyler. I try to focus on divulging things to Emma, though, but she interrupts before I can say anything else.

"Whoa, there kiddo!" Her joking voice is returning. "Don't move too fast – all I did was hold your hand and now you wanna marry me?"

"Ha ha, you're right, I shouldn't have told you..."

I feel a peck on my cheek, surprising me with how she was able to aim so well despite us both being invisible.

Maybe she was aiming for my mouth and missed? ... Wait – a girl just kissed me!!!

I really don't care whether or not a peck on the cheek counts – she kissed me!

I don't know how to react – should I kiss her back? So, instead I just awkwardly stand there for a moment. Thankfully, I'm invisible, as I don't think Emma notices my awkwardness.

"Well, how about this," she says. "If we make it out of this alive, I at least promise we can go on a date. Where would you take me?"

I blurt out the first thing that pops into my mind, and I don't even know why I say it – though probably because it's a place I'd seen all the high school kids meet up at on the weekends. "There's this ice cream shop down the street from where I live in Friday Harbor. It's *amazing.*" I'm instantly embarrassed by the simplicity of my answer, but surprisingly Emma's not.

"Sounds perfect."

"Really?!" I ask, my excitement obviously showing through my tone. I now feel like I could conquer the world.

Emma doesn't say anything immediately, and I can tell from what she says next that her train of thought has changed.

"Hey, you know what?" She asks?

"Yeah?"

"If that's what you saw in the future – then that must mean we survive this, right?"

I squeeze her hand back, seeking to give her confidence with what she just realized. I don't know if it's true of not, but it's enough to give us hope to overcome our fears.

"Well, then – what are we waiting for?" She continues. I love how Emma's tone throughout this entire conversation turned from nervousness to confidence, to now being excited. Her perspective is contagious, and I'd fight any battle alongside her.

"Ready if you are!" I exclaim.

She returns back to standing on my side, with our hands still clasped together. In a swift movement, we rise up above the ground and dart through the sky toward the tree-line where Mama Eagle and King Khachatur are.

As we fly from the beach to the forest, we pass next to one of the tyrannosaurus rex being captured and gutted by a hoard of animal-warriors.

Wait – that's Hard-Horn spearing the belly of it! . . . And there's the rest of the Safari Army taking it down!

I'm excited and empowered by seeing all of the gang still alive – war-torn, but still alive! Even old Shaman somehow has survived and is standing in his human form alongside the Safari Army. Undoubtedly, he's been using an array of his diverse range of potions and spells as his weapons.

When another tyrannosaurs rex is darting towards a group of unsuspecting wizards, I use my magic to make it freeze in place while I fly by. This allows the wizards to finish it off. But as we fly closer to Mama Eagle and King Khachatur, I'm careful not to use anymore magic, so as to not give our invisible position away to them.

We jet over the sand, careful to be high enough to not make any imprint on the sand from our movement.

My heart begins to race the closer we get to our old enemies – mainly because of how intimidating and scary the sight of such a large tarantula is. I'd forgotten just how petrified the very sight of him made me!

I'm again impressed by Emma's courage to be the one to take

him on, and I turn my focus to Mama Eagle perched on a branch up in a tree. I have to take her out swiftly to help out Emma's fight – so I can't screw this up.

We are about fifty feet from our enemies and approaching quickly – they don't seem to notice us at all. I squeeze Emma's hand one last time to wish her good luck, but then we break off our embrace to split up.

I can't see what happens to Emma, so I just have to have trust that she'll be successful in her fight. Rather, I need to focus on the predatory bird that has no idea I'm about to strike.

I glide cautiously higher into the sky to the eagle's altitude, but trying not to alert her keen senses to my presence. Mama Eagle is perched toward the very top of a tree, staring out at the hundreds of warriors battling below. I recall how an eagle's eyesight is unlike any other creatures – able to see for at least 5,000 feet away with cunning detail. And a single strike of its razor sharp claw can kill its prey instantly.

I defeated you once, and I'll do it again!

I glide right up toward her branch, and I'm about ten feet under it when I raise my wand to kill her with one swift attack.

Here I come!

With the memory still fresh in my mind of Mama Eagle

killing Nabu, I let the power within me flow out through the wand. Instantly a thunderous clap bolts out from my wand, flashing toward Mama Eagle.

No!

Right before the lightning bolt strikes her, she darts off from her branch and plunges down around the bolt and right at me!

"It's a trap!" I yell, trying to alert Emma. I don't even have time to see if she's ok, though, as I have to lunge around Mama Eagle's retaliatory strike at me.

I don't know how – but they knew we were coming! . . . They must have been able to see us somehow. . .

I dive to my right avoid Mama Eagle's jab at me with her beak. The beak alone is an impressive weapon. With its strong hook being used to tear food apart, it could easily cut me like a fish.

"No!" I yell instinctively. I fly out into the sky to try and gain an advantage from being invisible to strike again. But she follows me! She knows exactly where I am – her keen eyesight was able to spot us all along!

Flying high into the sky, I increase my speed to try and distance myself from her so that I have time to swing around and strike her with the freezing spell. No luck! In fact, Mama Eagle *gains* ground on me, and I'll soon be within the grasp of her remaining claw.

As I continue to dart away from her, I turn around in the sky and haphazardly shoot spells of bolts at her. She thrusts from side to side, successfully avoiding my weak attempts to impale her. With every missed attempt, she gains ground on me until I see the angry, predatory look in her eagle-eyes wanting nothing more to end my life.

"No!" I yell again defensively.

"Diiiiiie!" She squeals out loud in a mixture of a crackling, deafening eagle cry and her human voice.

My ears bleed from the lasting shriek of her cry, and I instinctively go to cover them with my hands as I can no longer take the attack of the squeal. Right as I do, she lunges at me with her claw, striking my right arm and taking hold of my entire body in mid-air with her wings!

I can't move! She covers my entire body into hers, like an anaconda constricting its meal.

"Let go!" I yell out loud.

With me firmly in her grasp, she looks me right in the eye before striking at me with her beak. I rapidly move my head from left to right to avoid her repeated attacks. There's no end to her strikes, though. Once or twice, her beak glazes my eyes, cutting it with ease. Her one remaining claw takes hold of my arm and begins cutting into it.

"Ahhh!" I yell out in terror as I feel the razor-sharp claw cut into the bone of my right hand. "AHHHHH!"

With the wand in my left hand, I make one more desperate attempt to freeze her with my magic. I use every ounce of my remaining energy before I succumb to the weakness overcoming my entire body in pain.

Zap!

Mama Eagle freezes in mid-air! It works!

Oh no!

I'm still within her hold as she falls to the ground from our great height, like a large ice cube awaiting impact with the ground below.

Through my traumatizing pain, I use any energy I have to wiggle from her grasp as we fall toward the sand. I creep out from her wings' hold and manage to fall away from her a couple feet before Mama Eagle lands in the sand. I roll into the sand to avoid hitting it at the fast speed.

Thud!

Mama Eagle pounds into the sand about ten feet from me, and just lays there unable to move due to my spell.

I hobble over to her, bleeding from my head and arm. Holding my right arm in pain with my left hand, I approach the gigantic bird.

I first limp up to her eye and see the intense hatred still burning in it – she's alive and trying desperately to make any movement to break the spell. Having been under this spell a couple times myself, I know exactly how much it sucks to be in her helpless position.

My right arm throbs but I release it from my grasp as I hold up my wand and point it down at her one remaining claw.

"This is for my friend, Nabu." I say before cutting the claw off with a bolt of lightning.

Instantly, her eyes look like they want to pop out of her head in pain – being a caged bird unable to move or react in agony through any other movement than her eyes.

I must waste no time, as I have no idea how Emma's battle is going.

I turn away from her, telling her she's not even worth my time to watch her evil life come to an end. "Goodbye, Belle Gunness." I mutter her real name before releasing the final blow to one of Vesuvius's henchmen. Her final, deafening squawk manages to cry out and I turn to confirm it's her final sound she'll ever make. And it is.

Holding my searing right arm again due to its overtaking pain, I fall to my knees in exhaustion. The pain is so intense that my eyes can barely focus on the tree-line as I frantically look for Emma.

"Emma!" I yell out, desperate for any sign that she's alive.

"Acea!" She cries in response. From the desperate plea of her voice I can tell she's facing impending death.

With my eyes still unable to focus from the pain, I just stand up and jog with every ounce of strength I have towards the direction I heard her cry from.

"Acea!" She yells out again.

"I'm coming!" I try to yell back, but I doubt she can hear my pathetic attempt to yell, which barely comes out as much more than a whisper.

As I move closer to the trees, my heart drops. King Khachatur has her pinned against a tree, spun against it in ropes of his webbing. For a moment I wonder if it's a trap to lure me in like he did in his burrow inside the Terrarium room. But I know it's not this time. I don't know how he managed to trap her against the tree in his webbing, but he's now perched up against where she's entombed. His giant tarantula legs are raised into the air, as the fangs located under his head are moving toward her. I can tell from this deathly scene that King Khachatur had a plan to take down Emma – and that his battle against her was also very personal.

I'm much too far away, and much to disabled from pain, to be able to reach her in time.

"No!" I yell out to the arachnid with everything I've got, through my pain.

When King Khachatur reacts to my yell, I see his body turn to look at me briefly. To my horror, he ignores me and turns back to cast the final blow at Emma.

"NO!" I yell one final time at him, raising my arm and casting the first spell that comes to mind – hoping it reaches King Khachatur before he strikes Emma.

Instantly the cries of the giant tarantula fill the air as his entire hairy body is engulfed in flames. He moves away from Emma, moving in panic as he reacts to the immense agonizing pain overcoming him from the heat. But every movement he makes in reaction only makes the flames grow higher. It takes only a minute before King Khachatur's life succumbs to the fire. His large body overturns and haunches into the fetal position.

I try to focus on Emma to see if she's still alive, but - much like King Khachatur – I can no longer take the immense pain radiating throughout my entire body. Right before I crash onto the sand, a bright flash of light emanates from Emma's direction. But right after that, I fall back into the sand, waiting for my mind to drift off into the never-ending abyss of pain.

Through the ringing in my still-bleeding ears, I hear the faint sounds of multiple footsteps in the sand rush up to me. With my eyes cracked open in trauma, I see four silhouettes fall over me. Part of me wishes it was a dinosaur, ready to finally strike and end my pain. But deep inside, I really don't want to die yet. I have to kill Vesuvius. That one thought permeates my mind, preventing me from drifting off to death.

"He's still alive!" I hear one of the silhouettes speak. My conscious peaks when I recognize it as my mother's voice.

"Son!" I hear my father plea. "Stay with us – the Shaman's here."

"Emma?" I squeak out.

"I'm right here, Acea!" She says, while grasping onto my hand.

"Shaman," my father says in haste, "his condition is worse than we thought. Are you sure your potion will work?"

"Oh my," My mother says, deeply worried. "You can see the bone in his hand – and look! His skull can be seen by his ear, too!" She caresses the hair on the side of my head, and for a moment I remember Isis having done the same thing. For as much as I felt loved by Isis as she caressed my hair, the feeling is nothing compared to being surrounded by the ones I love – my family. I feel a tear trace down my cheek, both in pain and at the thought that I've worked so hard to be embraced by my family like I am now.

"I love you," I say faintly, looking up at my mother, father, and Emma peering over my worn-torn body.

"Well then!" Shaman interjects, obviously clueless as to the moment he's interrupting. "Will my potion work? Of course it will, William!"

Shaman goes to pour a vial down my throat, Emma's hand reaches over and stops him briefly. "Shaman – make sure it's the right one…"

I can't help but chuckle, remembering the time Shaman mixed up the potions before.

Shaman's absent-minded looking eyes widen in disbelief that someone would accuse him of being incorrect. Defending himself, he abruptly responds: "*Excuse* me, but I've been handing this potion out left and right to warriors on the battle field all day! … And even using a little for myself… so be glad I saved the last bit of it for your lover-boy!"

With that, Emma releases her grasp from Shaman's hand and winks at me. Shaman drops the potion down my throat and I almost gag. The pain quickly rescinds from my entire body, and I look down to see my arm wound magically heal. But even though I'm instantly healed – something still causes me pain.

Coughing, I can't help but react: "Shaman! This tastes horrible! Don't you have a way to cover the taste up! You've had six years to improve it, haven't you? What have you been doing all along?"

I'm glad to see my family laughing at my intentionally humorous reaction. Shaman, on the other hand, doesn't appear too thrilled.

"Oh come here," I reassure him. "I'm just kidding." He goes to shake my hand, but I instead pull him into a hug. While I embrace the old man, I whisper in his ear. "Thank you, old friend. I assure you that your role in casting the spell over the Animal Kingdom is long forgiven by your heroic loyalty to our army."

When our hug ends, Shaman looks me in the eye and straightens up before smiling. I can tell from his smile that my words meant more to him than I'll probably ever know.

My father's looking up at the top of Mt. Vesuvius while he speaks. "Acea, look up there." It's obvious to me that he's using one of the sense spells he'd learned in school growing up, and I instinctively do the same without even knowing the actual spell.

I glance to the top of the volcano. As if the spell is innate and natural to me, my eyesight zooms in – probably much farther than even a bald eagle is capable of. Being zoomed in and focused on the rim of the volcano, I see lava and ash spewing out from the volcano's interior crater.

There he is.

At the rim of the volcano, not even facing the war being fought below, is Vesuvius. He stands facing the pool of lava at the top of the volcano. I can't see exactly what he's doing, but I don't need to. I know he's creating a bridge from Terra Fabula to the human world – and is in the process of destroying Terra Fabula as it merges into the human world. The destroyed Seven Ancient Wonders is evidence of this cataclysmic plan.

"He's mine." I say out loud, still spying on Vesuvius through my enhanced eyesight.

"I know," my father says, as if he knows there would be no way to prevent me from facing off against him. But what my father says next surprises me. "It has to be you."

I return my eyesight to normal, and look at me dad. "What? What do you mean it *has* to be me?"

"It was always meant to be you," he responds. "But now, you're the only one who can take him down. I'd be no match – my brother is much more powerful than I could ever be. He knows the way of wizardry *and* sorcery. That's why it has to be you – you do too."

"Are you saying that wizardry alone isn't enough?" I ask, surprised to hear what my father is saying. "But doesn't the power of good always overcome the power of evil?"

"It does," he says – but this doesn't make sense to me. "And that's why it has to be you."

"But, why?" I ask still confused.

"To learn absolute truth – to learn how to be the ultimate good in the world, such powerful knowledge comes from understanding how evil exists – and yet still *choosing* to embrace the light of all that is good." My father reaches his hand out and places it on my shoulder. "You've done this. I have not. And besides, you have the upper hand – your wand. Trust it."

The look my father gives while explaining this to me tells me he's admitting that my powers make me more powerful than him. His honestly and humility are traits that I admire, and great examples to me.

And what he says rings true inside of me. Not only have I studied both sides of magic – wizardry and sorcery – but I hold onto the virtues of wizardry with every thread of my being. Having seen first-hand how Vesuvius turned from good to evil, I know what I'm up against. I look up at the volcano where Vesuvius stands.

"But don't think you're going alone. I'm still coming with you." My father says.

"Me too!" My mother quickly interjects. I jolt to look at my mom in surprise.

"But mom, you're not a Wizard – you'll…"

My father smiles as if he knew his wife wouldn't let her two boys go off to battle alone. "She's not coming to fight Vesuvius," he says. "And neither am I."

"What? So why are you…" I trail off.

"There's still one other foe who must be defeated. And where Vesuvius is, she is surely lurking as well." Explains my mom.

"Circe." I exhale in disdain for that witch. I look at my parents lovingly, knowing they're coming with me to stave off Circe so that I'm not battling in a fight where I'm outnumbered two-to-one. "Thank you," I say lovingly to my parents, who are obviously willing to fight to their death not just for the survival of Terra Fabula, but for me.

Turning and looking at Emma, I plead. "Emma, please don't come with us." The thought of losing her to Vesuvius or Circe if the battle goes awry is more than I want to endure.

She must understand that the battle against Vesuvius is not hers to fight. Looking back at the war still being fought by both of the armies' wizards, as well as the remaining dinosaurs and animal-warriors, Emma smartly calms my nerves. "What? Waste my time fighting just one Sorcerer?" She cracks and walks over, holding my hand again. "You don't need my help with that do you? I think I'll stay back here and help defeat his army instead."

I can't help but stand in awe of her – not just her beauty, but her strength. In the six years while I was absent, she not only grew to be a skilled Wizard and warrior on the outside, but also on the inside.

"Besides," she continues. "We come out of this alive, don't we?" She again reassures me before the largest battle in Terra Fabula's history. But what she does next both confuses and motivates me.

She leans in and kisses me on the lips!

When she pulls away, she whispers in my ear. "I'll see you after, just like we discussed – good luck, Acea."

She doesn't even wait for me to say goodbye to her, instead turning around and flying off to rejoin the battle happening down the beach.

I look at my parents, still in shock by what Emma just did.

Though I should probably be embarrassed that she kissed me in front of my parents, that's the last thing on my mind. I still feel like I could defeat *anyone* right now!

My father, mother, and I all turn and look up to the top of the death-imposing, ominous volcano that is Mt. Vesuvius. Though it's normally what I would be thinking right now, my mother says it instead.

"Here we go!"

Chapter 26

Mt. Vesuvius

Lava and ash fill the air above where Vesuvius stands at the top of the volcano, engulfing the sky in red shadows. The crater at the top of the volcano boils over one edge of its rocky cliff, like a cauldron of hate seeping down to poison the remainder of Terra Fabula. The massive volcano towers over the entirety of the wizard world – casting a tall shadow of fear and intimidation to the Kingdoms below.

"I didn't see Circe up there…" I remark.

"Oh, she's up there." My father assures. "Remember, this entire war is because of what happened to her – there's no way she'd be anywhere else."

"Mom, are you sure you want to come?" I ask, looking desperately into her loving eyes. She knows I worry for her safety, even though she's become an impressive fighter and commander over the last several years.

She puts aside her commander-persona for a moment and gives me the warm, motherly look I recognize from the night she put me to bed as a twelve year old in my constellation-adorned bedroom.

"Oh, son – haven't you realized by now the endless sacrifice I'd make for you?"

Just her very words ring true inside of me, filling me with the same feeling I'd felt when touching the Family Tree in the Animal Kingdom's Aviary room. It's love. From my mother, from my father – we're here together now, and nothing can take that away. *This* moment is what it's all for. *This* moment – this *feeling* – is what gives me the advantage over Vesuvius. It's something I have that he doesn't.

My mother continues, coyly steering the subject to what's next for us. Her glance changes from looking into my eyes to fixating on the top rim of Mt. Vesuvius. "Now, William and Acea – when this is all over, where should we meet?"

I like my mother's confidence – not even questioning whether we'll come out of this alive. It's empowering. But also, her question is the first time I even have ever thought about what it would be like with my family together and the threat of Vesuvius extinguished. My mind drifts for a moment to the last memory I have of true comfort – the memory I'd initially desired to retreat to when I had awoken in the Animal Kingdom.

"I . . . I'd like to live as a family at our home on Friday Harbor." The fact this is my answer is somewhat ironic – I had, after all, wanted nothing more than to venture off the island the last time I had been on it. But now that I find myself dreaming of even the mere possibility of stability and safety again – that's where I'd like it to be at.

"This place – Friday Harbor. It sounds wonderful. I'd like to visit the home you both had – even if it is in the human world. From now on, my home is wherever my family is." My father says.

My mother leans over and kisses her husband, and I just smile at seeing their loving affection for one another.

When it ends, my mother looks at him in the eye, and then turns to me. "Are you both ready?" She asks when turning to look at the top of the volcano.

Neither me or my dad even need to respond, as we all know our fate lies at the top of the volcano whether we're ready or not.

My father takes my mother's hand, looks at me, and speaks: "Whatever happens son, know that I'm proud of you."

With that, he's about to dart into the sky along with my mother. But he pauses when I say the one last thing I need to tell them – knowing there's a possibility it's my last chance to say it. "Mom – Dad, I love you."

My father and mother smile and nod, hand-in-hand. And with that my parents lead the way in flying up the side of the towering

Volcano to where Circe and Vesuvius are. I cast off upwards right behind them, eventually reaching where they're at and flying beside them.

The flight up seems never-ending – which makes sense from just how *tall* the volcano is. As we ascend closer and closer to the top, the dust becomes heavier and heavier – itself becoming a form of defense for Vesuvius. We notice that those areas where lava flows down the side seem to have cleaner air above it – possibly due to the lava having incinerated the ash from the surrounding air. We naturally steer over to those areas, but as we do the immense heat is felt intensifying as we get closer. Instinctively, my father and I recite the *calorstragulum* spell to protect us – thankfully, my father has the ability to cast the spell so that it also protects my mother.

The flight over the streams of lava are treacherous. Random flares of molten lava randomly shoot into the air – as if meant as an additional, intentional form of defense. We jolt from side to side while intensifying our speed in an effort to finally reach the top and end this dangerous path.

The fleeting thought occurs for us to turn invisible – but just as it enters my mind, I dismiss it. I've been invisible before while confronting Vesuvius in the Animal Kingdom, and it did no good. Indeed, that experience tells me just how incredibly powerful he is.

We finally crest the rim of the volcano. Vesuvius is no longer standing on its edge, having instead moved toward the inner edge of the crater. Inside that crater, the pool of lava boils, as if it's a cauldron in which he is creating a large potion. Only this potion isn't for some normal magical ability – I know that somehow he's creating the direct path from Terra Fabula to the human world – bridging the two worlds without the need for Lemuria.

Circe stands beside her husband – both of them turned toward their volcanic creation brewing below in the inner crater.

As my parents and I land on the outside rim of the volcano about fifty feet from them, we walk suspiciously over to our two enemies – unsure of whether or not they know we've arrived. But the next sound that booms into the air quickly tells me not only that they know we're behind them, but that they've been expecting us.

"And here he is!" Vesuvius yells. He and Circe turn around, staring at us from afar. Vesuvius slowly claps in sarcastic applause. "You finally made it here, *son.*" The sound of that word no longer holds any threat to me. Rather, it makes me cringe more from it being a reminder of how much I had helped Vesuvius get to this point for the last several years. "Welcome to my Kingdom – did you like the additional security?"

Circe shrieks in laughter, while fixating her look on the three of us like she's been anticipating this evil moment even more than her husband. It's been years since I've seen her, and still I can't stand the sight of her ghastly broken teeth, sickly greenish skin, or shrill voice.

Now only about twenty feet from us, Vesuvius continues in a mocking tone. "It took you longer than I thought – especially for being such a *great* Wizard. Why, I can even smell the foul stench of Shaman's *rememdium* potion on you all the way from here. What happened did a dinosaur cut you, or was it Belle Gunness?" The tone in Vesuvius's voice tells me he knows the answer. But his tone of mockery quickly transitions to degrading anger as he continues: "You swore an oath to me, and an oath to sorcery, son!"

My father is about to interject in objection to Vesuvius still calling me his son. In anticipation of this, Vesuvius looks over to him, ready to quickly rebuke his brother. However, I stop any confrontation from happening by speaking up to verbally combat my foe.

"I haven't forgotten the ways of sorcery, Vesuvius - I've just overcome its *limited perspective of magic!*" I yell back in confidence. My use of the same derogatory phrase to explain sorcery that Vesuvius had used to degrade wizardry obviously angers him. But before he can say another word, my father's voice exudes with the force of a weight falling to the ground.

"Enough is enough, Vesuvius!"

Vesuvius looks right at him, as if he sees his brother as nothing more than a collateral road-block to his ultimate goal of destroying Terra Fabula. His glance is brief, though, before staring straight back at me. Vesuvius's next words fly out of his mouth at the same time - and just as fast - as he takes off flying right at me "You're right!"

The quickness of Vesuvius's attack is surprising! I react with the first thing that comes to mind - flying right back at him!

In mid-air Vesuvius and I both release a bolt of magic at each other, and the clap which sounds when they collide crackles throughout the entire land. I don't have a moment to pay any attention to my parent's actions, but it's obvious that they've begun attacking Circe the moment I took off in the air.

Our streams of lightning bursts collide as we both fly closer to each other in mid-air. Surprisingly, I haven't felt a cringe of pain at all from anything shot at me from Vesuvius.

My wand is incredibly powerful!

With our streams colliding while we draw closer to each other, the force pushes us slowly up – being a foot away from each other.

Vesuvius stared directly into my eyes in animosity.

"If you are no longer my son, than I have no use for you." His snarling statement is pathetic – the only reason he ever truly wanted an heir is to do his bidding. That's not love.

Still rising high into the sky while our streams of lightning push toward each other, it's obvious we're evenly matched. Even with my powerful wand magnifying my powers, Vesuvius has obviously grown in power himself. I don't back down from his predatory stare, though, and instead continue to look deep into his eyes.

I see hate. I see pain. I see animosity. That is not the full array of emotions which Vesuvius described sorcery embracing. It's only a limited, damaging scope of them. For the first time out of all the times I've seen Vesuvius face to face – I feel pity for him as I stare deep into his eyes. Pity for such lost potential, as he is undoubtedly capable of significant power. And pity for such a waste of a person.

"Well," Vesuvius says, still staring into my eyes angrily as we ascend high up into the clouds, "aren't you going to say something?"

"Why should I?" I respond, creating a look of shock in Vesuvius. "There is no rationalizing with evil."

Vesuvius's eyes light up, as if my words are the final nail in the coffin telling him I will never again join his side. He thus doesn't even try to tempt me to change my mind. Instead, his rage amplifies until he breaks away from our magical hold, darting up into the sky even higher.

I shoot a glance upwards, so as not to lose sight of him among the clouds. But it's too late. He glides somewhere among them, and I look furiously around for any sight of him.

But then his voice echoes from the clouds of soot and ash above, playing mind-games with me. "Look below you, you pathetic Wizard. Do you not see your precious Kingdoms have fallen? The Seven Ancient Wonders have crumbled – and this land has begun to merge into the human world! It will soon be destroyed. All you stand for is lost!"

I don't look down – I've already seen the devastation which he refers to. Instead, I continue to shift my focus among the ash clouds, looking for any sight of…

There you are!

I jet straight up into a cloud above me and pierce through it. Vesuvius notices my movement and darts away, but not before I've locked in on his path. The chase is on. He veers sharply, zig-zagging to try to shake me. He knows my position gives me the advantage, and I don't waste a moment of it.

Instantly, I draw my wand, releasing many different spells in his direction. My zapping lightning bolts, the freezing spell, and balls of fire all shoot at him sporadically, as I hope he'll be unable to quickly defend against them all. Shot after shot zooms by him as he manages to dodge them with his sudden, precise movements.

With every ounce of energy and focus, I increase my speed while continuing the barrage of shots toward the foul foe. I'm now only fifty or so feet away from him. Even though my spells miss actually impacting his body, I'm still close enough that they graze him, wounding him over and over ever so slightly. The repeated impacts from my spells of fire and lightning slowly overtake him, as his speed decreases. With all I have, I zoom up behind him and send one final, large wave of the freezing spell at him. Instantly, Vesuvius's body stiffens – unable to move at all – and then falls to the ground as Mama Eagle's had in my prior battle.

"Yes!" I cheer, finally having the upper hand in this battle.

I'm quick to react to the sight of Vesuvius's dead-weight body falling toward the ground from above the clouds. I fly quickly after it, not wanting it to leave my sight for a second. Just as I had with Mama Eagle, I'm going to finish off this fight quickly. I chase after him, ensuring that the fall through the clouds doesn't obstruct my view of the impending crash to the ground. Mama Eagle was lucky to fall into the cradling sand – but Vesuvius should have no luck with the volcanic rock laying below. His body should crumble upon impact. This will be a short-lived battle.

The death-blow of the ground quickly approaches and I can't help but smile in anticipation of the war's end.

THUD!

Finally, Vesuvius's stiff body slams into the rock at the rim of the volcano, just near the edge of the interior crater. I land safely on my feet just a couple of feet away. The ash and smoke from the landing clears and I run up to observe his broken …

"What?" I shudder in disbelief. His body is not broken, but instead lays there, like a brick on the rock – unmoving, but also unbroken. "How can this be?"

I move closer to his body, wanting to examine it with my own eyes for any reason that …

Suddenly, I can't breathe! I gasp desperately for my life, trying hard to inhale, but I can't! It's as though two hands have reached around my neck and are strangling me. I frantically look around for how this could be happening, wanting to find an easy target that I can zap before I faint. When I find nothing, I reach my hands up to my neck, instinctively wanting to loosen anything that could be around me.

The shrill, demeaning sound of Vesuvius laughing rises from his body. He stands up on his feet, brushes off the dust from his long black cape, and walks over to where I'm now kneeling, gasping desperately for air. I can't do it – I can't breathe. I *must* breathe.

Vesuvius now towers over me, holding his wand out at me to cast the final blow.

"You didn't think that the freezing spell would really work on me, did you?" He scolds. "Who do you think taught your father it? Wizardry would *never* embrace such a spell – it removes a person's free-will, which is against their pathetic virtues."

The grip around my throat tightens, and my eyesight blurs. I can't take it any longer and search for *anything* that could release me from the grasp of this evilness.

"But this strangling spell - I never taught it to your father." He looks down at me, and I cower in his sight.

My body has all but given up the fight, no longer able to overcome the physical weakness that has overtaken me. But my mind is still fighting, searching the depths of my memory for *any* spell, any strategy which could free me. My mind retreats to the comfort of my family. To my parents, Emma, and the twins I saw us having in the future. At the thought of them, the feeling of love overcomes me – the same feeling I'd been searching for throughout the entire journey that I'd felt many times along the way. The Family Tree, the stone table in the Animal Kingdom, the touch of Isis, my future with the cabin in the woods, and my parents telling me they love me – they all encompassed that same unbounded feeling of love. It radiates deep within me, strengthening every part of my body. It spreads rapidly, as if the power of thousands of generations of Wizards now fill me on the inside. Suddenly my body can't contain the overwhelming quantity of love and power.

It's working!

The feeling bursts out of my body, as if there's a force being expelled all around me, breaking the bound of Vesuvius's grip around my neck. But it doesn't stop there!

I watch as it radiates in waves of energy in all directions around me, flowing through Vesuvius and outward. I watch as it ripples over the crater of lava and across the other side of the volcano's rim.

Mom! Dad!

I see them still battling Circe on the far side of the volcano. Flashes of light flare back and forth from their battle, and my mother uses her sword to fight in what has been just as strenuous of a fight as mine against Vesuvius. When the wave of power cascades to their battle, Circe is instantly overtaken. I watch as her body crumbles in ash the moment that the wave flows through her.

Undoubtedly, such evil was unable to withstand the overpowering force of love.

My parents are elated that their fight is over. They look over to me, and my father yells: "Acea, hang on! We'll be right there!"

Still gasping for air, relieved to finally be able to breathe, I look back at Vesuvius's body. It lays motionless in front of me, obviously overtaken by the same power that delivered the death blow to his wife.

Relieved that this war is finally over, I turn back and yell at my parents. "It's over! Everything's okay now, he's de…"

Ah!!!

I fall to the ground in agonizing pain when something scolding hot burns me in the back. My wand comes loose from my hand and falls to the ground. I go to pick it up, but …

"Ow!!!" I yell out in pain when I'm instantly hit in the back of my head.

I turn around to see Vesuvius on his feet, limping in pain, but still alive nonetheless. In complete shock and disbelief, I have only a moment to ask "how?" out loud before I have to dodge for my life! Vesuvius is now commanding the pool of lava, raising ball after ball of fire from the crater and sending them my way. Somehow these balls of fire are so hot and powerful that not even my *calorstragulum* spell can fully protect me.

I'm weak from having almost died due to the lack of air, and now the immense pain from being hit by lava is running throughout me as well. Vesuvius laughs as he sees me weakly hobble to avoid being hit by several of his flaming fastballs of lava.

He revels in his position of strength and surprise, yelling at me while sending more balls of flame in my direction. "You didn't really think you'd be able to defeat me, did you? My power is *unlimited!*" I stumble on a rock as I retreat backwards to avoid being hit by the fire. I fall to the ground, hitting my head on a rock.

"Ow!" I scream out in pain. The pain only intensifies when a ball of lava lands on my leg.

Why isn't the calorstragulum spell fully working?!

"Ah, yes – my powers are even stronger than your pathetic heat shield." He says, anticipating my disbelief in this sudden change of circumstances.

Vesuvius walks slowly over to me while still orchestrating the lava toward my direction. I'm not just maimed, but lay vulnerable, unable to move through the intense pain. In my last remaining moment, I look to my parents and see them flying over the pool of lava. They're too far away – at this rate, they can't get here in time to save me.

Vesuvius catches my glance to my parents and smiles in despising hate. Suddenly his right hand raises – just like I'd seen Circe do when orchestrating the waters to raise at the Great Lighthouse years ago.

"NO!" I yell out loud. My heart drops and I want to die when I see the lava in the crater erupt in such force that the entire land of the wizard world is shaken. I desperately hope that the remaining wizards and warriors on the beach below find safety – they are the remaining citizens of this land.

My only hope for my parents is that my father's power to overcome the heat is strong. But as I lay helpless staring at the eruption, that hope is minimal. I don't see any hope of life from within the volcanic eruption of Mt. Vesuvius. The lava flows close to where Vesuvius and I are located on a taller rock.

He walks over to me to strike the final blow. "This is the end of the Order, and the *end of all wizardry!*"

He slowly raises his wand into the air, the reflection of the lava and intense hatred for good shining out of his flaming-red eyes.

His wand!

I see it raised in the air about to strike, but then look behind him quickly to where mine lays. With my very last ounce of energy, I command my wand to come to me. It shoots up from the ground, directly at me, like an arrow flying through the air at an incredible speed.

But I don't grab it – instead I command it to pierce through Vesuvius from behind him! The wand cuts through his body, right where his heart is, and flies out the other side. Vesuvius falls to the ground, and the wand flies into my hand. I stumble to my feet above where his dying body lies. With wand in hand, I raise it up to deliver the death blow to this evil Sorcerer.

"Ah!" I yell out, when the rumbling of the volcano trips me and makes me have to scramble again to my feet. I haven't a moment to waste – the volcano will erupt again at any second!

Raising my wand into the sky, I again summon the inner strength from the love I'd felt from my family. I have no idea if my parents are still alive, and I want to see them again so badly. I want to embrace them and tell them how much I love them. I want to see Emma again and do everything I can to put us on the path of the family I saw in the woods on Friday Harbor. With these thoughts, the love radiates from me and erupts out of my wand with such force that there is no way any person, Wizard or Sorcerer, could withstand it. This is undoubtedly the final blow to Vesuvius, who may not even need it since he lays dying on the volcanic rock.

But just as the death-blow impacts Vesuvius, I'm forced

backwards onto the rock! At the same time that Vesuvius is hit, the entire top of Mt. Vesuvius erupts in a historic, blinding flash of light.

FLASH!

Chapter 27

World History Class

"And *that,* class, is when Mt. Vesuvius erupted almost two thousand years ago. Now, this is the end of our unit on the Seven Ancient Wonders and the ancient Mesopotamian age." A female voice instructs.

Huh?

I groggily awake, finding my head laying on my folded arms at a desk. I bat my eyes for a moment, trying to figure out what's going on.

Am I . . . at school?

"Oh, why, hello Acea – nice of you to wake up just before the class is over." That same female says. I look up to the front of the classroom and see her standing with her arms angrily folded staring right at me.

Where am I? Was I dreaming?

"Class," the teacher continues, "you may all be seniors about to graduate in a couple months – but remember that you still need a passing grade to graduate. Alright, Acea?"

The bell rings, and I look up to see it's 2:55 p.m. Still groggy, and in complete disbelief for where I suddenly find myself, I look to my neighbor and ask him a question before he gets up to leave. "Hey, where am I?"

"What do you mean, where are you? Acea – you're about to graduate from Friday Harbor High School. You really need to start paying more attention." His tone isn't very helpful, and I'm still extremely confused.

"Well, what class was this?"

"Dude – it's AP World History – you've been out of it the whole class period. Couldn't you wait to fall asleep until you get home?" He stands up from his desk, and collects his binder into his backpack.

Before he leaves, I ask the unknown student one last question. "Hey – where are you going?"

He turns around reluctantly, and responds with an abrasive, disbelieving tone. "Home."

I also stand up and put whatever is around me on my desk into a backpack I find slumped against my chair. I'm guessing it's mine, but I honestly don't have the slightest clue about what's going on.

"Acea," the teacher calls to me. I look around for a reason to pretend not to have heard her, but all the other students have left. I reluctantly look up to her and see that she's waving her finger at her desk – summoning me to her impending lecture.

Not even saying a word – since I don't even know her name – I trudge up to where she sits staring unhappily at me.

"I'm serious, Acea, where were you today? This stuff will be on the final, you know. I wanna see you maintain your 'A' grade before you're cast off into the real world."

A large image of Mt. Vesuvius is projected onto the whiteboard right next to her desk. I stare at the imposing eruption being displayed on it, and I can't help but be confused.

Did I just make the whole thing up – dreamed it all while in history class? It couldn't be . . . it felt so real.

There's a moment of silence while I just stare at the poster in disbelief. Just the sight of Mt. Vesuvius cuts deep into me.

Before the teacher can continue her lecture, my inquisitive side compels me to question her. "Was today's lesson about Mt. Vesuvius?"

"Yes." Her tone is intrigued that I'm not responding to her admonition but instead wanting to know about the gigantic volcano.

"Could you tell me more about its eruption?" I ask while still inspecting the image.

She looks confused at my inquiry but answers it nonetheless.

"Well its eruption was the most powerful force ever felt in the world. It destroyed an entire civilization."

My heart sinks when I hear that. Though I don't know whether she's talking about the human world or Terra Fabula – if it really existed – my thoughts instead go to my parents. I last saw them flying over the pool of lava before it erupted at them. Whether it was a dream or not, I don't know – but I still have to ask the one question now on my mind.

I gulp before asking it – not really wanting to know the answer but nevertheless feeling compelled to ask it. "Were there any survivors?"

My teacher winces her eyes in confusion but still answers. "No … none that are known …" She's still curious about why I'd ask so much about the volcano despite all the other students having long left to go home. "… and the rest of the information on Mt. Vesuvius, as well as the Seven Ancient Wonders, can be read in your textbook."

It's obvious that she's trying to get rid of me. "Well, I'm sorry. I'll be more attentive tomorrow."

"Monday," she corrects.

"Huh?"

"I said Monday, Acea – it's the weekend. I'll see you Monday."

With that, I turn and walk to the classroom door. I open it to leave, but before I do, the teacher stops me to say one last thing.

"You know, though – there's something you won't read in the text book. There's an old fable that Mt. Vesuvius erupted when a very powerful Wizard dueled against a very powerful Sorcerer."

I jolt my head up in surprise, staring straight at her in disbelief. "What?!"

"… but that's just silly," she quickly retorts, "things like wizards, sorcerers, and magic don't exist." She looks back down at her desk and waves me away with the back of her hand. "See you Monday."

I shut the door to the history classroom and walk out of the high school in even more disbelief. I still can't get over the questions in my mind.

What is going on? Was it all a dream? It couldn't have been, it felt so real. But then again, I woke up in history class during a class about the same things I saw.

I look at the high school parking lot and just stop in my tracks. I don't even have a clue if any of the parked cars are mine.

Besides, the last time I drove a car was in Sarajevo – and I learned then I'm not a good driver…

Stop it, I tell myself. *Stop doing it. Stop pretending like what happened in*

Sarajevo or any of it was real. You don't know that.

I give the parked cars one last look before turning away and just heading down the road to where I live – or at least where I last remember living with my mom.

Eh – I'll just walk.

The walk home only makes things worse. Now I have plenty of time to question everything that just happened. But the abundance of time on my walk home doesn't help to resolve a single thing. I have no clue if it was real or all a dream. I feel like a complete idiot.

What is happening to me?

With how completely confused about everything I am, I decide to just go with what I know. I'm on Friday Harbor, and I'm alive. Where I'm at right now is at least real, so that means there's a good chance I just dreamed it all up from my environment while I was sleeping.

Honk – honk!

An old truck horn honks a couple of times from behind the remote road where I'm walking down through the woods. I turn around just in time to see it pull up next to me.

"Emma!" I exclaim.

"Hey, Acea – why are you walking?" Emma's driving an old

beat-up pickup truck and sticks her head out to talk to me on the side of the road.

"I … uh …"

"Well, either way, I'm just thrilled I *finally* found you!" Just the way she says it sends shivers down my spine, making me wonder if there is a second meaning to what she just said. And the look in her eyes pierce right through me. It's a look of wisdom but also one that has the same enthusiasm I saw in her while we were fighting on the beach …

Stop it! I again tell myself, trying not to mess up this moment with a cute girl.

"Are we still on for tonight? If your car isn't working or something, I could pick you up instead." Her beautiful eyes stare straight into me. There is no way I'm saying no to whatever she's talking about.

"Yeah!" I respond in excitement. "… where are we going again?"

"The ice cream shop – don't you remember our date?"

Ice cream shop?! Date?!

These familiar things are echoing in my mind, causing me even more confusion. I try to hide the inner war that's brewing from my confusion, and just want to be by myself for the rest of the walk home. I'd ask her if any of it is true, but honestly – with the high risk that I'm making it all up, I *really* don't wanna screw up a chance with Emma due to sounding like I'm crazy.

"No, no – I remember! Maybe around 7 p.m.?" I quickly try to give her confidence that I didn't forget the date, because I never would!

"Sounds perfect." She says cheerily.

With plans set in stone, I now want to be left alone to battle my inner turmoil. Not even realizing she didn't' even ask me if I want a ride home, I still just say what's on my mind. "Okay, then, it's a date! If you don't mind, I think I'll just walk home instead of getting a ride."

Emma bursts out laughing at me.

"Hey, what's so funny?"

"You are, Acea. You're always cracking me up."

"What???"

"You're already there – that's your driveway," she says pointing at the driveway through the forest right behind me.

My face flushes with embarrassment as I turn to see the driveway to my house. But what I see at the end of the driveway brings a rush of emotion that overwhelms me for a moment. Still staring at the end of my driveway in awe, I'm sure to respond to

Emma before she drives off. "Oh, yeah – ha ha – well I'll see you tonight."

"See you then!" She exclaims in excitement before driving off.

My home – the cabin in the woods.

A warm light flickers from inside, and I can't help but have the mental flashback of seeing this place in the snow on Christmas Eve – and peering through to see my future-self living in it with Emma and our twins.

Stop it!

My heart races with every step I take down the gravel driveway through the enclosed forest. I'm so nervous that I almost can't even do it. I close my eyes and just breathe for a moment, trying to muster up the courage to see what I'll find inside.

"A little boy woke up scared one morning," I begin singing quietly to myself out of habit, to calm my nerves. Once I begin the melody, I take a couple steps forward.

"Shiv'ring and cold – not knowing if he's alone." My mom's old melody is beginning to slowly work. I take several more steps forward, wondering what I'll find inside my house. If my mom isn't home then I know what that probably means – she could have died in the lava with my father and the whole thing was real. But if she is home, that alone doesn't mean anything – we could be living here like I was when I last remember or it could have been real and she survived. I suppose whether or not my dad is home would say it all – I've never been in this house with him.

All of this races through my mind as I continue singing out loud. "That boy's loving mom held him in her arms…." I'm now singing much louder while picking up the pace to see what answers may lie behind this door.

"Humming and singing, son, I'm here with you now!" I'm practically screaming out the last line of the song while I run up the wooden porch and burst through the front door.

There's a moment of silence which kills my heightened anticipation. But just as my hopes fade through the silence, my mom pokes her head around a corner from the kitchen.

Mom!

She smiles at me while drying a dish. "Oh hey, Acea – been a while since I heard that song." Just the sound of her voice is the sound of home. She puts the dish down and walks to greet me. She wraps her arms around me, swaddling me in the warmth that I would fight another war to be in.

Stop it!

"What took you so long?" She asks, and just as with Emma before – I can't tell if there's a second meaning to what she says. I can't tell if she's talking about why it took me so long to get home from school, or why it took me so long to come see her since the battle ended.

I decide to just focus on what I know to be real – this moment, being held by my mother.

"I … uh …" My answer to my mom is just as clueless and dumbfounded as how I reacted to Emma.

"Well, either way, dinner is ready, and your fa…"

My mom stops talking when the door opens behind me. My heart races at the thought that it's my …

"Hi, hunny!" My mom smiles.

I watch as my mother and father quickly move to one another and hug. "Just in time, William. Acea and I were about to sit down for dinner."

My father's look turns lovingly to me and I can't help but begin to tear up.

But if my father's here, then doesn't that mean it was all real?

I have no idea, and right now I don't care. I run over to hug him as if it was the first time I'd ever seen him. When I release my grasp from him, I move quickly to my mom. The three of us stand in the living room, not saying a word.

My mom gives a look to my dad that I just can't read before

saying to us, “Well, come on, then. You both could use a good meal after the day you both just had.”

It’s what *isn’t* being spoken that’s killing me. I can’t tell if I’m imagining it or not, but there’s not much being said at all.

Stop it!

As before, I want to only focus on this moment. *That’s* what’s real.

I pull out my chair at the dinner table and sit down.

“Ouch!” I can’t help but exclaim.

“Oh, Acea what is it?” My dad asks, concerned.

“I … I don’t know …” I say confused. I reach into my back pocket and my heart stops.

“Oh my, son – that’s my old pocket watch. How did you get it?” My mom says, while reaching over to snag it. “Wow, it’s been ages since I’ve seen this ol’ thing.” She looks at my dad before handing it back to me. “Keep it, I always meant to pass it down to you anyways.”

When she hands it to me, the top etching of ‘VB’ sparkles at me.

VB … Vivian Bishop!

My familiarity with the pocket watch rings inside of me. If it all was true, I always assumed those initials stood for Vesuvi…

Stop it!

But I can't. I just can't ignore the feeling I have inside of me. My parents watch as I slowly open the pocket watch to see what's inside. But unfortunately, my heart sinks.

There's no magical engraving inside. And worse yet, there's only three hands – just like in most normal pocket watches. Only this one has sustained much damage. I look dejected, hoping there would be a magical fourth hand, telling me it was all real. I go to close the lid, but just as I'm about to, something catches my eye. There's movement inside of the cracked glass!

I watch as that movement slowly materializes into…

"A fourth hand!" I exclaim at the dinner table. I jump out of my seat and smile to my parents while still celebrating in learning the truth. "A fourth hand – it was all …"

"Yes, Acea," my mother says, smiling back.

"You had to realize it for yourself – that way what you fought for would never leave you." My father explains, while looking lovingly at me.

I run over to my parents, repeatedly hugging them again in excitement. "Mom – dad, I love you!"

I stop for a moment and ask, "Wait – Emma?"

My mom nods her head, reassuringly, telling me that Emma

knew this as well when she stopped next to me on the highway.

"And Terra Fabula?" I ask, hanging on every word for the fate of my friends.

"There were survivors, it'll be rebuilt." My father comforts.

I look at my family – my family that I worked *so hard* and *so long* to reunite. Tears stream down my face like waterfalls. It was real. And it was worth it.

The End.

For more information on

Book One: *Acea and the Animal Kingdom,*

Book Two: *Acea and the Seven Ancient Wonders,* and

Book Three: *Acea and the Adventure Thru Time,*

please visit:

www.KyleShoop.com

facebook.com/AceaAndTheAnimalKingdom

Reviews are appreciated.

ABOUT THE AUTHOR

Kyle Shoop is the author of the *Acea Bishop Trilogy*. He lives in Utah with his wife and children. After spending several years volunteering in his wife's elementary classrooms, he was inspired to write this series.

Made in the USA
San Bernardino, CA
12 August 2016